THE WINNER OF
THE **BANJO**
PRIZE!

'*Taking Tom Murray Home* is a novel that sneaks up on you, and takes you by surprise – and before you know it, you're deep in its world and don't want to leave. This is a thought-provoking, feel-good novel like no other, and I'm just thrilled that it is our inaugural Banjo Prize winner.' *Catherine Milne, Head of Fiction*

'*Taking Tom Murray Home* is a charming, quirky, clever and extremely timely novel – I just loved it!' *Alice Wood, Fiction Campaign Manager*

'This is an absolute delight to read, and a great Australian uplit novel. And somehow it combines bush poetry recitals with Facebook social media campaigns. Genius.' *Thomas Wilson, Divisional Sales Manager (Fiction)*

'At its core, this is a story of grief – and of protest. Common sense would suggest it shouldn't be funny or uplifting, and yet it is. It is rousing and hopeful and deeply down to earth, like the Australians it so keenly and sensitively portrays.' *Nicola Robinson, Senior Editor*

'Could not put it down. It is a funny, moving, bittersweet Australian story. In parts it made you laugh and cry, but what a climax at the end.' *Doug Armstrong, Mailroom Supervisor*

'It's a timely story, with characters so endearing you will become their biggest cheerleaders on their incredible journey. Destined to be an Australian classic.' *Sarah Barrett, Fiction Campaign Manager*

'A quirky Australian tale of unlikely situations and drought-dry humour, *Taking Tom Murray Home* is touching, bittersweet, and very, very Australian.' *Shannon Kelly, Editor*

Tim Slee is an Australian journalist with wanderlust. Born in Papua New Guinea to Australian parents who sprang from sheep country in the Mid-North and Far North of South Australia, he worked for several years for the *Stock Journal* in Adelaide before moving to Canberra and then Sydney, where he worked for the Commonwealth Attorney-General's Department. Since then he has lived in Denmark, Canada and Australia, and is currently in Denmark again, on contract with a multinational pharmaceutical company. Although, according to his favourite airline, he has been around the world with them twenty-two times and visited fifty-four countries, Australia is still his physical and emotional home base.

Taking Tom Murray Home

TIM SLEE

HarperCollinsPublishers

HarperCollins*Publishers*

First published in Australia in 2019
by HarperCollins*Publishers* Australia Pty Limited
ABN 36 009 913 517
harpercollins.com.au

HarperCollins*Publishers*
Level 13, 201 Elizabeth Street, Sydney NSW 2000, Australia
Unit D1, 63 Apollo Drive, Rosedale, Auckland 0632, New Zealand
A 53, Sector 57, Noida, UP, India
1 London Bridge Street, London, SE1 9GF, United Kingdom
Bay Adelaide Centre, East Tower, 22 Adelaide Street West, 41st floor, Toronto,
   Ontario M5H 4E3, Canada
195 Broadway, New York NY 10007, USA

A catalogue record for this book is available from the National Library of Australia
ISBN 978 1 4607 5786 4 (paperback)
ISBN 978 1 4607 1153 8 (ebook)

Cover design by Laura Thomas
Cover images by shutterstock.com
Typeset in Bembo Std by Kirby Jones
Printed and bound in Australia by McPherson's Printing Group
The papers used by HarperCollins in the manufacture of this book are a natural,
recyclable product made from wood grown in sustainable plantation forests. The fibre
source and manufacturing processes meet recognised international environmental
standards, and carry certification.

With thanks to Lise, Asta and Kristian
for inspiring and forgiving

Contents

Yardley

Jenny says, 'Hey look over there, fire!' and I say, 'No way, just throw the ball,' and she says, 'No, Jack, there's a fire over at our place!' and she's off running like a scared rabbit, so what can I do, I go after her.

She goes the long way from Ardyaka Farm, through the fences and gates, but I go straight up Goat's Head Rock and through The Gap and then down under the hay shed where she never goes coz she's scared of rats but I never saw one there.

So I get there before her and man oh man you never saw such a hullabaloo as there was that day.

First I have to tell you, there was tons of cops. I don't know why we never heard them but we never did. Should have heard them, all those police cars, or maybe they were trying to sneak up on Dad. We should have known they'd try to sneak up on him but old Mr Warn said he'd keep an eye out on Old Mill Road, they had to go past there, and he'd call Dad if he saw any cops, but I guess he never did or he was asleep or something.

I catch Jenny as I round the dairy. 'Oh holy moly,' she says. 'He's burning the house.'

'No way,' I say.

'Lookit, you idiot,' she points. 'It is. It's burning.'

'Awesome,' I say. Which I know is a dumb thing to say but first I was thinking, hey what about my stuff and everyone's stuff, but then I remembered we loaded it all into Mr Carnaby's ute the day before yesterday, and then I thought, where's Mum, but then I remembered she was visiting Aunty Ell so she was away out of it which she said was a good thing. So in the end all I thought was, good on ya, Dad, you did it. Awesome.

I bet you can see the smoke all the way to Portland.

We stand there at the edge of all these people. It's our house but you'd think we were the strangers here the way they're all over the place.

'Where is he?' Jenny whispers. 'I can't see him, wait there's Mum, I thought she was over at Aunty Ell's.'

And sure enough, there is Mum talking to that policeman who was here before, I can't remember his name but he gave me a peppermint. I walk over through all the people, most just walking around like they don't know what to do, because I bet they don't, a man burns his own house down, that doesn't happen every day. I'm counting six cars and three utes with neighbours in, more arriving all the time, they saw the smoke I guess. Should have brought a fire truck, is what I think, and less cops.

I put my hand in my mum's hand. I can ball it up so it's like she's holding a softball, like a swinger. She can really swing a ball my mum because her hands are so big and rough she's got a grip like a bear, like mine is going to be one day, she says.

'Hey Mum,' I say but she doesn't say hey and keeps talking to the policeman and the policeman is saying he's going to charge Dad with public nuisance when they find him, and Dad better say nothing public about how he's burning his own house down because that would only make it worse.

'He better not be in Portland talking to the *Observer*,' the policeman says and Mum says, 'I don't know where he is. Honest, I don't. I thought he'd be here.'

And the policeman is saying, 'No, well we warned you, and there's charges, here's the fire service they'll bill you for the call-out,' he says.

And Mum says, quiet as you like, 'There's no law against a man burning down his own house, you confirmed that. Plus, I never called the fire service and just because you don't like it is not my problem.' Mum has a good glare on her when she's like that and you don't want to be on the pointy end of that glare but just the same you don't want to miss it when she's using it on someone else, especially a policeman.

Pop is there, got his wheelchair out of his car and he's just sitting there, watching it all and smoking a cigarette. He's not really our pop, but everyone calls him Pop and it's like he's everyone's granddad all at once, the number of birthday parties and barbecues you see him at. I like him because he smells of aftershave and always has gum in his pocket and a story to tell and I can already imagine the story he'll be telling about today.

Jenny comes up too and takes Mum's other hand but she doesn't say nothing just stands there staring around, mostly watching the house coz the fire is really taking now. The Country Fire Authority blokes stand around and a few of them are starting to get the hoses out but Mr McKenzie the CFA chief, he looks at Mum and Mum shakes her head at him so Mr McKenzie does this sign with his hand to his men and they go a little bit slower, seems like to me, getting their hoses all rolled out. Going to let that house burn.

'You lot are crazy,' the policeman says to Mum and waves at the fireys as well like 'you lot' includes them. 'I have to get instructions on this,' he says and goes back to his car, and the other cops they lean up against their cars and just then the roof at the corner above where the old kangaroo dog slept before he died, it caves in and the sparks go so high I start to worry, how long do they stay alight and might they reach the town before they burn out and might Dad start some other fires, which he doesn't want. Him and Mum talked about it and decided it was enough to burn down the house, they didn't want to damage the dairy, or start a fire that could spread to other places.

Mr McKenzie sees the cops go to their cars and he jogs over to us and what I like, Mum doesn't let go of Jenny or me, in fact she probably grips a bit tighter. I guess she knows we are a bit scared, which we are even though Dad has been telling people for weeks that if he can't get a fair price for our cows he's going to shoot them and then he's going to burn our house down and take the ashes to State Parliament and tip them on the floor there, see if he won't. And *then* the bank can have it.

'You want to just let her burn?' Mr McKenzie asks.

Mum says, 'Yeah, it's just stone and wood now, we got everything out.' And Mr McKenzie watches and his men they just watch too, waiting for him to say go or something, which he doesn't. Then he says, 'You should have got the cameras in, Dawn, this would have made the news all over,' and Mum says, 'Oh, we'll make the news all right but not with me looking like some old lunatic getting dragged away by the police.'

Jenny laughs, kind of, and Mum pulls her onto her hip. Jenny's way too big for that but Mum she's a big woman with good dancing hips Dad says, and Jenny grips her like her pony, when she had a pony, before we had to sell it. The wind changes and the smoke from the house starts blowing right at us. Jenny lets go of Mum and we sneak in behind her and put our faces in the small of her back and Jenny is looking at me like, *wow, it's really happening, isn't it?* Then Mrs Turnbolt comes out from her car and says, 'Dawn, I should take the children, right? Best for them to get back of all this, yeah?'

And Mum says, 'You cleared it with Harold?' asking if Mr Turnbolt is OK with it, and Mrs Turnbolt says, 'Yes, Harold is all right,' and Mum says, 'Right, then,' and I'm saying, 'No way, I don't want to go back to Turnbolts', we just came here from there. I'm staying!' But a lot of good that does, pretty soon I'm looking out Mrs Turnbolt's car window at the house, what's left of it, and Mum, and the cops, and the fire crew and the neighbours, and the smoke's all the way up to the sky now like a big pointing finger that says something bad happened here.

Right *here*.

The Turnbolts' place is OK I suppose. They got a gravel driveway that makes a good cricket pitch – you can use their garage door as a wicket as long as you don't use a real cricket ball or even a hard rubber one, or else Mr Turnbolt gets cranky. Last night I slept on the couch in the Turnbolts' kids' old room which still has posters from when Gary Ablett was captain of the Cats. Jenny got the bed the first night, but tonight we swap, because that couch smells of their dog Dusty.

We're out back playing cricket and I can still see smoke over where our place is, or was. Maybe it isn't our place any more, maybe it's the bank's by now. Jenny says she can't see smoke, it's been like a whole day, they put it out, but I can. I got better eyes than her and she's shorter.

And then Mum comes bowling out the back door and there's a wild terrible look in her eyes and she grabs Jenny and she runs over to me and she's crushing us and she's saying, 'He's dead. Your dad's dead.'

And Jenny starts dry wailing and I'm like, 'No, what?'

And Mum is saying, 'I'm sorry, I'm sorry, the bloody fool, the mad stupid bloody fool ...'

Direct Action

'The young'uns,' Mr Turnbolt says, looking across the kitchen table and nodding at me. Jenny's in our room, moping, but I want to hear what's going on. They're all in the Turnbolts' kitchen – Mum and the Garretts and the policeman, now I remember his name, it's Senior Sergeant Hussein Karsioglu, of the Portland Police, but he grew up around here and they all call him Karsi.

Usually they stop talking whenever Jenny or me come into the kitchen or lounge or wherever they are, but now Mum just sighs and says, 'Don't mind him, he's a big lad. He'll hear what he hears and he can ask me if he has any questions, can't you, luv?' And I nod and go and stand next to her because there isn't room on her lap between her bosom and the table. She gives me a tired smile.

Karsi is leaning up against a wall with his arms crossed and he says, 'Well anyway. We're going to need you to come to Portland, Dawn, I need another statement.'

'What statement?' Mr Turnbolt says. 'The woman's husband is dead, man. There's your statement.'

'I'd like to speak with Mrs Murray alone, if I could,' Karsi says. 'I can insist.'

'What you need to say, you can say here,' Mum says. 'In front of these people.'

Karsi sighs, looks at me with this kind of *what the hell* look on his face. 'You'll all need to be interviewed again,' he says. 'I want to keep a lid on this but I need to know, did anyone help Tom set the fire, because then they could be accessory to his death.'

'Accessory to a suicide?' Mrs Garrett asks. 'How does that work?'

Karsi says quickly, 'Don't go throwing that word around. Dr Watson told me he had heart troubles. I'm treating it as natural causes, unless I find there's some reason I shouldn't.'

A few of them laugh at this, and Mr Turnbolt says, 'Natural causes? The roof of the man's house fell on his head!'

'*Ssh,*' Mrs Turnbolt says, looking at me. She's got this way of talking out of the side of her mouth when she's saying something she doesn't want you to hear, but it's a bit pointless because when you see her doing it you listen harder.

Karsi looks at Mum. 'It's my call, and I don't want to involve the coroner in this if I don't have to. Emotions are high enough, without dragging this thing out for weeks. But questions have to be asked.'

'Why does she need to go to Portland?' Mr Garrett asks. 'Do your bloody interrogation here and be done with it.'

'I'm not conducting interviews here in Yardley,' Karsi says. 'Come up here with a bunch of uniforms, upsetting everyone.'

Mr Garrett is about to say something else but Mum pushes back from the kitchen table, stands up. She pulls me to her side. 'When do I need to give this statement?' she asks. She's got something like glass in her voice. Something strong but like it could break any moment.

'Today if possible. This afternoon would be good,' Karsi says.

'Except there's the meeting at Yardley Elders tonight,' Mr Turnbolt says. 'No one's going in to Portland today.'

'What meeting's that?' Karsi asks.

'Farmers First Dairy Crisis Meeting,' Mr Turnbolt says, all capitalised like that.

'Oh that, yeah. I forgot about that,' Karsi says. 'I was supposed to be there.'

'Maybe you should,' Mr Garrett says. He's got a face that's all knuckles. I've never seen it smile. 'Any politician shows their face there, they're in for an earful. Maybe more than an earful.'

'Is the bank man going to be there?' I ask.

'Is he my arse,' Mr Turnbolt says.

'Trevor!' Mrs Turnbolt says, looking at me.

'He might, actually,' Mrs Garrett says. 'I saw him in town the other day and asked was he going and he said do I think it's a good idea or would it just inflame things and I said no, it would show some guts, some caring spirit, if he turned up.'

'He won't,' says Mr Turnbolt. 'He's foreclosed on three properties in the district this year already. There's people will be there who he's put on notice.' Mr Turnbolt looks at Mum, 'Like you.'

Karsi squints a bit, then asks Mum, 'Are you going to this meeting, Mrs M?'

She looks down at the kitchen table. 'We were going to. I probably should. For Tom. He'd have wanted to be there.'

'Too right he would,' Mr Garrett says. 'Too right, Dawn.'

Mum looks up again, at Karsi. 'We'll go to this meeting tonight, then I'll come into Portland tomorrow and give you your statement, is that all right?'

Mum spends most of her life in jeans, boots and different jumpers and she only has one decent coat which is in a box somewhere, so she has to borrow one of Mrs Turnbolt's which doesn't really fit because Mrs Turnbolt is skinny and tall and Mum is … not. Her brown curly hair is a bit flat and she tries to fluff it in the Turnbolts' mirror.

'How long are we going to be living here?' Jenny asks. She's sitting on the spare bed. 'I want to go home.'

'We can't go home, moron,' I tell her. 'Dad burned it down. Besides, it isn't ours any more, it's the bank's.'

'Not yet it's not,' Mum says. 'Not officially. And don't call your sister a moron.' She finishes fussing with her hair

11

and turns to Jenny. 'We won't be here long, pet. A few days more, until we're finished with the police and the insurance assessors. Then we'll go to Melbourne and stay with Uncle Lou.'

'What about the cows?' I ask. 'Is Mr Garrett going to milk them? Who's milking them?' I ask, because I've just realised, with all this hullabaloo, no one is looking after the dairy. The cows will be fair exploding.

'Don't worry about the cows,' Mum says.

'Dad shot the cows,' Jenny said. 'He said he would.'

'He didn't shoot them,' Mum says. 'He sold them.'

'To Mr Garrett?' I ask.

'To another dairy,' she says. 'Now listen, you two, we're off to this meeting in Yardley. You just stay here, watch some telly. We'll be back before ten.'

'What time is it now?' Jenny asks.

'Seven,' Mum says. She crouches down and cups Jenny's face in her hands. 'We won't be long, but we gotta get going. All right?'

Soon as the car pulls out, with Mr and Mrs Turnbolt up front and Mum in the back, Jenny says to me, 'You right?'

'You bet,' I tell her, and we both run for the door.

Our bikes are out the back. We are out of there like dogs chasing sheep, ears flat, nothing but dust behind us. We get to the Garretts' in about ten seconds flat, or anyway, no more than five minutes. Jenny was the one said Mr Garrett is always late, he'd leave after Mum, and she's right. The Garretts are still inside, turning off lights, getting ready to leave.

I knock on the door, thinking what I rehearsed I would say.

Mr Garrett comes to the door, 'Well. What are you two doing here?'

'Can we come with you to Yardley?' I ask him. 'We were late getting back to the Turnbolts' and they left without us and Mum is going to kill us.'

'I don't know if it's a meeting for kids,' Mr Garrett says, sucking on a tooth like he's not sure.

'Mum didn't want us to be alone,' Jenny says. I smile at her. Genius.

Mrs Garrett sticks her head out of her bathroom, 'Come on, John. We'll give them a lift. Dawn wouldn't want them stuck at Turnbolts' alone, after … you know. People would understand.'

'I'll call her,' Mr Garrett says, reaching for his jacket on a peg by the door and patting the pockets. 'Where's my bloody phone?'

'I don't bloody know where your bloody phone is,' Mrs Garrett says, all tetchy. 'You should have it on a string around your neck, you doddery old …' Which is funny because they're both pretty doddery. And you know how there are competitions for people who look like their dogs? Well if there was a competition for couples who look like each other, the Garretts would win it easy because from the back they both look the same when they've got their raincoats and hats and rubber boots on.

'We're really late,' I say quickly. 'They probably left ages ago.'

Mr Garrett stops patting the pockets and puts the jacket on. 'You're right, you're right. Come on, Mrs G, we'll sort it out when we get there.'

And then we're in the back seat of the Garretts' old Ford and Jenny is grinning at me because no way were we going to miss it if the bank man shows up to this meeting. Because Jenny and me, we know it was the bank man who killed Dad and we're going to accuse him of it.

There's hundreds of people in the Elders office when we get there, or at least a hundred anyway. Mr Garrett had to park on the side street by the public toilets there were so many cars. We run ahead of the Garrets, coz they're old and slow. Inside Elders they've pushed back all the desks and got a bunch of chairs in from the school, which I'm thinking is where they should have held the meeting so they didn't have to move all the chairs, but whatever.

'Holy moly,' Jenny says. 'Where's Mum?'

But Mum sees us first and she comes piling down on us like she's a hammer and we're nails.

'*What* are you two doing here?' she asks.

'Mr Garrett gave us a lift,' I tell her. Hoping that will explain it.

'You should be home watching telly, not cadging a lift with Mr Garrett, you stickybeaks,' she says, and Jenny is kind of hiding behind me a bit, but then she comes out because she can hear in Mum's voice we aren't going to cop it.

'Is the bank man here?' I ask her.

She looks at me suspiciously. 'What is it with you and the bank man?'

'Is he here?' I ask again, trying to look around.

'Not yet,' she says. 'Maybe not at all.'

'He killed Dad to get the farm,' Jenny says and I give her a death look. She just can't shut up, that girl, but now she's said it and it's out there. I look at Mum, to see does she know it too, like we do?

Mum grabs me by the shoulders and leans in so I can smell sweet tea on her breath. 'You will not say that out loud to anyone, you hear me?'

I nod.

'You won't even say it in your own head,' she says. 'Because it's nonsense. Your dad died in an accident and was no one to blame but himself. I know you don't want to hear that, Jack, but it's true. All right?'

'All right,' I say, but I'm not actually agreeing. In my head, I say, *No he didn't. It wasn't no accident.*

'All right, miss?' Mum says, looking around me to Jenny hiding behind me again now she sees Mum is annoyed.

'Yeah, Mum,' she says. But I bet she doesn't mean it either.

15

Mum stands and looks around, and the Garretts have finally come in after stopping to talk to everyone in town on their way through the door, and Mum points, 'Now you go and sit over there by the wall and not a peep out of you.'

'Can we get a cup of tea and a biscuit?' Jenny asks, looking around and seeing everyone else has one.

'All right, be quick,' Mum says.

The biscuits are gingernuts, but not even the real ones.

We shouldn't have come because the meeting is really boring and the bank man isn't even there. Karsi is here like he said, with a policewoman, standing up the back drinking tea and eating gingernuts. There are lots of people talking about the banks, but no one from the banks is answering. I thought maybe Mum would say something about Dad, about what happened and how it was a shame and all the bank's fault, but she doesn't. It's kind of weird how a couple of days ago it was always him and her, everywhere we went. Now it's just her. Just us three. They take a vote on something and she puts her hand up with all the others is all.

It looks like it's all over, then something happens, I don't know what, and suddenly people go from very loud to very quiet.

'Who's that standing up?' Jenny asks. 'He looks angry.'

I look where she's looking and I see it's Don Aloisi, the coach of the Lions. Mum won't let us play AFL yet so I don't know him that well, but he's been around our place a few times and whenever he has, he's banged his head on something, like the doorway, or a hanging light, or a tree branch.

Everyone else seems to know what he's going to say except me and Jenny and they kind of hunch their shoulders a bit, like it's about to rain.

'You think, you really think the Parliament is going to care that a hundred people in Yardley have voted on a motion and signed a stupid petition?' Don asks.

'It's not a hundred people,' this man from Farmers First says from the front of the room. 'It's thousands, all over the State. In meetings like this.'

'We held a rally in Federation Square, mate. Two thousand of us. That achieved nothing or we wouldn't be here, would we?'

The man from Farmers First goes to say something else, but Coach Don holds up his hand. 'Save it, mate,' he says. 'Save your breath.' He looks around the room and he says, 'You are all kidding yourselves if you think anything except direct action is going to get anyone's attention.'

And then he says it.

'A man died here the other day,' he says, and I figure he must be talking about Dad because who else? 'A man *died*,' he says again, 'because he chose to burn his own house down rather than let the bank have it. The bloody supermarkets and the co-op and the banks are literally killing us and you all sit here voting to sign an online petition, you can't think of anything better to do. Well, I can.'

'Here now,' says someone next to Mum, putting a hand on her shoulder. It's a teacher from school. 'You're out of line, Don.'

'I'm out of line?' Don says, and I think maybe he's going to blow, but instead he slowly picks up his things. 'Well then, I'd better be going,' he says. 'I'll be over at the pub if there's anyone else in this room who thinks a petition is a bit bloody weak.' And then he walks out.

Everyone is quiet and I see Karsi is kind of hopping from one foot to the other like he doesn't know should he go and speak with Don or should he stay here and see what happens. Then he says to the policewoman, 'You stay here.' And he goes outside after Don.

The Farmers First man says, 'Righto, back to business. This is about more than a petition, so the next item on the agenda ...'

Mum stands up. She's a big woman ... well, like wide, not tall. So people either side of her have to lean away when she does and it's like a rock in a pond, everyone in that row each leaning a bit away but still trying to see her, what she's going to say. But she doesn't say anything. She just picks up her coat and her handbag and shuffles down the row of chairs to the end, and then she looks at me and Jenny like, *right, you two, we're going* and we both hop up and follow her out the door onto the street.

I'm thinking, oh boy, Coach Don is going to cop it now. Talking about Dad like that in front of Mum. But Don is already copping it. Ha. I just made a joke. Because he's getting an earful from Sergeant Karsi right in the middle of the street on the median strip between Elders and the Yardley Hotel.

'No, I'm asking you, and it's an official bloody question, what you meant by Direct Action,' Karsi is saying, and he's using capital letters like that. Direct Action.

Don is looking over Karsi's shoulder, down at us. 'Tom Murray wasn't the only one who realised actions speak louder than words,' Don says.

'Tom Murray is dead, Don,' Karsi says, right as Mum steps up behind him.

'Yes he is, Sergeant,' Mum says quietly, standing alongside Coach Don. 'Stupid bloody man.'

I think she's going to cry but then I realise she sounds more angry than sad. Angry at Dad? That just doesn't make sense.

Karsi looks like he's been caught drinking milk straight out of the carton. 'Sorry Mrs M,' he says. 'I didn't realise you were –'

'Shall we have that drink, Don?' Mum asks Coach Don. 'Over at the hotel, you said?'

Don nods at her and takes a step to turn around. Mum puts a hand on Karsi's arm. 'Three's a crowd, Sergeant, I hope you don't mind,' she says. By which I take it he isn't invited over to the pub with us. Even though we are more than three, we're already four.

'No,' the sergeant says. 'You go ahead, I guess.' And he stands there looking a bit lost as we cross the road into the hotel and I'm looking back at him and he waits a minute and then when no one else comes out of the meeting, he decides he looks a bit stupid standing on the median strip and walks back into Elders.

Pubs have this kind of bad delicious smell. The smell of the beer is sour and bad, but the smell of the schnitzels and chips is awesome. Except we already ate at the Turnbolts' so I know there is no hope of Mum buying us something now. She's fishing in her purse though and pulls out a few fifty-cent pieces and drops them into my hand. 'You two go and play some pinball or something,' she says.

'Pinball?' I ask. 'Where's that?'

She looks around. 'Didn't there used to be pinball machines and Space Invaders here somewhere?'

Don smiles. 'While since you've been in the pub, Dawn?'

'I don't hold with drinkers,' she says. 'So a good while, yeah.'

He fishes in his pocket for a few gold coins, because like, Mum gave us nothing. 'Here,' he says. 'There's an air hockey table in the lounge bar.' He gives us a ten as well. 'Get yourselves a fizzy drink,' he says. 'Through there,' he points out the back.

After an hour of sitting listening to grown-ups hold speeches, and tea without enough sugar and gingernuts that weren't even real and Jenny looking all mopey, I'm going crazy for anything to do, so air hockey sounds great. 'Race you!' I yell at Jenny and I'm off.

Apart from the air hockey, it's a nothing night. Mum finishes talking to Coach Don and the Turnbolts are waiting outside Elders for her and the Garretts have to drive us home because Mum won't let us all in the Turnbolts' car, there aren't seat belts enough, she says.

Not that it matters because we would have missed it anyway when the bank burned down because that happened sometime around three in the morning according to the news on the radio.

'No way,' says Jenny at breakfast. 'You reckon it was Coach Don? You reckon that was what he meant when he said Direct Action?'

'Could of been,' I agree.

The radio said the bank in Yardley had its window smashed in with rocks and then petrol bombs thrown in through the window by someone in a ute with its numberplates taken off. Someone in a mask. Police have pictures of the ute taken by a shop camera and are looking for a silver or blue Hilux 2010 or 2012 and good luck with that, that's about every second car around here.

'You don't reckon it was Mum?' Jenny says later, whispering. We're out in the paddock behind the Turnbolts' vats, whanging a cricket ball off the steel, listening to the different noises it makes depending on where it hits. Trick is to try to whang it so the other person can catch it. I suck at that part, Jenny is much better, but my noises are better than hers.

'Who?'

'At the bank. Radio said they were wearing a mask,' Jenny says. 'It could have been Don, or maybe even Mum, right? One smashes the windows, the other throws the petrol bombs. The two of them in the pub talking?'

I look at her like her head fell off. 'You reckon Mum has been riding around in Coach Don's ute throwing petrol bombs at banks?'

'Maybe.'

'You're mental.'

'Let's go in then, maybe we'll hear something.'

'Detective Jenny Murray.'

'I'm going, you can stay out here,' she says.

It's a boring game with only one person so I have to stop and go in. The reason she wants to hang around the kitchen is that the adults are all in there. Half sitting, half standing because there aren't enough chairs, so it's lucky Pop comes with his own chair built in. They started arriving in the middle of the morning and by lunchtime our driveway was full. Most had cakes or biscuits with them.

'Mum, can we have a cup of tea?' Jenny asks.

Mum is listening to Mr Maynard talk so she turns to Jenny, 'Sure, pet. Make a new pot, would you, this pot is empty.'

'And a biscuit?' Jenny points at the yo-yos on the table. 'Can we have a biscuit too?'

'No, those are for –'

'Go on, Dawn,' Pop says. 'Give the kids a yo-yo.' He pushes the plate over to her.

Jenny is a genius sometimes because of course the teapot is empty, they've been at it for an hour already. And making a new pot means we can both hang around in the kitchen like we're making tea instead of there to eavesdrop.

'Good on 'em,' says Mr Maynard. 'Banks are putting us out of business, now someone's put them out of business. Take months to clean up that bank after a fire like that. Weeks anyway.'

'Achieves nothing,' says Mr Garrett. 'Banks aren't the problem, it's the bloody supermarkets. What they pay for milk, you know that. Co-op's going broke. Blaming the bank is like blaming the real estate agents selling everyone's properties.'

'Then we got to take it to the supermarkets,' Mr Maynard says. 'Like someone took it to the bank. Direct action.' He's got a body like a beer barrel on a tripod and it jiggles when he's excited, like now.

Jenny elbows me in the ribs, nodding at Mr Maynard like, *do you reckon it was him?* But Mr Maynard is about seventy. I can't see him chucking petrol bombs any more than I can see Mum doing it.

'There's direct action that doesn't involve burning anything down,' Mum says, kind of quiet.

'They'd notice if that big Woolies in Portland suddenly had to shut down, wouldn't they?' says Mr Maynard.

'What did you say, Dawn?' Mr Alberti asks.

'I was talking to Don, last night,' Mum says. 'He gave me an idea. Asked me where I'm going to bury Tom. I told him I don't know, we never talked about it. But I called his sister last night and Tom's people are buried in Carlton.'

'What's that got to do with –' Mr Maynard asks.

'I'm thinking,' Mum says, 'I'll take him there to be buried.'

'Ah, right,' says Mr Alberti with a smile. He's the only one in the world I know with a gold tooth and you can't hardly see it because it's on the top up the back but if the light is right, like now, it shines when he smiles. I heard Mrs Alberti tell Mum once it's lucky he's got a good smile because he's short, wrinkly and the only hair on his head is in his ears.

Mr Maynard looks confused. 'I don't get it,' he says.

'Like, take him there?' Mr Garrett asks. 'How?'

'Back of a flatbed, I'm thinking,' Mum says. 'Maybe put some signs on the doors. *My husband died so you can drink cheap milk*, kind of thing.'

'No, *he died* and *you keep drinking cheap milk* is better,' Mr Alberti says.

Mr Maynard goes a bit red. 'Someone going to tell me what the hell you're all talking about?' I'm glad he's asking because I have no blinking idea.

'I'm talking,' Mum says, 'about putting Tom's coffin on the back of a truck and driving it to Carlton at about twenty kilometres an hour, as a protest. As a way to keep the protest going, without burning anything down.' She looks fierce, like she wants someone to tell her it's a dumb idea. Like she's daring them to.

Mr Garrett takes the bait. 'You don't want a truck, that won't work.'

'And why not?' Mum asks, ready for him. Knowing Mum, she's got her three good reasons all lined up. Sure enough. 'Give me three good reasons,' she says.

'Give you one,' Pop says. 'Karsi will arrest you, driving so slow. He'll give you some made-up traffic fine for driving too slow.'

'Arrest a widow?' Mr Maynard says. 'He'd never.'

'You saw him,' Mr Garrett says to Mr Turnbolt. 'Last night he would have had Dawn in the back of his car and locked up in Portland if we wasn't there. Am I wrong?'

'Yeah, he was already riled up about the house,' Mr Turnbolt says. 'Imagine how he'll be after the bank too.'

'You want my draught horse,' Mr Garrett says. Mr Garrett has a few horses, but I know the one he's talking about. It's got legs as thick as fence posts and I can walk clear under it without hardly ducking.

'That old nag?' Mr Maynard laughs, spraying biscuit crumbs out of his mouth.

'That old nag won the RASV Best Harness Clydesdale Alan Evans Memorial Pull,' Mr Garrett says, getting shirty.

'What, ten years ago?' Mr Maynard says

'Five,' Mr Garrett corrects him, sharp.

'Wouldn't make it to Melbourne even if you put that Red Bull gear in his drinking water,' Mr Maynard says.

'He'd make it to Melbourne and back again!' Mr Garrett says and he turns to Mum. 'It's a good idea, Dawn, but if you're in a truck, the cops can pull all sorts of stunts to get you off the road. I'll lend you my milk cart, the one with the road tyres I just got certified for renting to tourists.'

'And who'll drive it?' Mum says. 'You?' She's pulling on her earlobe. She does that when me or Jenny ask can we stay over with someone or can we go into Portland on our own.

'Yeah, course,' Mr Garrett says.

'Helen?' Mum asks Mrs Garrett.

'If John says he will, he will,' Mrs Garrett says. 'I'll cope.'

Mum stops fiddling with her ear, drains her tea to the bottom of the cup and drops it back on the table. 'All right then. By horse.'

'I know the rules of the road for horses better than Karsi does, I bet.' Mr Garrett is really warming up now. 'There's hardly nothing for them to get you on, the cops. Not like a truck where they can defect everything from brakes to your exhaust. Mostly it's just do you have a brake, lights front and back and like I said, I just got it certified. It's roadworthy, there's nothing to defect. Can hardly fine you for driving too slow behind a horse!'

'You can't take the freeway,' Mr Alberti says.

'No.'

'Then it's four hundred ks to Melbourne by the Great Ocean Road. You'd take days, maybe a week.'

'That's the point, Carlo.'

'Oh, right.'

Pop rolls himself to the back door to have a smoke while the others keep talking and I help him bump down the back steps to the dead grass and he shows me how to put on the brake. He rolls his own cigarettes and I sit on a step watching.

'You want one?' he asks after he licks the paper and seals it.

'I tried once,' I tell him, which is a lie. 'It made me chuck. Besides, Mum would smell it on me.'

'She would, she would,' he smiles. Then he lights his smoke and watches the match burn for a second before he blows it out.

'Your old man was always a bit of a firebug, did you know that?' he asks. 'There was this time he was knee-high to a grasshopper, maybe five years old, he was seeing if chicken feathers would burn and when they didn't he put a little kerosene on them and, poof, the feathers went up in a flash and took his eyebrows with them so he went in to his parents, all soot and tears and trying to explain what the hell had happened, and they said to him, hey mate, that's OK, the important thing is that you came to us and told us what happened. Honesty beats stupidity every time, they said. Should never have said that. Next thing you know, their damn hay shed is on fire and he goes running in, looking pleased as the cat that got the cream, saying how he accidentally set the hay shed on fire and

27

expecting praise for the telling of it. They gave him a damn belting, I tell you. That cured his honesty problem.'

I can't imagine Dad being five. He was always this tough, wiry grown-up with cracked hands and a big laugh, as long as I could remember.

Pop eyes me through his smoke. 'So it's just the ladies and you now, eh?' He pulls a bit of tobacco off his lip, which is the gross thing about people who roll their own smokes. 'Someone's got to tell you this, might as well be me. Your mum's a tough cookie, no doubt of that. Only woman in Victoria who coulda tamed your dad. But she's going to need you more than ever now, with your dad gone.' He leans forward, elbows on his knees. 'Women need their men to be strong, Jack. There's going to be crying and wailing and they're going to make you feel like it's the end of the world, mate. But you need to be the one who keeps people going when they fall in a heap, all right?'

I nod and he reaches out and pats my shoulder.

'I seen a lot of death,' he says, looking out over the brown grass and dry paddocks. 'You can mourn all you like, have your funerals and your wakes, but then you get up the next day, and the day after that, and there's still work to be done. And people like you and me, we just get on with it.'

The police station in Portland is a big cream and grey concrete place, set back from the street behind dead trees and brown grass, and as we jump out of the car the wind comes up and blows a whole lot of dried-up leaves off the street and into the air and me and Jenny shelter under the porch so we don't get whipped by the leaves and sticks while we're waiting for Mum and Coach Don.

The guy at the reception desk has a big smiling face with a fat moustache and I recognise him from coming to our school to give a talk about farms and guns. He calls Senior Sergeant Karsi who comes and gets us and puts us in a small room with water in plastic cups.

'We'll talk with Dawn first,' Karsi says. 'Then each one of you separately, including the twins.'

'I won't be with them?' Mum asks, sounding worried.

'Shouldn't they be accompanied?' Coach Don asks. He sounds worried too.

'These aren't criminal interviews,' Karsi says. 'You're all here of your own accord, no one is charged with anything yet. And this is not about the bank fire, let's get that clear. That's a problem for CIB in Geelong. Today is about helping us decide whether to notify the coroner.'

Mum looks at us. 'Is that all right with you two?' She's pulling on her earlobe again.

'Will it be you we talk to?' Jenny asks Karsi.

'I'll be speaking with your mum and Don. So it will be someone from our youth services unit,' he says. It's Jenny's question, but he says to Mum, 'They're good with juveniles.' Karsi looks around the table at us all. 'OK, if that's all the questions, we can get started. We'll speak with you first,

Dawn, the rest of you can … well, you can wait here.' He looks around at the bare walls of the room, 'Or look, Don, why don't you take the kids next door to the arts centre? They have this creativity room …'

'You want to go to the arts centre?' Don asks, like it isn't his idea of a good time.

'Not really,' Jenny says.

'For sure!' I tell him. Sit in this boring room with a cup of tap water for who knows how long? No thanks.

'OK, mister, you comfortable there?' the police lady asks. She came and got Don and me after we'd only been at the arts centre a few minutes. She's really pretty, with black hair pulled back into a ponytail and big dark eyebrows and brown eyes. 'I'm really sorry. It was terrible, what happened to your dad,' she says.

'Yes, miss,' I say. I don't know where to put my hands. She has hers folded on the table, so I do that with mine too. She has a pen and pad in front of her, plus this form I filled out when I came in. 'Are you going to record this?' I ask.

'Well, let's just chat first,' she says. 'There's a camera up there in the corner,' she says, pointing to the ceiling where a little black dome sits. 'For now I'll just make some notes, OK?'

'Yeah.'

'Now, I'm going to ask you a lot of questions and you might think some of them are dumb, or strange, but I just want you to answer with the truth, all right?'

'Yes, miss,' I say.

'My name is Leading Senior Constable Suarez,' she says, smiling. 'Or you can call me Maria, whatever you like.'

'OK.'

She takes up her pencil and looks at her pad where some stuff is already written. 'OK. Tell me about you, young man. How old are you?'

'Thirteen and a bit. It's on that form …'

'Thanks, just checking. And you go to Yardley Secondary?'

'Yeah.'

'Play soccer?' she asks.

'Yeah.'

'What position?'

'On the wing usually, or up front if Toby is away.'

'Toby?'

'He's our best goal scorer but he's lazy and doesn't turn up half the time. I'm faster than him, but he's a better shot.'

I'm thinking, OK, she warned me there would be dumb questions, but I'm waiting for her to get to the ones about my dad. On TV they go straight into the hard stuff, they don't go soft like she is. 'Don't you want to ask about Dad?'

She smiles. 'Yeah, sure. Tell me about your dad.'

'Like, how he died?'

'No, I mean, what sort of person was he?'

'Oh, OK. He was a pretty normal dad, I guess.'

'He was a dairy farmer?'

'Yeah.'

'Always been a farmer?

'Yeah, pretty much. Well, he was in the army for a few years but then his father died and left him the farm about the time he married Mum. So that was before I was born.'

'OK.'

'He also volunteers with the SES, when there's emergencies,' I tell her. 'Like floods and fires. Or, he did.' It's unreal, talking about him in the past.

'So, a pretty active guy?'

'I guess. Not so many floods lately.'

'Was he religious?' she asks.

'Like church religion?'

'Is there another kind?' she asks, frowning.

'He always used to say Geelong Cats were his religion.'

She laughs, a little one.

'He played a few games in their reserves. Then he got a heart problem. He says ... he said ... at the start of every footy season, he said he should have his heart checked, maybe he could make a comeback. I used to think he was serious. I bet he could have.' She's nodding, but she's not writing anything down. 'Are you going to ask some police questions?' I ask her.

She tilts her head and looks at me kind of sideways. 'Like what?'

'Like did he have any enemies and did he have a death wish and who maybe would have wanted him dead and if it wasn't Gary from the bank who once went out with my mother who would it be then and can I remember if there was anything dangerous in the house and did I see him go around putting petrol cans all over the house yesterday, which I did, and did I hear him say anything unusual yesterday and did him and Mum ever have big fights. Kind of thing.'

She looks at me, mouth kind of hanging open.

'Because they never did. They only had little ones,' I tell her. 'About money, mostly.'

I think I should maybe tell her more, but it feels like it's Mum's business, not mine. She used to sit up nights. Doing the banking, is what she called it. She had an old computer we bought second-hand from the school, and all these red and blue folders divided into quarters of a year. We'd do our night routine and then if we came out to the toilet or for some water, we'd see her at her computer desk, these piles of folders next to her and stacks of bills. Or you'd be lying there trying to sleep and the printer would be clacking away. You knew they were headed for an argument if she had one of her folders on the dinner table when we got home from school. They weren't stand-up fights. Just like two tired people hitting each other with pillows, without the laughing. Wet pillows.

She agrees with me that we can't rule out Gary as a suspect because maybe he was jealous of Dad once and it was his bank where we owed money. But she knows Gary and she thinks he's not the killing type. And the bank has already got the farm, or nearly anyway, so that's not his motive. The thing she is most interested in is what Dad did the day before he burned down the house.

I tell her we went around the place putting cans of petrol in every room the night before he set the house on fire. I was following him around. Mum had gone to the Turnbolts' by then, with Jenny. But I bugged him about it and he let me come with him. Mum said she was too tired to argue.

Constable Maria asks what we talked about and I tell her I asked him wasn't it dangerous to leave the petrol cans out overnight and he laughed. He said he was leaving the caps on the cans for now, but when he came back in the morning he would just open them up and kick them over. He said a lot of people thought petrol cans would explode like bombs, but they don't. He learned that in the army. They just smoke until they get real hot, and then they go whoosh, but it takes a long time. It was easier to kick them over and let the petrol spread but you had to be sure you were well clear before you lit a flame or made a spark or the fumes would ...

I guess they did.

Mum and Coach Don were in with Karsi a lot longer than me and Jenny were in with Constable Maria. While we were waiting we checked our stories to see if she got asked the same questions, which basically she did, except Jenny didn't see any of what I saw when I was walking around the house with Dad getting it ready to burn. Plus she didn't hear the conversation from the night before that, because she was asleep and I was up getting a glass of water so Dad and Mum didn't know I was listening.

I didn't think about it as a special conversation at the time, so I didn't tell Constable Maria.

Mum had said, 'What if someone gets hurt?'

'You'll all be over at Turnbolts', Dad said. 'Somebody who?'

'I don't know, the CFA? Won't a fire truck come?'

'Not if we don't call it,' he said. 'And even if someone else does, house will be half gone by the time they get here. But it's a good point, I'll call McKenzie, let him in on it. We can trust him.'

They were quiet, then Dad said, 'What?'

'Nothing.'

'Don't nothing me, Dawn Murray.'

'The twins, is all,' she sighed. 'What it will do to them.'

'I know.'

'They'll be destroyed by this.'

'No, don't say that.'

'I'm not changing my mind, don't worry. Or do worry. Worry about them.'

'I do worry about them,' he said, sounding annoyed.

'Then worry more. Worry about them more than you ever did in your life because if you go through with this, it's going to set them on their heels, at least for a while. Especially Jenny.'

'I know.'

'A long while.'

'OK, Dawn. I know.'

'Do you? The counsellor said she does things to herself because she's trying to get our attention and she's thirteen and she's going through everything that every thirteen-year-old girl goes through and on top of it you pile her analgesia and then the fact we're bloody broke and arguing all the time and now this ...'

'What do you want me to say? We're doing this, right?' And he looked at her and she nodded and he reached out and grabbed her and pulled her to him and she buried her head in his shoulder and I went back to bed.

There are some things you don't tell the police, I know that. Like how it made sense they were worried more about Jenny than me. Because there was only one of us who was cutting themselves with a box cutter and pushing nails in their skin and it wasn't me.

'OK, Jack,' Karsi says. He's asked can he go for a little walk with me, just around the block. Maybe down to Maxwell's, get an ice cream. Mum looks at him like, *what?* but then she just nods. Outside it's sunny and warm. I remember this street from when Mum once backed into someone else's car and she went and turned herself in to the police. But they let her off and we went and bought summer clothes for Jenny and me. We had more money then. And the trees were green, not dead and brown like now. Karsi points down the street, 'Let's just walk.'

He's quiet. I'm thinking maybe it's a police technique, waiting for me to say something stupid, so I stay quiet too.

'Constable Suarez said you walked around the house with your dad the night before the fire?' he finally asks.

'Yeah,' I tell him. I'm not sure what I can get in trouble for now, but I'm thinking maybe I shouldn't have said all that to Constable Maria. That she got me, with the nice cop routine. I'm so dumb.

'I'm so sorry, Jack,' he says. 'I'm just ...' He leans up against a fence, holding on above the dead hedges. He's rubbing his eyes like he's choking up, but he's not sobbing or anything. If he's crying, he's crying like I reckon Pop would cry. Dry tears.

He straightens up and takes a big breath. I pat him on the back.

'It's OK,' I tell him. 'It sucks.'

He laughs a bit shakily, 'We went to school together, did you know that? Me and your dad.'

'Really?'

'My family came here after the Second World War, my gramps started a building company.'

'Yeah?' I hear birds singing. I think, funny there are still birds when there are no leaves. But I guess it's easier to build nests when everything is just sticks and twigs and grass.

'Your dad worked for us when he was like, seventeen or something,' he says. 'Holiday job. We had that whole summer together. He taught me how to chug a beer.'

'Yeah.' He looks like he wants cheering up so I smile at him.

He looks at me. 'You don't seem too … you're OK?'

'You can't really see when I'm upset,' I tell him, kicking at a rock, looking down at my boots. They used to be shiny but they're not so shiny any more and the toes pinch. Mum said I could get Jenny's blue sneakers that have the metal toecaps. She's a size ahead of me, which is kind of weird considering she was only born like ten minutes earlier. 'And Mum makes us wear these stupid things,' I tell him, stopping and wagging a foot, 'with the gloves, so we don't hurt ourselves.'

'I know,' he says. He starts walking again. 'What's the name for it?'

'Analgesia,' I tell him. 'It runs in Mum's family but she doesn't have it.'

'You don't feel pain, right?'

'Don't cry, don't sweat, don't feel no pain,' I tell him, like I've said a million times. 'You want to pinch me?'

He stops and looks down at me. 'What? No.'

I keep walking. 'Kids do, when I tell them. They don't believe me. In fifth grade Tommy Barstow pinched my arm really hard and then when I didn't react, he punched me in the head.'

'That's not right,' he says.

'He said, "*Now* you're going to feel it." But I didn't.'

'You know people aren't allowed to do things like that, even children.'

'It's OK. We got him back,' I tell him. 'People forget there are two of us. They usually don't try it a second time.'

He smiles. 'And you're both … Jenny doesn't feel pain either?'

'A bit more, in her insides. Like, she can feel her periods. Or says she can. But I feel a bit more than her in the feet and hands. Once she broke her foot jumping off Goat Rock and didn't even know.'

'Ouch. I guess you have to be careful,' he says and points over the street to Maxwell's. 'You good with ice cream?'

'Yes please. We're pretty careful. We check each other all over, twice a day. For cuts and bruises and things. When we were little Mum used to check us both, and then we would check her just for the practice, but now we do it ourselves, lunchtime and every night before bed. I do Jenny and she does me.'

I don't tell him everything though. Like how Jenny has got herself two mirrors now, a big one and a small handheld one, and she made us take those to the Turnbolts'. How she's gotten all funny about me checking her lately and I can only check her if Mum is watching, and how she tells me I should start checking myself, like she is.

'You're going to have to one day,' she said last week. 'You might as well start.'

Which is stupid because how are you supposed to check that you don't have a cut on the back of your head? Or between your shoulder blades? And why should I check myself when she's right there, doing nothing?

'Do you mind me asking about it?' Karsi asks. There's hardly any traffic today, because it's after September holidays. A few people on the street. Everyone says hi to Karsi or gives him a little wave. I feel like people are staring at me, but I know that's my imagination. He holds the door open and I go inside and it's cool and it smells like pies and bread and coffee.

'No. Everyone asks.'

I get a sugar cone with a single scoop of chocolate with Maxwell's Special Dip, which is just Milo powder but they say it's special Milo powder, so I don't know, maybe it is.

'Your skin is just numb?' he asks, sitting down on a chair opposite. The chairs aren't very comfortable but at Christmas they put big fake Santa hats over them which makes them softer.

I like the first licks of ice cream, when you get the Milo powder and ice cream together. 'I don't know,' I tell him. I reach over and push down on his arm until it goes white. 'I feel that,' I tell him. 'But if you used a needle and pushed it in, it would feel the same. What did you get?'

He looks down at his cone. 'Natural vanilla.'

'Boring.'

'And … you don't get sad either?'

'Sure I do,' I tell him, going for my last chocolate ice-cream lick. 'I'll be sad at the funeral. But then you wake up the next day, right, and there's jobs to be done.'

He looks at me a little funny. 'It's okay to be upset, Jack,' he tells me.

I'm trying to tell him but he isn't getting it. 'Yeah, but I don't *do* crying. Don't sweat either. So I get hot really easy. Like fevers, so I have to stay inside on hot days. Mum takes us to the cinema in Portland if it's a real hot one.'

'I guess that's a mixed blessing,' he says. 'Not crying.'

'Mum says to be glad as long as it lasts, because there will be plenty of time for tears,' I tell him. 'That's what she says anyway. Can I try yours?' I point at his ice cream, where there's still a half with Maxwell's Special Dip he hasn't licked yet.

He hands it over. I try to taste the little specks, but apart from it's a bit more creamy and soft, it seems just like normal vanilla to me and you can't taste much through Maxwell's Special Dip anyway.

'Why I wanted to talk to you,' he says, taking back his ice cream, 'I want to know if you heard anything else your mum and your dad might have talked about, apart from what you told Constable Suarez.'

'OK.' This is good, like proper police stuff at last.

'Like, did they talk about their money problems?'

I lean forward. 'Sure, lots of times. They weren't like, secret about it.'

'OK. You told Constable Suarez they had a fight.'

I shake my head. 'Not a fight, Mum just told Dad he should care more about what would happen to us after.'

He reaches out, stops me licking my ice cream, 'After what?'

'After the fire I guess,' I tell him. 'After burning down the house.'

'That's it, that's all you heard them say about it?' Karsi asks.

'Sure. I mean, he'd been talking about it forever. Jenny was like, he'll never do it, and I was totally convinced he would, even before we did the walk-around the night before, laying out the petrol cans. You want to hear about that?'

He picks out a napkin, dabs his mouth. 'I know about that. No other fights, no discussions about anything else, anything strange, didn't make sense at the time sort of thing?'

'Like what?'

He looks at his ice cream and I get the feeling he's trying to make it look like it's not really an important question he's asking and you can tell it really is. 'Well, like, I don't know, other things your dad might have planned?' He lifts the cone and takes a bite. 'Not the fire?'

I think about it. Burn the farm down, shoot the herd. Except he didn't shoot the cows. I told all that to Constable Maria. 'No. Well he did say once he'd like to blow up the bank. They had a fight about that too. Your cone is dripping.'

Karsi is pretty quiet on the walk back. He tells me he thinks I should keep it between him and me, what I heard Dad say about the bank. Let him follow up on it. I tell him I can ask around, see if he said it to anyone else, but he says no, I should let the police do the police work, OK?

We go back to the Turnbolts' after that and me and Jenny swap stories but hers are boring and she's acting depressed, but she's just mostly annoyed she didn't get ice cream.

We swap beds and I get the spare bed and she has to sleep on the dog sofa. In the morning we kick a soccer ball around and we try to find our marbles but they're in a box somewhere so we make a circle in the dirt out the back and get some little rocks and we each get a big rock and make this game where you have to use the big rocks to smash the little rocks out of the circle and I'm so winning but then Jenny smashes her big rock into a little one that flies back and cuts her shin and we have to go inside and tell Mum so she can put disinfectant on it because that's how we could die.

The Turnbolts and Mum are sitting at their kitchen table and Karsi is there. Jenny looks at me like, *did you know he was here?* and I look back like, *no, he must have just arrived.* They stop talking while Mum goes out to the bathroom and comes back with cotton pads and some stuff the Turnbolts had in their bathroom cabinet. It's not like the stuff we have at home. Had.

They're all watching like it's some sort of TV documentary.

'Brave kid,' Mr Turnbolt says. 'That's a nasty cut.'

Jenny looks at him like, *whatever.*

Mum finishes up and puts a little bandaid on it. 'Don't pick that off,' she says. She sits back at the table and pulls

Jenny to her side. Seriously? She's so dumb she cuts her leg, but she gets a hug like it's some sort of reward. I go to the Turnbolts' fridge, see if they have any Coke.

'So … I put in my report,' Karsi is saying.

'And …' Mum asks.

'Natural causes,' he says.

Mrs Turnbolt sighs and puts her hand up to her chest. 'Oh good. That's good, Dawn. For the life insurance. They don't pay out for suicide.'

'Might not pay out anyway,' Mr Turnbolt says. 'You don't have to notify the coroner?'

'Not for a death by natural causes,' Karsi says. 'It's simpler this way, things can settle down quicker.'

'Dying in a house fire is natural causes now?' Mr Turnbolt asks.

'Doc Watson will sign that he had a heart attack, before the fire took hold …' Karsi looks down and then back up at Mum. 'He was already dead when the roof caved. Sorry, Dawn.'

'Just say it,' Mum says. She's got that same voice on she uses when Dad comes home after losing money on the horses. Kind of dead, kind of dangerous.

'It looks like he ignited the petrol in the front room …'

'Parlour,' Mum says.

'Parlour, and then maybe one of the other rooms. We figure the flames got ahead of him, or the smoke did. Probably he was running for the back door but the fire got there before him, and his heart gave out as he reached the laundry.'

'Well then,' Mum says. 'So now we know.' She sounds funny.

'It would have been instantaneous,' Karsi is saying. 'He wouldn't have felt the fire.'

'That's a blessing, I guess,' Mum says.

'Oh Dawn,' Mrs Turnbolt says.

'What do you want me to say, Catherine?' Mum asks her. 'Oh the *poor* man? It's good he didn't *suffer*?' She stands up and pushes Jenny down in the seat where she was sitting. She looks at Karsi. 'Have you released his body? Can we bury him now?'

'Body's at the hospital in Portland,' Karsi says, shrinking into himself a bit. 'Funeral home can pick it up any time.'

'Good,' Mum says, then she looks at Jenny and me. 'You two. I haven't seen you doing your checks today. Off you go.'

And Jenny looks at me like, *I'll do myself, thanks,* and I spend the next ten minutes in the bathroom standing on the bath on one leg so I can see my back in the Turnbolts' little wall mirror and thinking that I need binoculars if this is going to work and agreeing with myself she's being a real dick lately.

Dad has been ... had been helping me do my checks lately, with Jenny acting funny. We were doing the routine one night and I asked him what does that saying mean, no pain, no gain?

He had this wavy black hair that was always in his eyes and he'd push it out of the way with fingers that looked like he'd just dipped them in diesel. 'Means you want something, you have to work for it,' he said.

'OK. I thought it was more literal,' I told him.

'Literal?' he snorted and shook his head. 'Professor Jack.'

'What?'

'Nothing.'

He patted my back and handed me my shirt, and told me there are different types of pain. And he said, don't you worry, you live long enough, you're going to feel it all. He said there's the pain when you get something you don't want. Might be simple, like a kick in the head. That's the easiest to deal with, because mostly it's your pride gets hurt. Or maybe you get sick and maybe there's nothing you can do about it, like cancer. There's saying goodbye to a friend or girlfriend, like if you're moving to a new city, or you're just over them or they're over you.

That there, that's the pain of losing something. Life, love, security, friendship.

The worst, he said, is the pain of losing someone. That's the worst pain of all. Not money, though that hurt too, when you were suffering for the want of it.

It's losing people. One day they're there, you're having a laugh, the next day, gone. Car accident, farm accident, heart attack.

And that really hurts. That's real pain and one day you'll feel it, he said.

I can see Mum's feeling it, and Jenny. I'm feeling it too, but maybe it's my analgesia, maybe because mine is a bit worse than Jenny's, but it's like I can build a dam against it. I think about how Dad is dead, and I feel this heat rising in my gut, up through my chest and into my throat. Heat like you want to punch something, throw a ball through a window, catch a chicken and choke it. But when I feel that, I can take a breath and push it back down, right back down into my gut, and I can just tell myself it's nothing and forget it and distract myself.

It's a power I never knew I had until he died.

Danny Boy

You should have seen the mayhem as we were leaving town a couple of days later. First, we had to get Dad's coffin on the milk cart. Mr Garrett wanted to do that out at his place but Mum said, no, if we're going to do this, we're going to go for max publicity. We'll do it in the main street or nowhere.

'Max publicity,' Mr Garrett grumbled. 'With the *Portland* bloody *Observer.*'

I look over at the reporter from the *Observer* who was also there when Dad burned the house down, and he's hopping around like a grasshopper, clicking away with his camera as Mr Alberti and Mr Turnbolt and Mr Garrett and Coach Don lift the coffin onto the milk cart right in the middle of town. Sergeant Karsi has given up trying to talk Mum out of it and he's got three cars up from Portland for 'traffic control'. Jenny and me painted the signs on the side of the milk cart. Jenny likes hers (*My Dad Died For Your Milk*) but I like mine (*Your Low Milk Prices Killed My Dad*) after Mum said if we're going to Do This, it has to Have Impact. So I said to her maybe I should paint my face with red paint and she said no, that would be going to too far, luv.

When we were painting the signs last night, I was singing this rap song I was trying to memorise the words for and Jenny lost it and I said, 'What?' and she said, 'Nuthin.'

Then she said, 'Dad's dead, you know that, right? He's not just gone to Melbourne or interstate. He's not coming back one day. He's dead. D. E. A. D.'

'I know, Jenny,' I said. 'I'm not stupid. I know he's dead.'

'Yeah, but you act like it's nothing.'

I felt that heat boiling up from my guts. 'Someone has to be strong!' I told her. 'We can't all go around sniffing and moaning!'

She laughed. 'Oh, you're being strong? That's what you're doing?'

I picked up a paint brush, felt like slapping her face with it, but I just took a big breath instead, pushed it back down. 'Forget it, all right?'

'You want to see strong, Jack?' she said, her chin sticking out. 'I'll show you strong.'

I knew that look. 'Don't,' I said. 'Don't do it. *Please*, Jen.'

'Stop me,' she said. She reached over and took one of the nails we were using to fix the signs to poles so we could hang them on the milk cart. I could have wrestled it off her I guess, but she just would have done it when I wasn't looking.

She took the nail and pushed it into the back of her hand, between the bones. She didn't hit any veins I could see, but there was a lot of blood came out suddenly. She turned away. 'You do it.'

'No. It isn't sterile!'

'I know and I don't care. Here, I hate blood,' she said, holding out her hand. 'So you have to.'

The blood was dripping down her hand into the dirt between her legs.

'It never works,' I told her. 'You won't cry.'

'I nearly did once,' she said, sounding angry again. 'Just stop talking and do it.'

I grabbed the nail and jerked it back and forth, so she could at least feel it moving. It was pretty gross, because I think it hit a bone. She wanted it to hurt, to make herself cry. It was pointless, but try telling her that. After a couple of tries, I stopped and she took her hand back and looked at it.

And she wasn't crying, she was just angrier than before. She pulled out the nail and looked up at the sky and she screamed and threw the nail away and stomped off to the bathroom. When she came back out she was holding a handkerchief against her hand and Mum saw it and came running over and looked at her and looked at me and said, 'What did you do?'

'Nothing!' I told her. Then I realised with her hand bleeding like that, we were both going down anyway. 'I was hammering a nail and she was holding the sheet and she slipped and it went in her hand.'

'You drove a nail in her hand?'

'It was an *accident!*' I told her.

'It was,' Jenny said, looking at me like *thank you.*

'Oh for goodness ...' Mum said and took Jenny off to the toilet. When she came back she just walked up to me, held my shoulders and put her forehead against mine for a second. It's a thing she does. Us against the universe, always.

When they came back, we had to get the talk about injuries. And how it was lucky we both had our tetanus shots a few months back. How it was life or death, septicaemia. How we should just paint the signs, leave someone else to fix them to the poles.

After our lecture, Jenny sat down next to me again. Flexed her fingers.

'Feel better now?' I asked her.

'Yeah.'

'I mean, your purple fit.'

'Yeah, drop it.'

'You should try a different spot,' I told her. 'Maybe your leg.' I pointed to the soft part of my thigh. 'Like here?'

She looked at her hand. 'That one time I nearly cried ... that was my hand.'

'The *other* hand,' I told her.

She looked at both hands. 'No. Really?'

'Yeah, that was your left hand that time. You did your right hand this time,' I pointed out.

'Damn, seriously?'

'Yeah. Come on,' I tell her. 'We got to get this done.'

'Yeah, you're right,' she said, and stopped obsessing about her hand. 'What are you writing?'

'We need a hashtag,' I told her, trying to get the brush right. Painting on sheets isn't easy. 'Everything needs a hashtag these days. I just thought ...'

'Hashtag,' she said, looking at what I wrote. 'Hashtag BURN?'

I looked at it. I thought it looked cool. 'Yeah. It's pretty simple; like our house burned down and the bank burned down.'

'That's cool,' she said. So we put that in the corner of the signs. *#BURN.*

Karsi got the extra cars up from Portland after the thing with the bank. There's a cop parked outside the burned-out bank (like someone is going to firebomb it twice?) and another two cars in the street where the hearse is pulled up and they're dragging the coffin out the back of the hearse and putting it into the milk cart.

Danny Boy is up front, and even though I thought maybe he wouldn't look as big because I've probably grown up a bit since last time I saw him, he does. He's all excited and blowing air out his nostrils like a he's a steam train with a mane.

'That horse isn't even going to make it to Tyrendarra,' Karsi is saying to Mr Garrett.

'Don't you worry about Danny,' Mr Garrett says. 'Probably outlive you, the amount you fret.'

'Someone's got to fret,' Karsi says. 'Lunatics, the lot of you.' He goes over to Mum. 'I'll escort you part of the way,' he tells her. 'Highway Patrol from Geelong will meet you somewhere up the road; until then it will just be me, with some help from Port Fairy and Warrnambool.' He looks up the road. 'They're not loving this. When did you say the funeral service is?'

'Seven days,' Mum says. 'Sunday mid-morning. Best timeslot they had and quickest we can get there, according to Garrett.'

Karsi looks at the men lifting the coffin and carrying it toward the milk cart. 'I'm going to get questions from the Health Department.'

'And you know how to answer them,' Mum says. 'You know it's all legal.'

Then old Mr Alberti's legs go and the coffin tilts over and Mr Turnbolt yells, 'Shit! Grab his corner someone!' And Karsi dives in and he grabs Mr Alberti's corner of Dad's coffin and together they heave it into the milk cart and the reporter from the *Portland Observer* gets a photo of Karsi helping load Dad's coffin inside the milk cart.

The reporter's a tall skinny guy, all elbows and cheekbones, and he crouches down next to me as he's changing batteries and he says, 'That's going to go bloody viral, that is. That was a bloody beauty.'

'You said that out at our house,' I remind him.

'Yeah, but this time I mean it,' he says. 'Totally freaking viral. That was like the flag at Iwo Jima,' he says and shows me on his camera. 'See?'

'What's the flag at Iwo Jima?' I ask him.

'Forget it,' he says. 'Trust me, it was like that.'

I go to Mum and tell her and she says, 'That's good, luv,' like she doesn't believe him either.

The rest of the morning is boring. We try to get a tent onto the milk cart but there's no way to secure it so they just put a tarp over Dad. People are bringing us food and water and loading that on, and the guy from Home Hardware gives us real swags, the ones with the hoods like little tents, and a camp stove and gas bottle. People bring camping gear and chairs and stuff, tons more than we can manage, so they set up a flea market in the street and sell the stuff we can't use, to give the money to Mum. And Mr Garrett gives Coach Don lessons in how to hitch the milk cart and how to drive Danny Boy, so they can share the driving.

Jenny says to Mum, 'Are these people coming all the way?'

'We'll see,' said Mum. 'They'll want to come along for the first bit. That's OK, right?'

'Whatever,' Jenny says.

Mr Turnbolt brings out his big barbecue, the one he takes to the footy matches, and starts selling sausages and steak sandwiches and after he gives all the money to Mum but I don't know how much it is, she just sticks it in a box under the seat on the milk cart. Everyone from the whole town is there. None of them use social media so I have no idea how any of them heard about it but they are all here.

Jenny is going around saying, 'This is totally mental, can you believe it?'

And I'm like, 'I know, it's crazy. This is a funeral?'

But it isn't. I know that. The funeral will be in Melbourne and at funerals everyone wears black and people are all quiet and not all chatty like today. The pub brings a beer keg out into the street and starts pouring beers for people and I see the manager from the pub giving money to Mum too afterwards. 'It's not much,' he says. 'Maybe a feed or two.'

'It's something,' she says back. 'It's amazing,' she says, and she starts crying and Mrs Turnbolt gives her a hug and Mum wipes her eyes and then sees I'm watching her and she says, 'What? Go make yourself useful; the horse feed needs loading.' So I go off and help Mr Garrett put feed on the back of the milk cart. We have to pack it in around the coffin but Mr Garrett says we have to get it in under the tarpaulin to make sure it stays dry.

I'm under the milk cart with Jenny figuring out how the steering works when the bank man comes over to Mum. All we can see is their legs, but we can hear their voices.

'This is for the trip,' he says.

'We don't need your blood money, Gary,' Mum says.

'It's not from the bank,' he says. 'It's out of my own pocket. Here, take it. I grew up here too, right?'

Mum's voice softens a bit. 'I'm sorry about your bank. The fire.'

'Not your problem, Dawn. It's insured. I'm not sure though ...'

'Not sure about what?'

'Just, whether they'll reopen. This branch hasn't turned a profit in three years. There's talk in Melbourne they want to close it, just put in an ATM, make people go to Portland.'

'What about you?'

'Probably take a package. I'm thinking of taking up dairy farming.' He gives a little laugh.

'Ha ha. Well, there's plenty of cheap properties around here. You oughta know.'

'Yeah. Anyway, safe trip. I might catch you up further down the road, if that's OK? See how you're all doing.'

'It's a free country.'

'Yeah.'

'No, that sounded bitter,' Mum says. 'I'm not bitter, Gary. You'd be welcome.'

'Thanks.'

'Righto, all aboard!' Mum yells out. 'Where are the twins?'

Then comes the awesome part. The milk cart is something Mr Garrett calls a 1947 William J. Knight Bendigo Milk Wagon, and it has four big wheels with green hubcaps like on an old motor car, a seat for three people up the front, and a place to stack milk crates in the middle, or in our case a coffin put on sideways, and another seat for four up the back. Jen and me sit up on the back seat facing backward to the road so we don't have to look at the coffin. Up front on the right, driving, is Mr Garrett; in the middle is Mum and on the left is Coach Don. He used to be a ruckman, so he's got long legs, and he tries to put them up on the polished brass railing of the front board but Mr Garrett smacks his shins with his whip and frowns at him so he has to take his feet down again.

Danny Boy, the Clydesdale, is a bit slow on the pull so Mr Garrett has to tap him on the backside with his whip, but a few of the people in the street give a hand getting the milk cart rolling and Danny Boy gets the message and pretty soon we're clip-clopping along and the best part, everyone in their cars makes a convoy and they put on their blinkers and the convoy stretches out about ten cars ahead and about twenty behind with Karsi out front with his flashing light on, and one of the other cars behind. Once we're rolling, the other police car takes off back to Portland.

The reporter from the *Observer* is driving up and down the convoy in his car, leaning out the window taking photos.

'Viral!' he calls out to me and winks as he passes for the last time and then heads off back to Portland nearly as fast as the cops.

'Is he going to do that all the way to Melbourne?' Jenny asks. She almost has to shout, the sound of Danny Boy's hooves on the road is so loud.

'Doubt it, luv,' Mum says. 'He'll probably turn back once we get to the coast road.'

'Karsi wanted us to go back roads all the way to Melbourne,' Mr Garrett says.

'Did he just?' Coach Don sounds annoyed.

'Asked which route we'd be taking. I told him Warrnambool, Apollo Bay, Lorne, Geelong, then up. He said we should cut straight across from Warrnambool, go through Colac. Big dairy towns, he said. More sympathy. Less traffic.'

'Sympathy my arse,' Coach Don says. 'He's worried about your horse backing up traffic on the Princes Highway.'

'That's what I said,' Mr Garrett says. 'But he's right that we'd pick up a bit of momentum going through Colac — whole town would be with us.'

'You want to go Princes Highway from there though,' Coach Don says. 'You want traffic backing up behind you. You want people writing letters, calling talk shows, complaining about that bloody eejit on his horse and cart.'

'*Her* horse and cart,' Mum says. 'If the talk shows want to talk to the right bloody eejit.'

'They will,' says Coach Don. 'I guarantee you that.'

Tyrendarra

About half the people in their cars turn back when we get to the highway, but the rest stay with us all the way to Tyrendarra. It's all pretty mad; we still have a police escort all the way to the reserve. Some people toot their horns at us and Coach Don says we should put a sign on the back of the milk cart saying, *Honk if you support dairy farmers*, but Mr Garrett says that would drive his horse bonkers. At Tyrendarra we all pull onto the reserve and the party starts over. People have food in their cars and barbecues and eskies and everyone pulls into a circle on the oval with their car lights shining in.

'You can't all bloody camp here,' Karsi says. 'And I'll do anyone who tries to drive under the influence, you can trust me on that.'

But he sends the other police car back to Portland and he pulls up a chair and he has a beer. Him and Coach Don both played footy together in the Geelong Reserves, then he came back and played for Yardley Lions, Dad said. So he's got a soft spot for Yardley, you can see that.

Jenny comes over and shows Mum her phone. 'Look, I set up a Facebook account for us,' she says.

'That's nice, luv,' Mum says.

'You know, so people can follow us.'

'Show me,' I say, grabbing her phone off her. She chases me around the cars but I'm thumbing through the photos and I stop up where Mum can't hear us. 'You can't put those pictures on there,' I tell her. 'Mum will go mental.'

'Mum doesn't even have a Facebook page,' Jenny says, grabbing her phone back.

'Yeah, but those are pictures of our house burning,' I tell her. 'Dad is in there somewhere.'

'Is he?' she asks. 'You know that, do ya?'

I look at her like she's really lost it. 'Yeah, I do. Dad's dead.'

'Is he? You've seen the body, have you?'

I point over to the milk cart, which Mr Garrett unhitched. There's lights on the side that run off a battery and you can see the coffin under the tarp, the top and the bottom sticking out over the sides of the milk cart. 'Duh,' I tell her. 'Haven't you?'

'And how do you *know* he's in there?' she says, and runs off.

She thinks I'm thick. I'm not falling for that.

Really? Nah.

* * *

I get my first taste of sleeping rough, and I don't like it much. Even though I'm dead tired and it isn't even raining, I can't sleep. Jenny is sleeping, after about a half-hour of her stupid fake sniffing. The grown-ups are still off talking somewhere. Mr Garrett, Mum, Coach Don, Detective Sergeant Karsi and Mr Alberti. I can hear them arguing about something. Mum told Jenny and me to put our swags under the milk cart so we wouldn't get soaked in dew in the morning. We've been camping plenty of times but always in our tent. Once we loaned Aunty Batt's caravan.

That was a great trip. We went all the way down to Cape Otway, this campground where they had an outdoor cinema. Which sounds more than it was, because really it was just a big sheet stretched between two gum trees and a DVD player with a projector, but we'd never seen a movie outside before. And me and Jenny went around at night playing Koala Spotto with this kid called Dean and he started a fight with this old man who told us to pipe down and take our torches somewhere else and when Dean gave him a mouthful he tried to take my torch off me and Jen was like, *you touch my brother one more time and I'll kick you in the bum with my steel-toed boots, you old pedo.* And Mum heard her yelling and she came over and she made us say sorry to the old man but Jen showed me she had her fingers crossed and I crossed mine too so it didn't count. And that night when we did our checks in our tent, maybe that was the first time Mum wasn't doing it with us, and neither of us could sleep because we had this buzz in our heads like we could take on the whole world.

Sleeping under the milk cart is a bit like the times I slept outside our house on hot nights, on a La-Z-Boy, with just a mosquito net over me and looking up at the stars. But now is just like back in Cape Otway; my thoughts are racing cars zinging around in my head and so it's like sleeping at a race track.

Dad is dead. Really dead, right? Or what? It's true, I never saw his body.

I forgot to ask how long is it to Melbourne from here. A day, a week? What?

Should I tell Mum I think it's totally creepy to sleep under the milk cart, which means we're sleeping under Dad's coffin? Unless he isn't actually in there. Which maybe explains why she thinks it's OK for us to sleep under it.

What does someone's body look like anyway, after a roof falls on them and they're left in a burning house?

What if Dad did it on purpose and it was a suicide? A kid told me once suicides don't go to heaven. But if you kill yourself by accident, is that the same? And if Dad isn't in heaven, where is he?

Another thought strikes me. Are horses like dogs and we have to pick up the poop all the way to Melbourne? And do we have enough bags for that? Because Danny Boy does monster poops.

* * *

I guess I must have fallen off to sleep because next morning
Jenny wakes me. Well, I'm already awake from the sound of
the magpies, but trying to stay as still and warm as I can as
long as I can, almost like I'm still sleeping. 'Hey, stupid,' she
says. 'Come and help me find power for my phone.' I hadn't
thought of that. My phone is in my bag and I pull it out. It's
dead, but it's always dead these days, stupid battery.

I'm still dressed from last night so I pull on my shoes and
me and her run over to the sportsground clubrooms but
they're locked. We kick around a bit in case there's a power
outlet on the outside of the building but there isn't, then
Jenny sees there's an electric barbecue next to a playground
and we look there and on the side of the barbecue is a power
outlet and it works. She checks her Facebook.

'I've got seven followers!' she says. 'For the new account.'

'You've got seven friends,' I tell her. 'Big deal. Check the
Observer site.'

'Why?'

'See are there any photos from yesterday on their website,
that reporter was there.'

'OK.'

'Show me.'

'Stop grabbing, it takes forever to load. Whoa.'

'Whoa what?' I ask her, and she shows me the *Observer*'s
page and there's pictures from yesterday and the reporter was

right. One of the big photos is the one of Karsi helping push Dad's coffin onto the milk cart and the caption says, *Portland police help load the body of dead Yardley dairy farmer, Tom Murray, into the protest wagon.* It's got about three hundred likes already and it's only six o'clock in the morning.

'Wow, he said it would go viral,' I tell Jenny. 'Three hundred likes!'

'Three hundred likes isn't viral, dummy,' she says. 'Three hundred thousand, that's viral.'

'I know,' I tell her, annoyed she thinks she's the only one knows anything. 'But three hundred is pretty good. You never got three hundred for any of your dumb photos.'

'I'm going to share it,' she says. 'On Facebook.'

'To your seven friends?'

'Shut up. It's a start.' Shows me at the top of her screen where the profile photo says *#BURN* over a picture of our house.

'Cool hashtag,' I say. 'Wonder who thought of that.'

She writes, *Sergeant Karsi helping to load my dad into the milk cart as we leave Yardley. Next stop …* Then she asks, 'Hey, where is our next stop?'

'Mum said Port Fairy, if we don't mess about,' I tell her. So she writes, *Next stop Port Fairy. If you want to support dairy farmers, like or share!*

'That's so uncool,' I tell her. 'You don't ask people to like your Facebook page. Who does that? Desperate.'

'It's a protest, thicko,' she says. 'Not my personal Facebook. People always ask you to like protests. Go get me some breakfast, I need to stay here so my phone can charge.'

Breakfast is porridge with a handful of raisins, cooked on Mr Garrett's camp stove. Looking around I see most of the other cars must have gone back to Yardley last night. Mr Alberti looks like he slept in his car, and Pop must still be sleeping in his because I can see his skinny legs and feet in dirty socks propped up against the window on the back seat.

'Where's Sergeant Karsi?' I ask Mum.

'He went back to Portland last night,' she says. 'He had to talk to some detectives from Geelong about the bank fire. Here, take this bowl to your sister and while you're over there, the two of you have a wash.' She throws me a towel.

'Is he coming to escort us again today?'

'I don't know,' she says. 'He's got better things to do than bother with us, I'd expect.' She's got a cup of instant coffee and she looks like she didn't sleep much but she looks about ten years younger than usual. Her hair is messy and it's hanging round her shoulders and across her forehead and she hasn't got her lippy on (that's what she calls lipstick) but her cheeks are all red and her eyes are fired up and she's looking like she Means Business. I give her a hug.

'What was that for?' she asks.

'Nuthin.'

'You still got to have a wash,' she says, pushing me away. 'You pong.'

But then Karsi arrives in his car. He doesn't have lights flashing or anything and he drives over nice and slow, like he doesn't want to wake anyone. He gets out of the car and reaches back in and comes out with a tray with some steaming coffees in paper cups and one falls off the tray and onto the ground.

'Shit,' he says and kicks the cup under his car. He walks over and puts them up on the front seat of the milk cart. 'Those are for you,' he says. 'But now I'm one short ...'

Mr Garrett sniffs and takes one. 'You bring sugar?' he asks.

'No I didn't bring bloody sugar,' Karsi says.

'What, no blueberry muffins either?' Mum asks, a little smile in her voice.

'No bloody blueberry muffins. Nice and chilly last night, was it? You still going through with this?'

'Hell yes,' Coach Don says, coming up on the conversation from somewhere behind the milk cart. 'Aren't you, Dawn?'

'Yeah,' says Mum. 'Yeah I am.'

'*We* are,' Mr Garrett says.

'I thought so,' Karsi says. 'So, I got instructions last night, from the regional commander.'

'Ooooh, the regional commander,' Mum says. 'What did the commander say?'

'You want it verbatim or do you want the child-friendly version?'

Mum looks at me. 'Give us the child-friendly verbatim version.'

'Is he awake yet?' Karsi asks, nodding over at Pop's car.

'Don't think so,' Mr Garrett says.

'Good,' Karsi says, and helps himself to the last coffee. 'The regional commander,' he says, 'said to me I should follow you dick– fools until you are out of the shire and I should radio ahead to Port Fairy and warn them you're coming and then I should leave you to your f– freaking ... fate and get back to my freaking real job.' He sips his coffee. 'And I'm to tell you, you all have to make yourselves available, if Geelong CIB wants to talk to any of you about that bank fire.'

'That's not so bad,' Mum smiles.

'He also said,' Karsi continues, 'if I get my freaking face in the bloody newspaper again assisting a protest action I'll be doing traffic the rest of my life.'

'Could have been worse,' Coach Don says. 'You were preventing an incident. Imagine if the coffin had broken open. Could have been a riot.'

'I pointed that out. Didn't help,' Karsi says. 'So when is this show going to hit the road?'

Just then five cars full of people from Yardley pull off the road and into the reserve. Yesterday it was twenty, but today it's five. I'm looking to see if there are more, but it doesn't look like it.

'Gang's all here,' Karsi says dryly. 'This candle will blow out before you even hit Geelong.'

'You, come and help me hitch Danny to the milk cart,' Mr Garrett says to me.

'He's got to have a wash,' Mum says.

'He can have a wash when we've got the horse harnessed,' Mr Garrett says. 'You don't want him getting clean then getting dirty again.'

'You can pick up that manure too,' Karsi says. 'People play footy on this reserve.'

Mr Garrett says it's like a proper funeral procession, the cars in front of us with their lights on and Karsi behind with his blue light turning. I don't know what I expected but I thought a horse and cart would go much faster than a person walking, but when Coach Don's hat blew off his head, he jumped down to pick it up and was able to catch us up again without hardly even breaking into a trot.

It's a boring trip; grey cloudy sky, not even anyone honking their horns at us, just people peering at us like they have no idea what's going on and it doesn't look that interesting anyway so they go back to their tablets and phones and books and conversations before they've even properly passed us. Oh, there was a tractor who tried to overtake us, but Mr Garrett said that's just not on. Overtaken by a John Deere? Not my Danny, and he geed Danny Boy up to a trot and the tractor driver gave up and settled in behind us, and Karsi dropped in behind him, so now the tractor looks like it's part of the protest.

As we get closer to Port Fairy, after Yambuk, we have what

Mum calls a rolling lunch, which means she climbs around in the back making sandwiches for everyone on top of Dad's coffin and Mr Garrett and Coach Don share the driving so they can eat. Not that you can really call it driving if you ask me, because Danny Boy basically drives himself. Jenny climbs in the back and puts down Danny Boy's blanket as a mattress and then some rugs and sleeps on that, which I can't do because of the smell, promise you that. I want to sleep though, and I must have, because middle of the afternoon I wake up and someone has put me on the horse blanket and Jenny is sitting up in my seat and we've stopped to give Danny Boy some water.

'Well, that's ten now,' I hear Mr Garrett say.

'Twelve!' says Jenny. 'There's another two.'

'Twelve what?' I ask, rubbing my eyes and climbing over onto the seat.

'Well hello, sleepyhead,' Mum says. 'Thought you were going to snooze all the way to Melbourne.'

'Twelve new cars!' Jenny says, 'In the convoy! They're coming in from Warrnambool! Must have read about us in the *Observer.*'

'More like over from Colac,' Coach Don says. 'Dairy country there. But wherever they're coming from, they're welcome.'

I look in front and behind us and it's true, there are about ten cars in front of us now and another five behind, plus the tractor. Karsi has made them all pull onto the side of the highway so all the other traffic can pass us, and there's a line of about a kilometre of cars backed up and they aren't happy. Well, some are OK, they wave and smile, but most just look grumpy and some even yell out rude stuff at us.

'Don't listen to them,' Mum says, putting her hands over Jenny's ears like that will help. 'They don't know what this is about.'

'And what *is* this about, Mrs M?' Karsi says, finished waving through the piled-up traffic now. 'You got some cold water there?'

'Sending a message,' Mum says, handing him a bottle. 'Making people notice.'

'Oh, they've noticed,' Karsi says. 'Noticed what a pain in the arse dairy farmers are.'

'You'd have ended up a dairy farmer if you hadn't failed Year 10, mate,' Coach Don says to him.

'Hell I would.'

'It was police cadets or the army for you, as I recall.'

'Yeah, but pulling on a cow's tits for a living, no thanks. I leave that to you smart blokes. Look, I'm going to have to ask Port Fairy for a car now to see you guys the rest of the way. I'm supposed to be getting back.'

'So?' Mr Garrett asks.

'So it's starting to cause problems, like I knew it would,' Karsi says. 'Your little stunt. You really should have a permit for a protest like this.'

'This isn't a protest,' Coach Don says and he smiles. 'It's

a funeral procession. You don't need a permit for a funeral procession.'

Karsi scratches his head. 'Oh, it's a funeral procession now?'

'See all them cars with their lights on? See this coffin?' Mr Garrett says.

Karsi looks at Mum like he's not buying it. 'Sending a message, you said.'

'With a funeral procession,' she says.

'Four hundred kilometre long funeral procession,' Karsi points out.

'Four hundred and twenty-seven,' Jenny says, getting lippy. Of course she knows exactly how far.

He's standing there and a little white car does a totally illegal U-turn on the highway and pulls up right in front of Karsi. A man is driving and a lady jumps out with one of those little hand recorder things and then dives back into her car for a camera. Then she suddenly realises there's a cop standing there.

'Oh shit,' she says. 'Geraldine O'Sullivan, *Geelong Advertiser*,' she says.

'Like that will get you out of doing an illegal turn over double white lines on the Princes Highway?' Karsi asks her.

'I'm hoping,' she says. 'Hey, are you the cop who helped load the coffin?'

'No,' Karsi says and starts walking back down the line of cars. 'You! Move that bloody tractor further in!'

'Which one is the widow?' the lady asks.

Mr Garrett looks like he's about to give her a serve for being so rude, but Mum jumps down from the milk cart. 'That would be me,' she says. 'And his name was Tom Murray. I'm Dawn.'

The lady blushes. 'Wow, sorry. Look, you're world famous in Geelong today thanks to your policeman friend here. Though I doubt he's very popular back in Portland.'

'World famous today, you say?' Mum asks.

'Yeah well, you know, today's news, tomorrow's chip wrapper,' the lady says. She looks up and down the highway. 'Would you mind if I ask you what it's all about?'

'Sure,' Mum says, pointing up to the seat of the milk cart. 'Come up to my office.'

'My god, is that really the coffin?' the lady asks as she's climbing up. She holds out her hand. 'I'm Geraldine, by the way.'

Mum shakes her hand back. 'Thanks for coming.'

I decide this is boring and I say to Jenny, 'Hey, do you want to see if the tractor guy will let us up into his cab?'

'Race you, fatty,' she says, and she's off.

Mrs Maynard breaks out a slab of cream cake so the stop turns into a picnic on the verge with people sitting down with cake and thermoses of coffee and tea and Mr Garrett wandering up and down grumbling about wasting time. I grab some cake and try to find a spot to sit but the only empty spot that isn't on the dirt is next to Karsi.

'Ha, you caught me,' he coughs around a mouthful of cake. 'I was just …'

'It's good cake,' I tell him. And I realise this is my chance. 'If I tell about a crime, does it have to be official or can it be off the record?'

He smiles. 'You watch a lot of *CSI* or something?'

'Yeah,' I tell him. 'But it's more a suspicion than a proof sort of thing.'

'You want to accuse someone of a crime?' he asks. 'You sure of that? That's a serious thing.'

'Yeah,' I say. 'No. But can it be like, just us, talking?'

He looks down the verge to make sure no one can hear us. Pop is the closest and he's looking away, smoking. 'Sure, we're just talking,' he says. 'Man to man. Off the record.'

'About a murder,' I tell him. There, I said it.

'Murder,' he says. 'Your father, I'm guessing.'

'The man from Mid Valley Bank did it,' I tell him. 'The manager.'

'Gary?' he says, not quite smiling. 'How do you reckon that?'

'It's all written down here,' I tell him, taking my notes out of my pocket. I've been writing stuff down ever since Jenny threw me that line, *How do you know he's in there?*

He takes the paper and tilts it toward the sun, turns a couple of pages then looks back at me. 'Why don't you just give me the short version?'

'He and Dad had a big argument a week ago,' I tell him. 'Dad would have hit him, except Mum held him back.'

'Well now, I know about that. Gary was shook up and told me about it, but that says more about your dad's temperament than it does about Gary,' he says. He leans over to look me in the eyes. 'He was there to tell your dad and your mum that they were out of time, they had to pay their debt or hand your place over to the bank. You know how bank loans work, right?'

'Yeah, I heard the whole thing,' I tell him. 'Me and Jenny were listening.'

'So, you know, he showed a lot of respect going out to your place to do that in person. Not just send them a letter.'

'I know,' I told him. 'He did it because of Mum. He had a thing for Mum.'

'A thing?'

'Him and Mum had an affair and Dad got Mum back,' I tell him. 'But he still loves her, so he killed Dad.'

He doesn't laugh at me like Jenny would have. He just hands back my notes. 'Now, that's a theory. I'll give you that. And when it comes to something like murder, it's usually always about either love or money. So I'll give you that too. But if you're going to be a detective, you have to think things all the way through.'

'I did, he –'

'First, Gary is already married – happily as far as I know. Second, do you think your mum is going to want to get with a man who threw her off her farm?' he asks. 'Even if he is just doing his job?'

I think about it. 'I guess not. But maybe he just didn't want Dad to have her, not that he thought he could ever –'

He taps my notes. 'And the other thing you have to do, if you're determined to be a detective, is keep asking yourself what's most likely, that Gary killed your dad or that he just had a heart attack due to all the excitement of burning his house down, like the doctor said he did?'

'I guess ...'

'It's important we keep our stories straight, Jack. But I'll think about what you said,' he says, standing up and brushing cake crumbs off his trousers. 'I don't believe you're right, but I'll think on it, OK?'

'Thanks,' I say.

'Now, we better get this show back on the road. Do I have cream on my chin?'

Pop asks me to help him put his chair into the back seat of his car. He has this cool old car with hand controls and he scootches in the passenger side and slides over on the bench seat and then he reaches over and pulls his chair up into the back seat while I push at it. He can't pull it up on his own, but he's still really strong from pushing himself around everywhere, so we get it in there pretty quick.

'Thanks, matey,' he says. 'Hey, Jack?'

I look up the verge. I don't want to miss out on riding in the tractor. 'Yeah?'

'I heard what you and Karsi were talking about,' he says.

'Oh.'

He puts his arm out the window of his car and waves his hand at people up ahead. 'There's plenty of people who've got a lot of not much good to say about Gary. But a killer? No way.'

'No, hey. I was just …' Now I *really* want to get away. Plus the tractor is starting up and Jen is climbing in. But Pop isn't in any hurry.

'Gary knew your dad since you were kids. Back when you two first got your diagnosis, you were what? Six years old?'

'Five,' I tell him.

'Yeah. You were in the same class as his kids, used to play together. He noticed it first, how you'd get hot just running around and nearly pass out. But your mum gave you an icepack and the temperature went away, so it wasn't a virus or anything.' He reaches into his car, comes out with the cloth he uses to wipe the inside of his windscreen. 'Here, wipe your jumper, you've got crumbs on it.' There's hardly any but I wipe anyway, and he keeps going. 'I don't know why no one ever thought to wonder why the two of you never cried, but we didn't. We just thought you were both tough kids, I guess. We didn't know that was all part of it. Can't sweat, can't cry, can't feel pain. Then Jenny jumped off Goat's Head Rock that time and came clomping into your kitchen with her foot all sideways and said there was something wrong with her shoe.'

I wince. Dad says … used to say … that you remember the drama, when you're a kid. I remember the doctor saying

Jenny had a greenstick fracture of her tibia and her telling him she couldn't even feel it. How they sent her to Geelong first and then up to Melbourne and then we both had to go and see the doctors at the university, have all kinds of tests. And there was a doctor there from Sweden and he looked at our DNA and said our genes were a match with this little village in the north of Sweden where they have this kind of mutation. And he said Mum has the same DNA but it doesn't affect everyone the same. Which is how we heard about Dorotea's.

'Problem was,' Pop says, 'the two of you were growing up fearless. Of course you were. Nothing and no one could hurt you. You were both like that kid in the cartoons standing on the roof of his house with a cape, thinking he can fly like Superman and not worried there's this thing called gravity. That was you two, at least once a week, one near disaster at a time.'

He's getting me angry. 'We're all right now,' I tell him. 'We're careful. We watch out for each other. You wouldn't even know about our analgesia if it wasn't for our stupid gloves and boots. Except Jenny has a bit of a limp.'

'Hey, I know, I know.' He looks away and up the line of cars to where Mum is talking with Mr Alberti. 'Anyway I just wanted to say something. You see all these cars, why do you think they're here?'

'Because of the funeral procession,' I reply, frowning, like it's obvious.

'Yeah, but why? These people have farms and shops and jobs. They've got plenty of other things they could be doing. So why are they here?'

Now he's really getting me annoyed, asking the same question twice. 'Because of Dad, I guess. They're his friends and neighbours.'

'Some of them,' he says. 'Some hardly knew him at all. But there's always a straw that breaks a camel's back and these people were up to their necks in drought and debt and misery. Then they heard about you. Everyone in town knows about you and Jen.'

'Yeah, because we're freaks.'

'Stop that nonsense, no one who knows you thinks that. And throwing you off your farm, that just wasn't right.'

'And *he* was the one who threw us off our farm!' I tell Pop. 'The bank man. That's why I —'

'See that car there,' Pop leans out the window and points further up the convoy. 'The silver-grey Holden?'

I look where he's pointing, where a lady I don't know is standing with her door open and just looking up and down the road, waiting like everyone else. 'Yeah?'

'That's Gary's wife. He didn't come himself, didn't think it would look right, but his wife has come along.' He pulls his arm in and looks ahead through his windscreen. 'Just thought you should know, mate. We came together because of your dad, but we're sticking with it for you kids.' He taps the steering wheel with his hands. 'Everyone's kids.'

Port Fairy

The tractor guy whose name is Trev decides being in the funeral convoy is more fun than pushing down an old wall which is what he was going to do, so he lets us ride the rest of the way into Port Fairy with him which is lucky because the reporter lady is sitting next to Mum which would have meant me and Jenny would have had to ride in the back with Dad which Jenny might be cool with but I'm not. It's more interesting than sitting behind Danny Boy all the way anyway, because the tractor has this awesome engine humming and it's got aircon in the cab and the dashboard has this big GPS on it, you can see exactly where you are right down to two metres so that if you're spraying crops you don't double up on a single drop, which is better for the environment, Trev says.

He says after he realised there was no overtaking us he turned on the radio and we were on the traffic radio, or there was a story about us, and the radio said to be careful there was a big funeral procession on the Princes Highway south of Port Fairy and Trevor said, no shit, Sherlock. Then he put two and two together and realised it was those dairy farmers and the suicide and Jenny says it wasn't suicide it was murder.

'*Murder?* Are you serious?' Trev asks.

'Jack thinks the bank man killed our dad,' Jenny says. 'As good as if he put a gun on his head.'

'To his head,' I tell her.

'Whatever.'

'Oh, right. I get you,' Trev says.

'No you don't,' Jenny says. 'You think I'm being metaphysical.'

'Metaphorical,' I tell her.

'Shut up. Coz I'm not.'

'You really think the bank manager in Yardley killed your dad?' he asks me.

'Yep. He must have tried to stop him because he didn't want the house to burn down, seeing as it would be his house when he got it back off us.'

Trev thinks about this. 'Wait, wouldn't he have tried to stop him before he set fire to the house?' he asks me. 'The radio said your dad was found inside the house, so it must have already been on fire.'

Jenny is with me on this and looks at him like he's a halfwit. 'Well, obviously they had their fight inside the house.'

'After he lit the fire?' Trev asks.

I shrug. 'Sure. But the bank manager interrupted him and they had a fight and he knocked Dad out or something and he ran for it.'

'He's a big guy, this bank manager?' Trev asks me.

Pop can say what he likes. I've still got the bank manager as top of my suspects list. 'Probably he snuck up on him,' I say.

Trev looks a little doubtful, I reckon. But around about then is when the Port Fairy cops stop the convoy.

Jenny and me run back up to the milk cart where there's a huddle going on with Mum, Coach Don, Mr Garrett, Mr Alberti, Mr Maynard (I never knew he was in the convoy), Karsi and two other cops who have just pulled up in their car and waved everyone in to the side of the highway again. The lady from the *Geelong Advertiser* is hopping around taking photos with her camera and so is the reporter from the *Portland Observer* who has turned up out of nowhere and they're busy getting in each other's way and growling at each other.

'What I'm saying, Karsi, is that this is as far as this nonsense goes today, and tomorrow Regional Command can decide what happens,' the older of the new cops says. He's got a beard and beer belly and his police hat pushed right back on his head.

'So what are you proposing?' Karsi asks. 'They all sleep on the side of the road?'

'The cemetery is just up the road,' the younger cop says. 'Might be easiest.'

Karsi and the other cop just look at him.

'Just saying,' the young cop says. 'Two birds with one stone kind of thing.'

'My husband is going to be buried in Melbourne,' Mum says. 'Not bloody Port Fairy.'

'Maybe you want us to set up camp in the middle of the Princes Highway?' Coach Don asks. 'We'd be happy to.'

'Don't even say it, Don,' Karsi says. 'They'll think you're serious and do you for public nuisance. What about the showground?' Karsi asks. 'Next left, then whip around to the showground, could get twenty cars in there no problem.'

'And a Clydesdale,' Mr Garrett says. 'Good facilities for horses at the showground. Won a blue ribbon there. It's where I would have suggested anyway – there or the caravan park.'

'I'm not having you scare the tourists with that bloody coffin,' the older cop says and sighs. 'OK, the showground it is.'

'Right, you two, up on the milk cart,' Mum says. 'Quick smart.'

It's another party like a Lions footy final, but without the party mood. Someone says it's like a rolling wake, which sounds better than funeral procession. All the cars pull up on the main oval at the showground and some people set up barbecues and someone rolls a keg off the back of a ute.

A Port Fairy CFA truck turns up saying the police told them to but they just scratch their heads a bit and then sit down and start eating sausages and drinking beer like everyone else.

Karsi has gone off with the Port Fairy police to do the paperwork, he says, which Coach Don says means get a schnitzel at the Royal Oak Hotel.

The sausages are a bit burned and there's not enough sauce. A man brings a crate of soft drinks but they're warm and I don't like taking ice out of eskies; sometimes there's beer labels floating around in them and the ice tastes like glue. So I'm looking around for ice and I see Trevor the tractor guy has pulled up a chair next to Pop and Mr Alberti and they're drinking the home-made stuff Mr Alberti always brings to parties in a paper bag. He mixes it with red wine and lemonade and adds ice, so I know he'll have some ice.

'Business all right then?' Mr Alberti is saying to Trevor after he hands me his ice bucket and I start fishing some out for my Coke.

'Plant hire?' Trevor says, laughing. 'After today's job I'd arranged to drive that one to Warrnambool anyway, sell it back to the dealer. I used to hire out by the day, then it became the half-day, now it's by the hour, and that doesn't keep the wolf from the door.'

'Stick with us then,' Pop says. 'All the way. Good for the TV news, having a tractor in a funeral procession.' He reaches out his glass and clinks it against Trevor's. 'You'll be welcome.'

We're hiding from Mum because we know any minute she's going to say, right, you two, teeth and bed, so we explore the showground a bit and play murder in the dark for two. Then I notice something.

'Hey, it's real quiet,' I say to Jen.

'Getting scared, scaredy cat?'

'No, shut up, listen.'

'I don't hear anything.'

'That's the point. Where's the voices?'

We run out from between the buildings and can see there's still lights on the showground oval, and cars, but all the people are gathered around the milk cart and no one is saying anything. They're all just standing around, looking down at the ground, and some have got their hats and baseball caps off and are holding them. The reporter from Portland isn't there but Geraldine from the *Geelong Advertiser* is.

We find Mum and go up to her and she takes our hands and holds them like a couple of softballs again and she's crying.

'Right,' says Coach Don. 'I'd like to say something.' And he climbs up onto the milk cart and stands on the seat behind Dad's coffin. Geraldine from the *Geelong Advertiser* lifts her camera to take a photo but the man next to her pushes it gently down and she doesn't argue, slings it over her shoulder again and looks up at Coach Don like the rest of us.

'Most of you knew Tom Murray, some of you didn't. He wasn't anyone special and I never paid him any attention at school.'

'Well, that's nice. I thought they were mates,' Jenny says.

'Shush,' I tell her.

'When he inherited Lazybones Dairy there were plenty who said he didn't have the backbone, and he wouldn't last a year, but he did. Then we decided he wouldn't last three, but he did. Because what we hadn't counted on was that he'd *married* a backbone, and that was Dawn here.'

'Nicest thing you ever called me,' Mum says quietly, but she's smiling.

'Sorry, you know what I mean. Dawn filled in the bits of Tom that were missing and together they were a hell of a team and Lazybones was … I think you won Dairy Farmers Dairy of the Year in 2006, didn't you?'

'And runners-up in 2007,' Jenny says real loud, then puts her hand over her mouth and a couple of people laugh.

'And runners-up, that's right Jen. But then the supermarkets started screwing the co-ops and the co-ops started screwing us and we went to the banks and the banks said they couldn't do anything, and the politicians and the media and the bloody Farmers Federation and well …'

'See, told you,' Jenny says.

'Told me what?' I ask.

'The bank manager is here,' she whispers. She nods across to the other side and I see him, standing there with the lady Pop pointed out. He must have come in the last hour or so. 'Look how *guilty* he looks.' She's being sarcastic, and OK, he doesn't look especially guilty to me.

I thought Coach Don was winding down, but he winds up again. 'And well, no one thought anyone was going to do anything but then Tom Murray said, "I'm buggered if I'm going to let the bank have my farm!"'

A few people cheer.

'He said, "I'll burn the bloody thing down before I let them have it!" And no one believed him, but he did, and it went horrible ...' Coach Don stops and sounds a bit choked, but he starts again. 'It went horrible wrong. And now he's dead, and I want to say a poem over his body.' He looks down at Mum. 'If that's all right, Dawn?'

Mum has wet cheeks and she just nods, so Coach Don fishes a piece of paper out of his pocket.

'This is by a poet, name of Henry Lawson,' he says. 'He wrote it I don't know, a hundred years ago, but it's just as true today. I changed it around a bit, but anyway ...'

'Is he the cricketer from that card game, Henry Lawson?' Jenny asks.

'Maybe, I didn't know he was a poet though.'

'Shush, you two,' Mum says.

Coach Don coughs and lifts his voice.

'The poor are starved, my brothers! Our wives and children weep!
Our women toil to keep us while the toilers are asleep!
Rise ye! rise ye! noble toilers! rise and break the tyrant's chain!

March ye! march ye! mighty toilers! even to the battle plain!
Rise ye! rise ye! noble toilers!
Rise ye! rise ye! noble toilers!
Awake! And rise!
Rise Ye! rise ye! noble toilers! claim your rights with fire and
*   steel!*
Rise ye! for the cursed tyrants crush ye with their iron heels!
They would treat ye worse than slaves! they would treat ye
*   worse than brutes!*
Rise and crush the selfish tyrants! Crush them with your
*   hob-nailed boots!'*

Coach Don yells the last line and the crowd cheers and a couple throw their hats in the air and a few clap, then we all clap and Coach Don climbs down and people start patting him on the back.

'What's hob-nailed boots, Mum?' I ask.

'Yeah, and who was Henry Lawson?' Jenny asks.

Mum pulls Jenny and me to her. 'You two have so many questions,' she says, 'and I've got no answers.' She starts shaking and Jenny grabs her harder and I just hold on a bit until it starts to get uncomfortable and then I pull away and just pat her back until she cheers up.

I'm learning nights like this, people when they're sitting around, they like talking about Dad. Do you remember this? Can you believe he did that? Half the stuff I've heard before, but some of it I haven't. So when I hear it's going that way, people with their camp chairs in a circle around a fire, I just sit behind them in the dark and listen. It's best when Mum isn't there too, like now.

'He never really did like farming, did he?' Mr Maynard is saying.

'Well he burned his bloody farm down,' Mr Garrett agrees.

'He burned his house, not his dairy, it's two different things,' Coach Don says. 'He liked building stuff. That was one thing he did like about farming. Fixing things. Fences, machines, walls, buildings.'

'Army engineer, wasn't he?' Mr Maynard asks. 'He should have stayed in. Good career, the army. Regular pay at least, and nothing to spend it on.'

Pop laughs really loud, then realises Mr Maynard is looking at him. 'What? You expect me to agree, after the army took my legs?'

'A rolled-over truck took your legs,' Coach Don says. 'The way I heard you tell it.'

'Rolled-over *army* truck,' Pop says. 'Anyway, he told me he got out before they sent him away to kill jihadis because he couldn't see the point of that.'

'Couldn't see the point of protecting our way of life?' Mr Maynard says.

'Fighting to protect Middle East oil is how *he* saw it,' Pop says. 'War is different now. It's all about money. When I went to Vietnam …'

'Here it comes,' Mr Alberti groans.

Pop ignores him, 'Yeah you can joke. We might not have won the battle in Vietnam, but we won the damn war. Tell me how many Communist countries you got left in the world now? Can you name any, except North Korea? Kids probably don't even know what a Communist is, growing up this century.'

'The Chinese are still Communists,' Coach Don points out.

'Communists my arse,' Pop says. 'They're all about the money too, like everyone now. It's not good versus evil any more, it's just us versus them. Tom saw that. That's why he left the army.'

They're all quiet. 'Are you sure he said any of that, or is it all you?' Mr Alberti asks. 'I never heard him talk like that.'

Pop takes a last pull on his beer and puts the empty can in the cup holder on the arm of his wheelchair and makes a grunting noise and starts to back out of the circle, then he rolls back in again. 'Tom was from good stock, a family of people who stood up to be counted, is what I'm trying to say. So when time came, he joined the Royal Australian Engineers and he put in his years.' He shoots a glare at Mr Maynard. 'Walking off that farm, it's not because he was a quitter, if that's you're trying to say. That wasn't an admission of defeat, it was an act of defiance, and there's a world of difference, unless you're too thick to see that.'

As he rolls away, Mr Maynard leans forward and kicks a log further into the fire with his boot. 'Jaysus. All I said was, he never really liked farming.'

* * *

I go off to sleep to the sound of someone doing burnouts on the road outside the showground. Far enough away it doesn't bother me. I wake up to the sound of yelling. It's still dark. I'm snuggled right down in my swag underneath the milk cart and have to crawl up to the opening and pull aside the hood. People are running around, cars are starting.

Mum's there. 'Ssh, it's OK. Stay in there.'

'What's going on?' I ask her.

'The bank on Sackville Street,' she says. 'Someone set it on fire.'

'Where's Coach Don?' I ask her.

Jenny sticks her head out from the swag beside mine. 'What?'

I hear the CFA truck starting up. Lucky a couple of them must have decided to stay the night and sleep in their truck, and they go roaring out of the showground, nearly taking a fence with them.

In my mind I see Coach Don standing beside Dad's coffin yelling out his poem. Mum stands up and is looking around like she wants to be doing something; luckily Mr Garrett gives her something to do.

'I'm going to town with a couple of the blokes, Dawn,' he says. 'Can you keep an eye on Danny? Just give him a feed and some water to settle him down; this racket has got him all stirred up.'

'No worries,' she says and goes around the back of the milk cart to get some oats for the horse.

Jenny and me look at each other and I grab my jumper out the bottom of my swag and she grabs hers and we wiggle our way to the front of the milk cart and we're off. We don't hardly know Port Fairy but we only have to follow the cars barrelling through town towards the fire and after a few minutes' running we see lights and smoke and then we find Sackville Street and there it is. Police cars, the CFA truck and a mob of people from the showground.

It isn't a very impressive fire. Like, our place burned up something fierce, and I didn't see the bank in Yardley go up but the damage made it look like a bomb had gone off in there. We get as close as we can to the bank before a firey chases us away. This fire looks just like a window got broken and someone made a fire on a desk with some papers. The fire is already out and people are standing around smoking.

I see the old cop from last night, the one who stopped us out on the highway, talking to some other police. 'You get out to the showground, no one leaves before I get there, all right? I want names and statements! And find that bastard Karsioglu. I'll get on to Warrnambool, get them to send some more uniforms ...'

Mr Garrett and Coach Don and Mr Alberti are standing on the street corner and we go over.

'Can we get a ride back with you?' I ask them.

Coach Don looks down at us a little surprised. 'How did you get here?'

'Ran,' Jenny says.

'Couple of Kenyans, you two,' Mr Alberti says, whatever that means.

'Can we though?'

Next morning Mum wants to get going but some detectives from Geelong arrive and they're still interviewing people. Mostly they're trying to work out who was there at the showground, who wasn't there, who might have left around the time of the fire, who's gone home since.

'It's a dog's breakfast,' Karsi says, coming over to speak to Mum. Me and Jenny and her are just hanging by the milk cart. Mr Garrett has Danny Boy all harnessed up and ready to go, and it's starting to get warm in the sun.

'We've got to get on the road,' Mum says. 'Got to get Tom to the cemetery.'

'I told them that,' Karsi says. 'They don't care. Say you could put him in a hearse and have him in Carlton by tonight if you wanted to.'

'They can't force me, can they?'

'Not unless they arrest you,' he says.

'For what?'

'Hell, I don't know, Dawn,' he says, sounding annoyed. 'Being a fuckin' stubborn old cow?'

'Language, Karsi,' Mr Garrett says, coming around from behind the milk cart. 'There's kids here.'

Karsi looks at us and takes off his policeman hat and wipes his brow. 'Sorry, getting hot I guess.'

'Yeah well,' Mr Garrett says. 'You can tell fat Detective Sergeant Wotsit over there that we're leaving in fifteen minutes unless he's going to start arresting people.' Mr Garrett looks ready for a fight.

'You want to think about that?' Karsi asks.

'Try me,' Mr Garrett says.

'We just want to get Tom to Carlton like we planned,' Mum says, a bit less fierce. 'None of this other business has anything to do with us.'

Karsi bats at the sheets hanging on the sides of the milk cart, the ones about Dad that Jenny and me painted, with *#BURN* in the corners. 'That's your story? Seriously?' he asks but he walks off to speak to the detectives.

Most of the people from Yardley who stayed overnight are still here and I reckon some more even arrived when people on the phone told them what happened last night. There's about fifty cars parked on the showground now and people have got chairs and Mrs Alberti and Mrs Maynard have set up a table where they're selling cakes and Jenny thumps me and points and we laugh because there's a group of Warrnambool police at her table buying lamingtons for their breakfast even though on the table there's a sign saying *All Monies Towards The Funeral*. Jenny takes a photo of them on her phone.

Mr Garrett sees it too and says, 'Good to see the boys and girls in blue doing *something* useful. Here, you two.' He hands us two empty feed buckets. 'Go around to all the cars and ask people if they'll give something towards the cost of the funeral.'

Jenny looks at me like, *do we have to?* but Mum gives me a little shove and so we go do it, and most people kick in a few coins and a few even throw some notes in there.

'This is so dumb,' Jenny says when we're halfway round.

'You mean embarrassing?' I ask her. 'Totally.'

'No, I mean, you want to raise money you should set up a GoFundMe page, people can donate properly.'

'Can you do that?' I ask. 'From your Facebook page?'

'I can share it on there. Except I need someone to lend me their phone. I got no data left.'

When we get back Mum's talking to Aunty Ell. She's not our real Aunty, but everyone in town calls her that.

'Look!' Jenny says. 'Got about a hundred bucks I reckon. Hello, Aunty.'

'Hello, luv,' Aunty Ell says. 'Good on you two. I was just telling your mum I've been on the phone to the Wathaurong mob to let them know you're on your way. Asked them to do you a welcome to country when you get to Geelong, you just have to give them some notice. Set it up.' She hands a piece of paper to Mum with a phone number on it.

'We'll call them,' Mum says. 'Thanks, Aunty, really.'

Aunty Ell smiles and pats Mum on the shoulder.

'I made this for you,' this voice behind me says and I turn around and there's Aunty Ell's son Darren. He's a year ahead of us in school, but our dads played footy together. He's holding out a white wooden cross the size of a tennis racquet. 'I made it,' he says, 'For your dad.'

I take it from him. 'Thanks,' I say. I mean, what else? What am I supposed …?

'Let's go plant it,' Jenny says, taking it off me. 'By the road.'

'Wait,' I say, jumping up onto the milk cart and grabbing the schoolbag Mum made me bring. I grab a fat marker pen out of it and write *#BURN* in the middle.

'Right,' I say, jumping down. Me, Jenny and Darren run out to the main road and Geraldine from the *Geelong Advertiser* sees us and follows us out. We try to shove it into the ground but it won't go because the dirt is hard and dry.

'You should have made the end pointy,' Jenny says.

'Yeah,' says Darren. 'Give it.'

He takes the cross and scrapes it up and down on the road until the end of the long bit is sharp. 'There.'

'Use this,' says Geraldine, handing me a rock. Darren holds the cross and I pound it in with the rock and she takes pictures.

When we're done, Jenny looks at me. 'We should say something.'

'Like what?'

'We could do a prayer?' Darren says, shrugging.

95

'Yeah.'

Then we all look at each other. 'Do you know one?' I ask the lady.

She smiles. 'I'll teach you the Hail Mary,' she says. So we all kneel by the cross and do a Hail Mary.

Then there's all sorts of movement and Mr Garrett yells at us to get up on the milk cart and Mum's already up there. We wave bye to Darren. Cars are lining up at the exit to the showground like an honour guard. Out on the road a police car has its lights on and is blocking the exit. Karsi's car is parked next to it.

'Are they going to stop us?' I ask Mum as we take off.

'No, luv,' she says. 'They're going to escort us to Warrnambool. They just want us out of Port Fairy.'

'Are we going to get in trouble for that fire?' Jenny asks.

'Someone will,' Mum says, sounding funny. 'You can't burn a bank without someone getting the blame. But we didn't do it so we got nothing to worry about. OK?'

Jenny looks at her for a second too long, like she's going to say something else, but then she changes her mind. 'Hey,' she says. 'You want to play Yellow Spotto?' So we climb into the back of the milk cart and sit there watching cars overtake us and waiting for the yellow ones. Sometimes people make rude signs at us or shout something dumb, but mostly they just wave.

On the way out of Port Fairy Mum takes a call from the *Geelong Advertiser* lady, Geraldine, asking how to spell our names and can she hop up on the milk cart for a bit more and talk.

Mr Garrett doesn't like her, that's obvious. She's standing on the side of the road up ahead of us where her car dropped her off and he doesn't even slow down for her so she has to jog to catch us as we go by. She's a bit chubby and her boobs jiggle as she grabs Coach Don's hand and he pulls her up. Once she's in, Coach Don jumps out and walks back to one of the cars behind to get a lift, and the reporter gets up next to Mum. She smells a bit hot but has nice perfume and brown curly hair and a big smile. She says thanks for talking to her again, and me and Jenny sit up close in the milk cart so we can hear.

'You said yesterday you want to make a point about your husband's death. If it isn't too painful, can you tell me exactly how he died?' Geraldine asks. 'I read the Portland paper account but it just said it was an accident.'

'If he's dead,' Jenny whispers and I hit her.

'Shut up.'

Mum looks thoughtful. 'The police and the doctor say he had a heart attack,' she says. 'All the excitement. He had a dodgy heart.'

'Right, but he set fire to your house,' Geraldine says.

'Yeah.'

'Because ...'

Mum shrugs. 'Bank was going to take the farm. We were six months behind on the loan and had run out of options.

Already sold all the stock, wasn't a going concern any more. There was just debt left.'

'But a farm is more than a house. Why burn down the house?'

Mum laughs, but not a happy laugh. 'He called a lawyer, asked him was there any law about burning your own house down? The lawyer said no, no law he knew of, if it was done according to local bylaws, and not on a fire ban day. So Tom filed with the council to demolish the house and started telling people around that he was going to burn it. They didn't believe him.'

'But he did it,' Geraldine says.

'That he did. Fool.'

'You didn't approve?'

'Burning the house, I didn't care. We'd lost it all anyway. You have to understand we've been trying to keep our heads above water for years ... Tom said it. "I've run out of shits to give, Dawn," he said, "Let's get out of here."'

'Some people are saying you burned your house down for the insurance,' Geraldine says.

Mum laughs, 'Some people don't know much. House insurance was one of the first bills we had to stop paying. Besides, you think an insurance company would pay out on a house fire when Tom was walking around for weeks telling everyone in Yardley he was going to burn it down?'

'So what was the point?' the reporter is frowning. 'Spite?'

'No. A punctuation mark,' Mum says. 'End of one life, start of a new one. Just walking off, that would be admitting defeat. But burning the house down, that showed it was a deliberate choice. Our choice. He was a poet, my Tom. *From fire, new life* ... like with gum trees.' She shrugs. 'That's how he sold it to me anyway.'

'And this funeral procession ...' Geraldine says. 'That's because?'

Mum shrugs again. 'His people are from Carlton. He always said if he went first, I should bury him there.'

'No, I mean, why like ... with the horse?' She looks behind her, over the top of us, at the coffin.

'We're sending a message,' Mr Garrett says, butting in. He sounds angry, waves his hands to indicate a couple of cars overtaking us. 'Let these people know their cheap milk has a price. It's costing people their properties, their livelihoods, even their lives. Like Tom, right, Dawn?'

Mum's voice isn't angry. She sighs, 'Yes. Like Tom.'

'And the banks,' Geraldine says quietly, like she's sneaking up on it and knows it. 'Is that part of the protest, people burning the banks?'

'That's got *nothing* to do with us!' Mr Garrett says. 'Are the police saying it is?'

'No,' she says. 'They just said they're "pursuing inquiries". But it's the second bank arson in three days ...'

'They can pursue inquiries all the way to Melbourne, no one of us is burning banks,' Mr Garrett says.

'That speech last night by the Yardley football coach.'

'Don.'

'Yeah, Don. He was quoting one of Lawson's rebel poems. Is that how people feel? Is this some sort of popular uprising? A country rebellion? First the banks, and then ...'

'It's not just country folks,' Mr Garrett says. 'People are fed up everywhere. There's riots in Melbourne, soccer fans going each other, cars being torched, people putting *needles* in strawberries. Strawberries! The government blames everyone but themselves, but people are just sick of being screwed. By the banks, by the churches, by big business, by politicians who forgot their job is to bloody run the country, not just win the next election. Look around you, this country is dying!' he says, sweeping his arm out to take in the dead brown paddocks around us. 'We're the ones who can see it. We're the ones who are feeling it, but they'll be feeling it in the cities soon enough. When they're paying more for water than they pay for electricity, when prices go through the roof because their milk comes from New Zealand and their bread is made from dough shipped from China made from wheat grown in bloody Siberia. I bet you then you'll see a rebellion, and not just a country one.'

'It's not rebellion we're about,' Mum says, putting a hand on Mr Garrett's arm. 'It's not city versus country versus banks or politicians. It's a funeral procession. We just want to get my husband to Carlton, get him buried and along the way let people know what's happening out here,' Mum says. 'That's all.'

'Oh really, that's all?' Jenny whispers.

'What do you mean?' I whisper back.

She shakes her head. 'Do you ever listen to anything or do you just run around looking dumb and kicking at rocks?'

'Are you writing a story for the *Advertiser*?' Mr Garrett asks Geraldine.

'I already filed the first one, yesterday, before the Port Fairy bank arson. Filed the second one this morning about the Lawson speech and the bank. I told my editor I think this story has legs,' she says. 'I'm going to stay with you all the way to Melbourne.'

'Are you now?' Mr Garrett says, frowning, like it's up to him to decide.

'My dad was a dairy farmer,' Geraldine tells him.

'Yeah? Where at?'

'Riverland. My brother is still there.'

'Not hardly objective then, are you?' Mr Garrett asks, raising one furry eyebrow.

'Not hardly,' she agrees, grinning.

'Good to have you aboard.'

'Yellow spotto!' I yell and punch Jenny as a bright yellow station wagon overtakes us, dog in the back barking at us mentally as it screams past.

Warrnambool

We go through Dennington on the way into Warrnambool and there's a few people parked at the side of the road to watch us drive through. I mean, it isn't exactly *Justin Bieber The Crowd*, but I guess about ten cars and maybe fifty people. Most of them look like farmers but there's a couple of people in shirts and skirts and trousers like office workers from Warrnambool who've come out. Two of them look like what Dad used to call greenies, a guy and a girl with long matted hair, both of them, and baggy clothes. The girl is holding a sign that says *Multinationals Killing Dairy Farmers!*

'Ferals,' Coach Don says, shaking his head as they wave at us going past. The girl has a pretty, round, smiley face and I wave back.

The police car up front leads us off the highway down a side road to a showground again. There's already another police car there and two police standing by the showground entrance as we pull in. One of them has a camera and is taking pictures of numberplates. He snaps one of Pop's car and Pop gives him a peace sign out his window.

'Can they do that?' Coach Don asks.

'They're doing it,' Mr Garrett says. As we pass them, he points at Danny Boy's bum. 'Get a picture of that!' he yells. The policeman smiles back but it isn't a real one.

It's a bit more organised this time. Someone from the local council has come down and unlocked the toilets and change rooms. There's electric barbecues and a few people start setting up for dinner. A guy with a mobile coffee van comes in and starts selling coffee to people and Mr Alberti goes over and tells him to nick off, this isn't a bloody festival, but Mr Garrett smooths it out and says if the guy donates a hundred bucks to the funeral fund, he can stay. Jenny is going around telling everyone she's setting up a GoFundMe page and giving them the address.

The two ferals we saw in Dennington have put up a tent on the edge out on their own and nobody is talking to them. The girl sees I'm looking at them and gives me a little wave and I wave back. No one is watching, so I walk over.

'Hey, buddy,' she says.

'Hey,' I say. She sounds American.

Her friend is cooking something in a billy and it smells good. He looks up. 'You want some?' He's Australian.

I look around, but Mum is talking to the police and Jenny is off selling her web page. 'What is it?' I ask.

'Rice, canned corn, vege stock cube, nothing flash,' he says. 'Fill you up though. Hungry?'

'Yeah.'

He pulls a little stool out the back of their car. 'Here you go then. Be about ten minutes.' Holds out his hand. 'Ben.'

'Hi.'

'I'm Deb,' the girl says.

'You're American.'

'Canadian,' she smiles. 'Everyone makes that mistake. Love the look with the gloves and boots by the way. You rock it.'

'Why are you here?' I ask them.

Deb smiles. I love her smile. She's probably the prettiest girl I ever saw anywhere, even on the internet. Even though she smells a bit woody.

'Wow, get right down to it, don't you?' she says. 'I'm sorry about your dad by the way.'

'Mum says he was a bloody fool.'

'Or a bloody hero,' Ben says, stirring the rice. 'Depending how you look at it.'

'Yeah. Why are you though?'

'We were camped down at Cape Otway,' Deb says. 'Went into town to check email, read about your dad, this …' She waves her hand.

'Rolling wake,' I tell her.

'I like that,' she says, ruffling my hair. '*Rolling wake*. It made me cry, what happened to you and your family. Ben said why don't we go and join in. Give our support.'

'So here we are,' Ben says. He looks over at the others, cars in a circle, all sitting with their backs to us. 'Not that we're all that welcome.'

'Coach Don says you're ferals,' I tell him. 'Ferals always protest against dairy farmers. They cut Mr Alberti's fences and let his cows out onto the highway.'

He frowns. 'Not all of us are vegan, or extremists.'

'Dad used to call people like you greenies, what's that even mean?'

He takes the rice off the burner and tips some water out and I think he's not going to answer me. Deb looks at him, 'Yeah, Ben, what's that even mean?' I can see now she has a little stud in her tongue, like a little blue ball.

He hands me and her a plate and spoons and sits down. 'Well, it's a word for people who care about the planet. An easy word for anyone who lives a bit alternative.' He leans over to me, 'Anyone who thinks the system is broke, you know what I mean? And tries to do something about it. Do you ever –'

'Does that hurt?' I ask Deb. 'The tongue thing?'

She sticks it out at me. 'Thith?'

'Yeah.'

'It stung a bit when they put it in,' she says. 'But not any more. You forget it's there.'

'So why have it?' I ask her. 'When your mouth is closed you can't hardly see it.'

That gets me a smile. 'You ask good questions,' she says. 'Anyone ever tell you that?'

'Dad used to say I drove him bonkers.'

'You keep asking,' she says. 'The world needs more people asking questions.'

'What you eating?' says this voice and I look around and it's Darren eyeing off my bowl. He's holding a footy. So I guess Aunty Ell is along for the ride too now.

'You want to have a kick?' I ask him.

'Yeah,' he says. 'But maybe we could eat a bit first, eh?'

'Sure, the more the merrier,' Ben says. He leans over towards the food and he stumbles a bit and he knocks the pot with the boiling water and rice in it and it starts to fall. I grab it just in time and go to put it back on the burner.

'Whoa!' Ben yells. 'Drop it!' and he knocks it from my hands. Rice and hot water go everywhere and Deb and Darren jump back. I look at him like he's crazy and then look down at my hand and see it's all red and a bit black from the soot from the bottom of the pot. The skin on my palm is a bit crinkly.

'Water! Cold water!' Ben is yelling and he's blowing on my hands. Deb runs over to their car and then comes back with a canteen and starts pouring water over my hand. As she pours, a couple of blisters start to come up.

'Oh my God,' Ben says, kneeling down and watching, then looking around. 'I'm so sorry! Where's your mother?'

'I'll go find her,' Darren says. He puts a hand on Ben's shoulder and rolls his eyes. 'Don't freak out, mate. This stuff happens to them all the time.'

Mum has this cream for burns. It's a while since one of us had a burn though, so it's out of date but people say it's probably still OK and she puts it on my palm and fingers. Even though it doesn't look so bad of a burn as I had last time, Pop tells Mum I should go to a clinic and get it looked at, but Mum decides we'll just put a bandage around it and see how it is tomorrow. The skin is a bit tight, but I can still move my hand just fine. Jenny goes to push on one of the blisters to see if it will pop but Mum bats her hand away.

'I'm really sorry,' Ben is saying. 'I knocked the pot and he just reached out and grabbed it and hot food went like ...'

Mum is looking down, still rubbing cream into my palm. 'Don't fret. It's not your fault, he just doesn't think sometimes.' Like I'm not even there.

'Yes I do,' I tell her.

'He didn't even yell out,' he says, still looking like he's worried he'll get blamed.

'Or cry,' Deb says.

'Duh, it's called *analgesia*,' I say, a little annoyed, trying to remind them I'm here. 'We both have it,' I tell Ben. 'Don't cry, don't sweat, can't feel pain.'

'Not the way other people feel pain,' Mum explains. 'It's genetic unfortunately, jumps a couple of generations. Dorotea's analgesia. I didn't realise, until after I had the twins.'

'My god, I've heard of that,' Deb says. 'Little children don't feel anything, they can bite their own tongues off ...'

'Dorotea's isn't as bad as that,' Mum says. 'It didn't kick in until they were about seven or eight, so they were old enough to learn how to deal with it.' She squeezes out some more balm onto my palm, massages it in. 'There's this village in Sweden, it's called Dorotea. My family came from there, way back. About four out of a hundred people in the village get this thing, so it's called Dorotea's analgesia. There's a gene therapy that might be able to fix it and we're saving for the twins to get it. Or we were.'

'I don't want gene therapy. I don't want to feel pain,' I tell them. 'I don't want to be able to hurt.'

'Hurting is how we protect ourselves, Jack,' Mum says, like always.

'How do you all cope?' Deb asks.

Mum gives me this face, but Deb doesn't see it. The face she gives whenever anyone asks that question. But she answers anyway as she softly rubs my hand. 'You need routines. Need to check them every day, couple of times a day. For cuts or bruises and the like. No such thing as just a fever because it could be a sign of something they can't feel, like a broken bone or burst appendix, so we get that checked every time. We just have to be careful.' Mum sighs. 'Really careful. But these two,' she shakes her head.

'Hey, don't put me in with him!' Jenny says. 'I'm not the one with the cooked crab claw.'

* * *

'I made you this,' Geraldine from the *Geelong Advertiser* says. It's later now and there's a big bonfire going and people sitting around in a circle drinking beer and port and coffee and tea. Maybe thirty are left, that's all. The local people mostly went home after Coach Don got up and said his poem over Dad's coffin. He made like he didn't want to and they were all forcing him, cheering, '*Hob-Nail Boots! Hob-Nail Boots!*' But you could see he didn't mind the attention at all and he gave it an extra big boost at the end there when he got to the boots bit.

Me and Jenny are sitting playing travel Uno with dice, but we're missing one, so it kind of sucks. I look up. Geraldine is holding a big white wooden cross.

'I thought it might be nice if we made a little prayer everywhere we stop,' she said. 'For your dad. Would you like that?'

Jenny is looking at her with her untrusty eyes, but I say, 'Yeah.' I look at Jenny. 'We should, right?'

Geraldine hands Jenny the cross. 'Only if you want to.'

'Mum should join us,' Jenny says, taking the cross. 'She'd like that.'

'Yeah of course,' Geraldine agrees.

'And Mr Alberti, he'd want to,' I say.

'Anyone could join,' Geraldine says. 'It's up to you. You could make it a tradition every day. Something *you* started.'

'I'll tell Mum,' I say. 'Like, now?'

'No, not in the dark,' Geraldine says. 'And people are

tired. Tomorrow morning, up on the highway before you start off?'

'Yeah,' Jenny agrees. 'That'd be good.'

We take the cross and go over the other side of the fire where Mum is half dozing, half listening to some of the others talking. 'What have you two got there?' she asks.

'A cross, like we had in Port Fairy,' Jenny says. 'We want to plant it out on the road tomorrow, for Dad.'

'I don't know,' Mum says.

'We write *#BURN* on it and say a Hail Mary,' I tell her. 'Geraldine taught us. You could join.'

'Geraldine?' Mum says and raises an eyebrow. 'Well, I guess.'

'Anyone who wants to can join,' Jenny says. 'Before we start the day. It can be a tradition.'

'A tradition, eh?'

'Yeah, we started it yesterday,' I tell her.

She reaches out her arms and grabs us both and pulls us to her. 'You two. You two little ratniks.'

She's not letting go, so I pull away. 'I'm going to ask Deb and Ben.'

'Who?' Mum asks. 'Who's that?'

'The greenies,' Jenny says, like Dad would have said it, rolling her eyes.

'They're saving the planet,' I say. 'And they're on our side.'

'I'm going to invite the cops,' Jenny says.

'They'd never join in,' I tell her.

'Sergeant Karsi would,' she says. 'And maybe some others.' She leans back and remembers something she meant to tell Mum. 'Hey, my Facebook page has a hundred followers!'

'Your what, luv?' Mum asks.

'My Facebook page,' Jenny groans. 'There's people I don't even know sharing it. And I got six sign-ups on GoFundMe.'

Mum shakes her head, looks at me. 'Do you know what she's talking about?'

'Don't even try,' I tell her. 'I'm going to find Ben.'

But Ben and Deb's campsite is empty, they aren't sitting around the fire. I check their tent, and they're not in there either. I thought maybe they might be listening to a radio or something but no. Then I notice their car is gone.

There isn't much else happening and the fire is dying down so Mum rounds us up and sends us off to have a shower and do our teeth and we bed down under the milk cart again.

Under Dad.

Or not.

I sleep through it. So does Jenny. I mean we were really knackered after the last couple of days and the thing with the bank in Port Fairy so I reckon a bomb could have gone off right over our heads we wouldn't have heard it.

You can't even see there's any special problem when we wake up. There are some people having breakfast and they've started the bonfire up again. Maybe there are a few more police, but it's hard to tell, I haven't been counting. I rub my eyes and look through the gum trees to where the sun is coming up. I don't have a watch, but Jenny has one on her phone. She's still lying in her swag, so I kick it. 'Hey, what's the time?'

'What?'

'What's the time?'

'Shut up, I'm sleeping.'

Now a police wagon pulls into the campground and four more police get out and there's definitely more than there were the night before.

'You want to get up,' I tell her. 'Something's happening.'

She crawls out of her bag and knocks her head on the bottom of the milk cart. I look for Mum. She usually has her swag at the end near our feet but it's already folded up, ready to throw in the milk cart. So are Coach Don's and Mr Garrett's. Mrs Alberti sees we're up and comes running over. She's in her nightie, with her bare skinny arms flapping as she runs. It's a bit scary, like watching a plucked chicken charge you full speed.

'Kids!' she says. 'It's OK.'

'What's OK?' Jenny asks.

'Where's Mum?'

'She hasn't been arrested,' Mrs Alberti says.

'She's been arrested?' I ask.

'She *hasn't* been,' Mrs Alberti says. 'She's just at the Warrnambool station, helping with inquiries.'

'About the bank in Port Fairy?' Jenny asks.

'Or the one in Yardley?' I ask.

'No, about the supermarket,' Mrs Alberti says. And she tells how the police were watching the people camping on the showground last night and they had a man on the gate checking on people coming in and out and they had a police car parked outside the bank just in case and how about 4 a.m. someone firebombed the supermarket.

And Jenny is all, well how do we get into town, and we should go to the police station too and tell them it isn't Mum, she was here. And I'm thinking how Deb and Ben's tent was empty last night.

Mrs Alberti doesn't let us go anywhere and the police aren't letting anyone on the campground leave and people are starting to get angry. It's one thing to join a funeral procession and spend a night around a bonfire, it's another thing to be penned up on the showground and not allowed to go home to your farms. But the Warrnambool police or the Geelong police or whoever they are, are ice cold, no one is going nowhere. Geraldine is taking lots of photos of angry farmers and police and interviewing people, but about what, I don't know – there's less action than a junior footy match.

So apart from standing around watching angry people yell at the police, there isn't much happening and Darren and I just start a kick-to-kick with some other kids and Jenny goes to get Danny Boy some feed and water and clean up his poops.

Finally Mum and Coach Don and Mr Garrett get driven back into the showground by Karsi in his police car and we run over.

'Mum?' Jenny asks, grabbing Mum and burying her head in her jumper. 'We thought ...'

'Don't you two worry about me,' Mum says, holding Jen with one arm and reaching for my hand with the other. 'Geelong has put Karsi in charge, at least until we get to Colac. Let me look at that.' She unwraps the bandage, which is a bit dirty now from the football game, and she prods a bit at the blisters with her fingers.

'Not too bad,' she sighs. 'I think you were lucky this time. Go get the medical kit, I want to dress it again.' She sounds annoyed.

'Are you mad?' I ask her. 'I'm sorry.'

'Oh, Jack.' She gives me a big hug, 'I'm not mad at you. It's the police and all this fuss, every single time we stop somewhere. It's not you at all.'

I go and get the medical kit and she washes my hand with antiseptic and then starts rubbing cream into it again. 'You know, your dad and me decided a long time ago there was no sense wrapping you in cotton wool. You have to live the life God gave you on your own terms. Sometimes the easy way, sometimes the hard way.' She takes me by the shoulders. 'If I get mad it's because you didn't check yourself, or Jenny. Or if you didn't tell me about something like this. OK? I'm never going to get mad if you tell me.'

'You did once,' I remind her.

'Testing each other by sticking pins in yourselves ...'

'Acupuncture pins!' I say. 'They're made for –'

She turns me around and pushes me off. 'Breakfast, now.'

Karsi goes and tells the other police to start letting people go and people virtually race back to their cars. Cars start streaming out of the showground and most turn left and head back to Portland and Port Fairy and Yardley where they came from. Only a few pull onto the road and wait for us. Ben and Deb's ute is one of them, I can see that though.

'That's them all gone,' Mr Garrett says. 'Whiff of trouble and they evaporate.'

'People will come and go as they please,' Mum says and then sees us. 'Hello, ratniks. Have you had breakfast?'

'Were you arrested?' I ask. 'Mrs Alberti said –'

'No, I wasn't arrested,' Mum says.

'I said you weren't,' Mrs Alberti tells her. 'But they hear the word arrested, that's all they can think of. What did they want then?'

'They wanted to put Tom's coffin in the back of a paddy wagon and drive it straight to Melbourne,' Mr Garrett said. 'But Dawny held her ground. You should have seen her.'

'Karsi was great too,' Coach Don says. 'The Warrnambool police were all for calling in the Health Department to force us to hand over the coffin, claiming it's a health risk and Karsi was like, I already got advice on the cadaver situation, we can talk about that in private and he disappears with them and whatever he says, it shuts them up.'

'What's a cadaver?' Jenny asks.

'It's a –' I go to answer but Mum talks over the top of me.

'It's like a coffin, luv,' Mum says. 'That's all. They wanted to take your dad off the milk cart and stop the procession.'

'Because of the supermarket?' I ask.

'And the banks,' Mum says. 'One of the police taped Don's recital of the Henry Lawson poem last night and they were trying to say it was an incitement to riot.'

Coach Don smiles. 'Maybe it was, a hundred years ago.'

'We're going to need to lawyer up,' Mr Garrett says. 'Karsi won't be able to hold them much longer. Some bully of a cop is going to step in and throw us all in the clanger and freight Tom off to Melbourne. We need legal.'

Geraldine has been standing up against her car, watching and listening and she says, 'He's right. But I wouldn't worry too much. *Herald Sun* is going to run the story today and they're talking syndication. They'll pay for a good lawyer for you, if you agree to go exclusive.'

Mum and the others look at her but Coach Don seems like the only one knows what she means.

'With you,' he asks. 'I'm guessing.'

'If you don't mind,' Geraldine says, moving into the circle. 'Or they can send someone else. Will probably want to anyway. Can't let a little girl from Geelong hog the story, can they?'

'What's it mean, exclusive?' Mr Garrett asks.

'Means we don't talk to any other papers, just the *Advertiser*,' Don says.

'Just the *Sun*,' Geraldine says. 'Through me. It'll go national though. Geelong, Sydney, Adelaide, Perth. Your husband dead, two banks and a supermarket burned down.'

'That Port Fairy bank didn't even catch properly on fire,' I say to Jenny and she shrugs.

Geraldine goes on, 'The horse and cart, the coffin in the back, police trying to shut you down. It's going to go ballistic, you know that? But you go exclusive, we can control it.'

Coach Don narrows his eyes. 'Exclusive print,' he says. 'Not television, and not radio.'

'Print and digital then,' Geraldine says back at him. 'Without digital we can forget talking them into giving us a lawyer.'

'Give us a minute,' Coach Don says, and the grown-ups get into a huddle. After a few minutes they break up. 'All right,' Coach Don says. 'When it comes to newspapers and news websites we'll only talk to you. But television and radio are still open slather. And we want to hear from a lawyer today and there'll be no nonsense with signing away rights or drawing up contracts, you got that? It's our word and yours.'

Geraldine reaches out her hand and they shake. 'Deal,' she says. Then she squats and says to Jenny and me, 'Now, didn't you two say something about planting a cross out on the highway this morning?'

* * *

There are about ten people out there on the road on top of the mob of us from the milk cart, Aunty Ell, Darren, Mr and Mrs Alberti and Geraldine with her camera and Detective Sergeant Karsi. There's four other cops but they don't join in. Jenny, me and Darren bang the cross in by the highway where the road exits from the showground and we all kneel.

'Now what?' Mum says to me.

I cross myself like Geraldine showed us. 'Hail Mary full of grace ...'

And that feeling starts crawling up out of my chest again, out of nowhere. So I concentrate on the words and I say them as loud as I can and Jenny is looking at me like, *why are you yelling?* but it works, and the words drown it out and push it back down where it came from.

Mum stands up, ruffles my hair. 'Pretty enthusiastic praying there, mate. You'll be dragging us all off to church next.

We get onto the main street and we can see the fire engines still cleaning up from the supermarket fire. Police have put up tape. Our procession is moving at a crawl and the cars aren't many but they all have their headlights on, and Karsi is still out front in his car and there's another police car behind.

People out on the street stop. There's some waving, but most just stare. Maybe they heard about the fire, maybe they heard about us, maybe even they made the connection. But it seems supermarkets aren't something they get riled up about because no one is shaking their fist at us like Mrs Alberti warned they might.

If anyone gets angry looks it's probably Ben and Deb in their beat-up ute which is painted pink and green and has their sign *Multinationals Killing Dairy Farmers* stuck to the back gate.

'What's a multinational?' I ask Mum.

'Companies you find all over the world,' she says. 'Like burger places.'

'Are burger places killing farmers?' I ask her. That would suck, if we also had to hate the burger places. I love burgers.

'Burger places are probably a bad example,' she says. 'I think they get their beef here in Australia. No, it's like the companies that make drugs. They make their medicines in America, sell them here and pay virtually nothing in tax.'

'So the banks and supermarkets are multinationals?'

'No, actually I think they're Australian. It's complicated ...'

'Hijacking our bloody protest,' Mr Garrett says. 'Bloody greenies.'

'It's not a protest,' Mum reminds him. 'It's a funeral.'

'Hijacking our bloody funeral,' Mr Garrett grumps and shakes the reins. 'Come up, Danny!'

We settle in for the long trek to Colac. Mr Garrett reckons we should break it into two bits. Get to Cobden today, stay at the recreation ground.

'No supermarkets, no banks,' he points out to Coach Don.

'There's a wotsit, an independent.'

'No one going to torch him,' Mr Garrett says. 'Bet *he's* not doing cheap milk.'

'Get someone to go on ahead and check?' Coach Don suggests. 'We don't want this to hurt the little people.'

'Probably a good idea,' Mr Garrett agrees.

I reach over and thump Jen's leg and point down the back of the milk cart behind Dad's coffin and we crawl down there where no one can hear us.

'There's some stuff you should know,' I say. 'I'm starting to think you were right.'

'What are you talking about?' she asks.

I make that noise with the back of my throat I know she hates. 'Like,' I tell her, 'did you know the bank manager and Dad once both went out with Mum?'

'What? No. What?'

'Pop told me. So obviously he'd do anything she asks. Right?'

'No. You're making that up.'

'Ask her.'

'Oh yeah sure. Hey, Mum, did you know the bank manager before he was bank manager?'

'True anyway. And before he was a bank manager, when he was at uni, he used to be a roo shooter in his holiday breaks.'

'Pop told you all this? So what?'

'And did you know that Coach Don has been to gaol? That's why he got kicked off the Geelong Reserves.'

'No way.'

'Way. They were on an end-of-footy-season trip and he got drunk and fell asleep and wouldn't get off the plane when they landed.'

'They send you to gaol for that?'

'No, they send you to gaol for hitting the man from the airline who was trying to wake you up. Sergeant Karsi witnessed for him but it didn't help. You learn things in gaol.'

'Like what?'

'Like how to make petrol bombs I bet. One more thing. Dr Watson was the doctor who delivered you and me when we were born. He's been our family doctor since before we even were a family.' I look at her like, *so, duh.*

She shakes her head. 'So what? Why are you telling me all this?'

'Freeby jaysus,' I say. 'You're the one said maybe it isn't Dad in that coffin! I have to spell it out for you?'

'The way your brain works, yeah, you do,' she says.

'The bank manager didn't kill Dad, but he still loves Mum and would do anything for her. He felt guilty about kicking us off the farm so he shot a roo and skinned it and put it in the house so it looked like a body. Then Dr Watson faked all the paperwork to make it look like Dad died in the fire and he told Karsi it was a heart attack.'

'Why?'

'So Dad could start blowing up banks and supermarkets,' I tell her, like it's poker and I'm laying down five aces. 'That car in Yardley, remember? I bet it was Coach Don who broke the window, but Dad threw in the petrol bomb. Now he's secretly following along behind us, doing these other fires and everyone thinks he's dead!'

She looks at me the way people look at zoo animals. 'I know what I said, but that is *completely* mental.' She crosses her arms.

I bang on the coffin behind me. It gives a very solid thud.

'What if it's not? What if it's just a dead kangaroo in there?'

She presses her back against the back rail of the milk cart and with all her might gives the coffin a shove with her foot, and hardly moves it. 'Or it could be dirt,' she says. 'Could be full of dirt and rocks.'

'Exactly.'

'Like your head.'

'So funny. We have to get a look inside,' I tell her.

The newspaper lawyer meets us in Cobden. There's not many who stay the night with us this time, maybe five cars, including Ben and Deb, who people are still not really talking to. There's one police car.

His name is Alasdair. With a 'd'. He says he doesn't work for the paper, he works for Cromwell Someone and Someone Else, which he obviously thinks people should be impressed by. He says he's an expert in criminals and law and he's done a lot of homework on this funeral procession thing. Geraldine is sitting beside him, but I can see she's trying to look like she isn't actually with him.

'I understand you have to be in Melbourne by Sunday,' he announces. 'So the clock is ticking. That works in our favour. Police know this thing has a limit.'

'Sergeant Karsi told us that much,' Mr Alberti scoffs. 'And he never worked for Cromwell F-nut and Sons.'

'They can go after your horse and cart,' Alasdair says. 'Defect it to take it off the road and force you to put the coffin in a hearse.'

'Just had it roadworthy certified,' Mr Garrett said. 'They'll find nothing.'

'Oh yes they will. The way this works is one morning you'll wake up to find your tail-light has spontaneously busted itself during the night. Or they'll pull you over, issue a notice to have the brakes checked, that's enough to get you off the road.'

'Let them bloody try it. I got contacts in the heavy-horse game. I can fix a tail-light in an hour, hell I can get another cart here inside a day,' Mr Garrett says, veins in his neck sticking out now.

'Good, that's good for them to know. We need to get them to see the best idea is just to keep you moving because if they do, this will all be over in a few days. Least, that's what I'll be telling them.'

'That's all we want,' Mum says. 'To get Tom to Melbourne, with dignity, while sending a message.'

Alasdair pats her knee, which I can see Mum hates. 'That's what we all want,' he says. 'But this business with the banks and supermarkets, that's got to stop.'

Mr Alberti goes red in the face. 'Are you accusing us?'

'No, no. But I spoke to the CIB in Geelong. They won't tell me anything about their investigation, but the way they spoke, it doesn't sound like they're close to being able to charge anyone. There are just too many people involved in this convoy of yours and it will take them months to sort out. They're used to taking their sweet time on arson, not working up against the clock like you're forcing them to, with the risk of a new bank or supermarket going up in flames every time you bowl into town. They want *you* to make a public appeal,' Alasdair says to Mum.

'Make a what?' Mum says.

'They want you to go on the radio and TV and ask people to stop. Tell them you're afraid someone will get hurt and you don't want that to happen.'

'I *don't* want that to happen,' Mum says. 'It's bad enough Tom killed himself, the fool. I don't want anyone else hurt, I don't want anyone going to gaol.'

'The police are willing to set up a press conference for you when you get to Colac. Geelong Command will send one of their top brass, and he'll do the hardball thing, say how they're going to come down on these arsons like a ton of bricks, then you'll get up and ask people to stop.'

'I can do that,' Mum says. She looks scared, but brave. 'I think I can.'

Alasdair looks happy as a cat dipped in cream. 'It would be a fantastic platform for your message,' he says. 'You'll have TV and radio there, and they'll probably broadcast live. Which leads me to this ...'

He has a bag with him and takes out a piece of paper. 'I know you said no contracts,' he says, looking at Coach Don. 'This is just a heads of agreement – some ground rules to be sure what we're agreed on.' He goes to hand it over to Coach Don.

'That wasn't the deal,' Geraldine says to him. She tries to grab the papers off him but he holds them out of her reach.

'This is what your bosses asked me to present,' he says to her. 'So can we just discuss it?'

Coach Don takes it and looks it over, then hands it to Mum. 'We're not signing that.'

Alasdair tries a smooth smile. 'It just says I'll continue to represent you in any matters civil and criminal for the duration of your trip to Melbourne. In return you assign exclusive rights to your story to the *Sun* and affiliates, just print and digital, mind. You retain TV and radio and any other rights. It's what you agreed on the phone.'

'I've met plenty of lawyers in my time,' Coach Don says, 'for better and worse, usually worse. There's always something in the fine print, especially the fine print that isn't printed. You've got our word, verbally. You can try to take that to court later if you aren't happy or you think we're not honouring the deal. But we're not signing away our rights to anything.' He looks at Mum. 'Right, Dawn?'

'Right,' Mum says, chewing her lip. 'We appreciate your help, Alasdair, Geraldine. But I also think we can probably muddle through without you.'

Alasdair looks like he wants to fight about it, but Geraldine is glaring at him and he changes his mind. 'OK,' he smiles, 'well, it's your funeral, as they say. I'll have to check with Melbourne if they're still willing to go ahead on the basis of a handshake deal. I'll get back to you after I call them.'

'You do that,' says Mr Alberti.

Cobden

The police have us staying at the rec ground in Cobden this time. It's not half as good as a showground, but there are change rooms where people can shower and use the toilet. We aren't allowed to park on the oval and the groundskeeper has come down and he's patrolling like one of those dogs at a car-wrecking place to make sure no one starts doing doughnuts on his turf.

Mum and Coach Don head into town to buy some stuff for dinner. Jenny's all wound up because she can't get internet and no one will lend her their phone, so she can't check her Facebook or GoFundMe pages and all she can do is ring some of her dumb girlfriends and ask them to check for her.

Three is such a dumb number. Four is so much easier. With four it doesn't matter if two people are off doing their own thing, there's still two who can hang out together. Like now. If Mum was in town and Jenny was obsessing with her phone I could be kicking a ball with Dad. Or we'd be setting up the barbecue, or sneak-listening to a footy or cricket game on the car radio and ducking down every time someone walked past in case they were looking for us. I look over at his coffin, thinking he'd better bloody be in there, leaving me hanging like this.

Aunty Ell is sitting by her car and waves me over. She's got a packet of a chips and a bottle of Coke. 'You want some?' she asks. 'Keep you going to dinner?' She hands me a cup and pours some Coke and gives me the chip packet.

'Where's Darren?'

'Off somewhere,' she says. 'We pull up, he's off like a greyhound that boy, hates being cooped up in the car. Maybe he could ride with you in the milk cart tomorrow?'

'I'll ask Mum,' I tell her.

'He'd love that,' she says. 'He's fascinated by that horse. Are you all right, love, you look a bit lost?'

I dive into the chips. 'No, I'm all right,' I tell her. We sit quietly for a while, just watching people set up their tables and chairs and tents. The Albertis have the best set-up, but they're full-time professional campers, go north every year. Their kids run their dairy, and they mostly just travel around Australia in their big campervan but they haven't got that, just their ute and a big stand-up tent. Mrs Garrett comes at the end of every day with food she's made during the day, usually a cooked chicken or roast beef and rolls and salad. Mr and Mrs Maynard have left their son to run their petrol station, and they've got some really basic picnic tables and chairs on Mr Maynard's Toyota flatbed and a little dome tent. Ben and Deb just have a little two-person tent and a couple of stools and their gas stove and they just make chicken, rice and beans and lentils and boil water for tea on it. They're also in town getting supplies, and asked do I want anything but I told them Mum has me covered.

'Do you think … nah, forget it,' I say to Aunty Ell.

'Think what, love?'

'Do you think there's any chance my dad is actually still alive?' I don't know what I expect. Maybe that Aunty Ell will look at me the way I looked at Jenny when she said it and tell me not to be mental. But she stretches out her legs and points at the ground next to hers. 'Pull that chair a bit closer.'

I scooch closer. I like how she smells, like camomile tea and soap. She's got some chip crumbs on the front of her blouse.

'I know exactly what you're feeling,' she says. 'You and your sister. My dad died when he was just forty. I was sixteen. He stepped out in front of a semitrailer going too fast through town, and that was it. I was in Melbourne at school and when they told me I didn't believe them. I tried to make them show me his body, prove he was dead. They wouldn't do it, said he was too badly banged up. He used to disappear all the time, he and Mum would have a fight and he'd go back to where his mob came from up near Lismore, months at a time. So I told myself they were lying to me, maybe he and Mum had a fight and Dad had left her and just gone back to Lismore. He was too angry to say a proper goodbye, he'd just taken off.'

'But he was dead?'

'Yeah, mate, he was. I took a bus to Lismore with my own money and went to my grandmother's place and she told me. He wasn't there. He was buried under a rock in Yardley cemetery, that's where he was.'

I look across at the milk cart with the coffin on it and she sees me looking.

'That's where your dad is, luv,' she says. 'And when we get to Carlton we're going to put him in the ground and put a rock over him and you can visit him there whenever you go to Melbourne.'

Jenny comes running over to us and she's waving her arms like a windmill.

'You've got to see this! You too, Aunty, come on!'

She's over at Ben and Deb's tent and they've let her log on to the net through Deb's phone.

'Sit, sit, sit!' she says.

Deb is smiling her awesome smile and Ben is sitting legs crossed, making a pot of tea.

'It's pretty cool,' Deb says. 'I recommend you get comfortable.'

'Is she surfing on your phone?' Aunty Ell asks, looking a bit worried.

'Don't worry,' Deb says. 'My dad pays the bill. He's just glad he can always get in touch, so he knows I'm all right.'

'OK then,' Aunty says.

'He'd be here with us if he could,' she says. 'He's seen what's happening here and he's with you a hundred percent.'

'Where's he live then?' Aunty asks.

'Adelaide. Works for a mining company.'

'They've heard about this in Adelaide?'

'Sit, look,' Deb says, and gives Aunty Ell her stool. 'Show them the news site.'

'There's us praying this morning! There's you, Aunty Ell, and there's Darren!' Jenny says. 'There's the signs on our milk cart! There's the milk cart, Danny Boy, wait, here it comes … There's me and you and Coach Don in the back. Look at the convoy, it looks like about twenty cars but it wasn't that many.'

'I can see, Jenny,' I tell her, 'I'm not blind. There's you two,' I say to Ben and Deb and point to their ute driving past the camera as it zooms in on their sign.

'Here's the best bit,' she says. On the screen with the newspaper logo is a picture of Geraldine talking into a microphone with a person in the street of Cobden. 'You can't hear him,' Jenny says, 'but this person thinks it's terrible about what happened with the supermarket in Warrnambool and there's people that will lose their jobs maybe because of it, but he can understand that people out here are angry. They've had enough and they're at wotsit. What is it?' she asks Deb.

'Breaking point,' Deb says.

'It's the same on the ABC, and the other newspaper is showing a video someone took from the side of the road. But they're not all nice,' Jenny says. 'Look.' She clicks on a link and there's a news page with a headline *DEATH CONVOY LEAVES BURNED BUSINESSES IN ITS WAKE.*' It shows a group of angry people waving their fists.

'I never saw those people,' I say, grabbing her phone to see if I recognise any of the faces.

'It doesn't say the picture was taken on this trip,' Ben says. 'Some media do that, they reuse old pictures and make it look like it happened today when it happened maybe years ago, or somewhere else.'

'Who cares,' Jenny says. 'Have a look at this.' She grabs her phone back and opens her Facebook page and shoves it in front of us.

'No,' I say.

'Oh yeah,' she says. 'Five thousand eight hundred follows! Only four angry faces on all the posts. My video of Coach Don saying the hob-nail boots poem got five hundred likes and twenty shares!'

'I didn't know you videoed that.'

'I video *everything*,' she says. 'If you had your own Facebook page you'd know that. I posted you and Darren kicking the footy with Danny Boy in the background and it got two hundred likes and ten shares!'

'That's good, Jenny, your mum will be proud, how you're getting the message out,' Aunty Ell says and Jenny beams, but she's still busting.

'That's nothing,' she says. 'You know my GoFundMe page?'

'No, dear,' says Aunty Ell.

'It's a fundraising page. I set it up to ask people to donate towards the costs of the funeral procession and the fight against the banks and supermarkets. I link to it from all the posts on my Facebook page.'

'Your mum isn't fighting the banks and supermarkets,' Aunty Ell says. 'She wants people to know they're strangling us, but she isn't fighting them.'

'What is it then,' Ben asks her, 'if the banks and supermarkets are driving people broke, kicking them off farms they've owned for generations, forcing people to suicide and desperation, sending small towns and businesses broke and finally someone like Dawn speaks out about it? What's that if it's not a fight?'

'It's a funeral procession, love, with a difference. But it isn't a revolution.'

'I can change what it says,' Jenny says. Then she looks up at Ben. 'They were Ben's words.'

'I think you should ask your mum,' Aunty Ell says. 'Let her decide.'

'Anyhoo,' Jenny says. I can hear she's frustrated. 'Have a look.' She points at a number in a table. 'This is how much people have given! One thousand and something people have given an average of ten dollars each!'

'That's ... Ten thousand bucks,' I say, doing the maths. 'Ten *thousand* bucks?!'

'Yep, wait. Ten thousand four hundred and fifty,' she says. 'I bet when I check back later it'll be more.'

I look at her. 'Could we pay off some of our loan with that money? If we gave it to the bank?'

'I don't know,' she says, and looks at Aunty Ell.

'I don't know how much you owe, pet,' Aunty Ell says. 'But I'd guess it's a whole lot more than that.'

'It'll pay for the funeral though, right?' Jenny says. 'It'll pay people's petrol to Melbourne maybe even?'

'Maybe it will,' Aunty Ell says. 'You clever girl.'

We're expecting Mum to be over the moon but she just looks worried when she gets back from the shops with dinner and Jenny tells her about the money.

'Where's all the money go?' she asks. 'When people donate it?'

'Into my PayPal account,' Jenny says. 'I had to write something so I wrote down my PayPal. It goes there.'

'You have a PayPal account?'

'Mum, you set it up for me so I could play Minecraft, remember?'

'Oh yeah. Do we pay tax on the donations?'

'You could ask your lawyer friend,' Aunty Ell says. 'See what he says.'

'What are we going to do with it?' Mum asks, like it's the biggest problem on earth.

We're sitting having dinner with Coach Don and the

others. It's just ham sandwiches and tea. I tried toasting mine over the fire someone lit in a barbecue pit, but that just made them smoky not toasty.

'Like she said,' Coach Don says. 'Just use the money for the costs of the funeral and if anyone asks for petrol money sure, you could give them a bit.'

'How do we get it out of PayPal,' Mum asks. 'I just don't know anything about how it all works.'

'Ben and Deb could use a bit of money,' I say.

'Did they ask you?' Mr Garrett says, getting ready to be annoyed.

'No, I just know they're living on rice and canned corn and they've only got enough money to get to Melbourne and then they'll be broke.'

'They've been with us from the start,' Jenny says. 'Like everyone else.'

'For a reason,' Coach Don says. 'They want to hijack this thing for their own ends.'

'And what ends are they?' Aunty Ell asks.

'I don't know,' Coach Don says. 'World bloody peace, save the forests, stop coal mining, reforest the bloody golf courses, all that rot.'

'Sounds terrible,' Aunty Ell agrees with a smile, which means she doesn't. 'Give 'em some petrol money, eh Dawn?'

'I reckon,' Mum says. 'If Jenny can tell me how.'

That's when Karsi comes up. 'I've been ordered back to Portland,' he says.

All the grown-ups stand, like they're getting ready to say goodbye.

'Highway Patrol will take it from here,' he continues. 'You'll have cars front and back to escort you from Colac tomorrow and they'll be with you all the way to Melbourne. I've also heard they're going to have uniforms outside every supermarket and bank in town the whole time you're there.' He smiles. 'So spread the word, will you. Anyone tries any silly business in Colac, they're going to get caught.'

I look at Coach Don, but he's smiling a smile like there's some sort of secret conversation going on only him and Karsi can understand. 'I'll do that,' he says.

'So, this is goodbye then?' Mr Maynard says, and he wipes his hand on his trousers to get the chicken grease off it and sticks it out.

Karsi doesn't take it. 'Not likely,' he says. 'You think I'd go home and just watch on TV to see how this all turns out? I told Geelong I'm taking a week's leave,' he says. He looks around and grins. 'If you'll have me?'

Jenny spends the whole night telling anyone who'll listen about her Facebook followers and GoFundMe page and that means she gets to bed way after me. So I have tons of time lying on my back looking up at the bottom of the milk cart. I thought a hundred times about dragging my swag out from under the milk cart and sleeping out in the open but it's that time of year where you never know if it's going to rain in the middle of the night and that would suck even more than sleeping under a coffin. We totally got burned like that one night when there was this total eclipse and Dad had us all sleeping outside on camping mattresses and it was cloudy so we didn't even see the eclipse and no one slept at all because if it wasn't bad enough with the frogs in the dam croaking away or the mosquitos biting, about three in the morning it started raining. We all ran inside and Mum was angry because our sheets and doonas were all wet but Dad was laughing and he made a pot of tea and then cooked drop scones, which are basically just flour and milk and eggs all whipped together and fried in butter. Because we were up all night, we didn't have to go to school next day. I was going to remind Jenny about that, but I must have gone to sleep before she came to bed.

We start so early the next morning Jenny sleeps the most of the next day in the back of the milk cart, curled up in her swag at the back behind Dad's coffin. I ask Mr Garrett can Darren ride with Mum and us, and he says sure thing, and so me and Darren spend the whole day in the milk cart playing Spotto and I Spy and Bullshit. We have lunch in a parking bay on the side of the highway where there are toilets and while we're waiting maybe another ten cars join us. Mr Garrett says they're farmers from Colac, come to join in for a while, and he knows some of them from the shows. There's whole families in the cars and they bring tons of cakes and biscuits and stuff and so we have a real feast. One even gives Darren and me a bag of Snakes but I have to share with Jenny because of course she wakes up for lunch.

I guess we're about twenty cars long, our convoy, with Danny Boy still going strong, even if he isn't very fast. As we get to the sign on the way into town, which says *Welcome to Colac*, we start seeing them. On the side of the road people are standing and they've planted little white crosses in the grass beside the highway. Actually some are quite big white crosses, up to their waists, some of them, and some of them even have *#BURN* written in the middle.

'Dairy people,' Coach Don says, waving to a bunch of people standing beside a bunch of crosses. 'They know what this is about. Some of 'em even knew Tom probably.'

The police direct us into the showground again and there's a bit of an argument when the guy who owns the caravan park next door wants to charge us for staying at the showground but the police sort him out and tell him he can't charge us for using the oval at the showground and that he's going to let us use his toilets and showers and he isn't going to charge us for that either. Mum is busy because the Victoria Police want to do a press conference on WIN TV with her, so we're free to go exploring.

You can't exactly see the lake from where they put us, but it's only a few hundred metres down the road and a bunch of us kids take off and go check it out. It's too cold to swim, but we chuck rocks and one kid goes in and dares everyone else but no one else does.

* * *

It's just one of those dumb things. Mum always says they come in threes. We've got time to kill, so me and Darren are playing this game we call Droppit, where you face each other about ten feet apart and throw a cricket ball to the other person, nice and easy. If the other person catches it, you both take a step back, then the other person throws, and you keep going until one of you drops it and see how far apart you can get. Our record is thirty-eight steps. Anyway we're at about thirty steps and Darren is throwing and he tosses it really high up and I lose it in the sun and it comes down out of the sky and hits me right on the cheek.

I pick it up and go to throw it back to him so we can start over, but he's looking at me strange, so I put my hand to my cheek and it's covered in blood. He comes running over.

'Oh wow, sorry,' he says. 'I didn't mean ... I think it split your cheek.' He reaches into his pocket and pulls out a handkerchief and holds it up to my face. He dabs a bit while I stand still looking up at the sky. 'Yeah, it's not too bad. Just a lot of blood.' He takes my hand and guides it to the cloth, 'Here, you hold it. Press tight.'

'Freaking annoying,' I say.

'You probably want to sit down,' he says, sitting down himself, so I sit next to him.

'We would have got the record this time, I reckon,' I tell him.

'Yeah. You know I think it's amazing, how you and your sister are,' he says.

I look at him. 'We're freaks.'

'No, really,' he says.

'You don't have to feel bad about it, just because I split my face open,' I tell him. 'It's OK. Everyone thinks we're freaks, even if they don't say it.'

'I don't think you're freaks,' he says.

'Right.'

'I don't. It's more like you have superpowers or something. Like you're some kind of superheroes,' he says. He lifts my hand away from my face, then puts it back. 'Keep the pressure on, you're still bleeding.'

'Superhero that's bleeding to death,' I say. 'Some superhero.'

'No, I mean, you know. You grab a boiling hot billy, you take a cricket ball to the face and you don't even react. Most kids would be lying on the ground, wailing, but you just pick the ball up, go to throw it back.'

I pull the handkerchief away and look at it. It's a green material, so the blood stains it black. I think the bleeding's slowing down now.

He goes on, 'You should play rugby or something. You'd be like, guys coming at you, hit you hard enough to knock down any normal person, but you'd be all, what? That's all you got?'

I laugh, which only encourages him more.

'Yeah, or be a cage fighter, like UFC. Some lunatic pounding on you, you just let him go until his knuckles are all broken and he's got no wind left, then wham, you bring that sucker down!' He mimes it as he's telling it.

'I reckon he'd knock me out with his first hit,' I tell him. 'Feeling no pain doesn't protect you from getting your skull cracked.'

'Yeah, OK. What does it feel like, to not feel?' he asks.

It's not as stupid a question as it sounds. 'I don't know. The nurse at the hospital said it must be like feeling the world through gardening gloves and woollen socks.'

'Except you hit someone's hands with a hammer if they're wearing gardening gloves, they're going to feel that, but you wouldn't.'

'Yeah, no. Dorotea's analgesia is supposed to be not as bad as other kinds, so I guess I can feel something. I mean, I haven't bitten my tongue off accidentally, or ripped off a fingernail without noticing. It just isn't what *you* call pain.'

He leans in and I freak a bit, thinking he's going to hug me or something, so I pull back, but he's just looking at my cut cheek.

'It's still bleeding,' he says. 'We're going to have to tell your mum.'

'Can we not?' I say to him. 'Not yet. Can we just sit here for a while?'

'Sure,' he says.

It's not too bad, sitting there in the late afternoon sun with Darren, all the commotion going on around us, but none of it touching us. Mum is going to go spare when she sees my face, but right now things are OK. They're almost normal for once.

'I've got an idea,' he says.

'Yeah?'

'Yeah, you could be like a boxer. And I'd be your manager. And we wouldn't make money on your fights, we'd make money betting how many hits you could take to the face.'

OK, so much for normal.

Colac

I can't avoid it forever so I go over to Mum to show her my face, but a man is putting a microphone on her. Like a rock star wears. He puts it over her ears and threads it down her back under her shirt and clips it to the waist of her jeans at the back.

'Say something for me,' he tells her, holding some headphones to his ear.

'I feel like an idiot,' she says.

'Perfect, thanks,' he says and goes back to his camera on its tripod.

'Dawn, I'm Stan Einfeld from FRX news, can I have a word?' asks a man in a suit with a blue tie and side-parted sandy hair and white teeth and white knuckles. He's holding a microphone.

Mum looks around. 'Well, I don't know, we have an arrangement with the *Sun*, for newspaper and digital …'

'We're radio, Dawn,' the man smiles. 'Won't keep you but a minute, I know you're about to go live.'

'Well, I guess …'

The cameraman swings his camera around too, just for the practice I guess since he isn't actually with the radio guy, and puts it on Mum.

'Thank you, Dawn. Our listeners are no doubt wondering, does someone have to die before you stop this pointless protest?'

Mum goes quiet. I know that look. I've seen people yell at Mum at the soccer, I've seen Jenny answer her back; it's the same look. She doesn't get bothered, she doesn't yell back. You take Mum on, she just goes quiet, but when she's done being quiet …

'A man already died,' Mum says to him. 'My husband.'

'And you have our condolences, Dawn, but people are burning down businesses in your name,' the man interrupts her. 'Your protest group is being accused of arson. If someone dies in one of these fires, the blood will be on your hands, won't it?'

'This is a funeral procession,' Mum says, 'not a protest. Now if you'll excuse me, I have to get ready.'

'Dawn, you can't hide from …' the man follows her, but she ignores him so he gives up and starts looking for someone else to bother.

There's a woman dressed in a blue skirt and white shirt running around trying to get Mum to stand in the right spot and also get all the other people to move out of her shot, and she shoos the radio reporter away. I give Mum a wave and she smiles a weak little smile but she's not really looking at me, she's looking behind me and I turn around and I don't know where they came from but there's about ten reporters there now, with microphones and hand-held recorder things on top of the two with big cameras on tripods and they're standing talking with each other but with one eye on Mum so they don't miss it when she starts.

There are two of those big vans with satellite dishes and some lights set up and I go look at them but it's pretty boring. Mum and the others are talking to some police who have hats and jackets on. One is talking with Geraldine and he looks like the boss.

Karsi is leaning up against Mr Alberti's car and watching with half a smile on his face as I walk past. 'Hey there, detective,' he says and points at a policeman in a uniform with a lot of buttons on it. 'The Big Cheese has arrived. Your mum is nervous as hell.'

'Is she all right?' I ask him.

'She'll be great. You want to get closer so she can see you, give her a thumbs-up or something.' He bends over. 'Wait, what's up with your face, mate?'

I'm about to make something up when it goes quiet as the woman in the blue skirt and a clipboard climbs up onto the back of a ute and shushes everyone. 'Hi, everyone. Regional Superintendent Dawson is going to address the media first, followed by Mrs Murray, and after that there will be the chance for questions to the Superintendent.'

'What about you, Mrs Murray?' one of the reporters asks. 'Will you answer questions?'

Mum opens her mouth but the lady steps in. 'Mrs Murray can speak with the media privately afterward if she wishes. She won't be part of the official question-and-answer session.'

They're not happy about that, but they don't have time to complain about it because the Boss Cop climbs up onto the ute, clears his throat and says, 'Ladies and gentlemen, can we begin?'

They've got a TV camera there pointing up at him and a bunch of microphones taped to a small stepladder. Mum climbs up beside him.

'Right,' he says. 'Firstly, I have to say the condolences of the Victoria Police go out to Mrs Murray here for the death of her husband following a fire on his property some days ago. We fully respect her right to transport him to Melbourne for burial in whatever manner she chooses, and as you can see we are facilitating the funeral procession in a manner intended to minimise disruption to traffic.'

'He looks annoyed,' Jenny whispers from behind me.

'Yeah, but I think that's his normal look,' I tell her.

'On the other hand, a number of serious incidents have taken place in towns which this funeral procession has visited,' the police officer continues. 'A bank was petrol-bombed in Yardley, another in Port Fairy and a supermarket was completely destroyed by fire in Warrnambool,' he says.

A small cheer goes up from the people watching on and the boss cop frowns at them. 'This isn't a matter for public amusement,' he says. 'Whoever is doing this is putting the lives of police, firefighters and the general public at risk through their reckless actions. Every one of these incidents is being investigated, and the criminals will be brought to justice, but I am making a public appeal today to whoever is doing this – you're not helping your cause, you're just hurting the very communities you probably think you're trying to help. Mrs Murray?'

He steps a bit to the side and makes space for Mum and she kind of shuffles into the middle of the platform.

'My husband Tom died burning our own house down so the bank wouldn't get it. I thought he was stupid for doing it, and I told him so, but he wouldn't be talked out of it and it cost him his life.' She takes a big breath and tells people about milk prices and farmers going broke.

The police officer tries to look like this has nothing to do with him, but after a minute he gives Mum a look and she takes her cue. 'This business with the banks and supermarkets being set on fire,' she says, 'has nothing to do with me or this funeral procession. Whoever is doing it, I want you to stop before someone gets hurt or put in gaol.' A bunch of cameras fire their flashes and Mum flinches, but she takes a piece of paper from her pocket and with her hand shaking, she unfolds it. 'There's a poem doing the rounds,' she says. 'It's by a fellow called Henry Lawson.'

'Good on you, Dawn!' someone yells, and there's some clapping, which dies down quickly as Mum clears her throat. The police officer is a bit unsure if he should stay up on the ute or step down and he looks at the lady in the blue skirt and she just shrugs.

Mum raises her voice:

'Rise Ye! rise ye! noble toilers! claim your rights with fire and
    steel!
Rise ye! for the cursed tyrants crush ye with their iron heels!
They would treat ye worse than slaves! they would treat ye
    worse than brutes!
Rise and crush the selfish tyrants! Crush them with your
    hob-nailed boots!'

Then she folds the poem and she stands there in front of everyone and she lifts her fist in the air and she holds it there and people start cheering and the media start yelling and now the police officer decides it's time for him to get off the ute and out of there and Mum just stands there with her fist raised and so does Coach Don and Mr Alberti and Mr Garrett and Ben and Deb and Aunty Ell and Darren and pretty much everyone else except the police.

The police aren't happy with Mum's speech. They say she was giving Mixed Messages and that her speech was bordering on an Incitement To Riot. But Alasdair is here and he points out that to his knowledge there's no law against quoting Henry Lawson and he'd like to see them arrest someone for doing it. The police officer says it's all about context and who the hell is Alasdair anyway so Alasdair has to explain who he is and go off and talk to the police while Mum talks to reporters and Jenny and me get sent into town to buy an ice cream to get us out of her hair.

We hear that the video of Mum reading the poem was on the seven o'clock news on the ABC and then she's on the radio soon enough. About eight o'clock more and more people start parking around the showground and Mr Garrett says they're all dairy farmers who've seen the news and are coming in to show their support. At first the police try to turn them away but people just park their cars on the side of the road and walk in, so the police give up and open the showground gates again and soon it's like a circus has rolled into town — there are tables and stalls and tents and people pouring beer from kegs in the back of utes and about a half-dozen bonfires going and kids everywhere running around. It's mad.

Mum gets a roll of white cotton from I don't know where and she set us kids to chopping it into metre-long lengths and a bit further down she has people with paint and brushes painting slogans on the flags and Deb and Ben are supervising people putting them on poles.

'What are we doing this for?' Jenny whines after a while when she gets sick of cutting up linen.

'You'll see tomorrow,' Mum says. 'Just keep cutting until we run out of cloth, or poles, or paint.'

Then she looks at me, looking at me properly for the first time that evening. 'Jack Murray, what the *hell* have you done to your face?'

'I did check him! Why do you think he has a bandaid on it?' Jenny is saying.

'Why didn't you tell me?' Mum says to me, really angry, peeling back the plaster.

'I tried,' I say, 'but you were talking to reporters!'

'If I can't trust you both with things like this, I'm going to send you up to Uncle Leo and you can wait for me there.'

'I checked him!' Jenny insists. 'I put disinfectant on and it wasn't bleeding any more and it wasn't deep, so I put on a bandaid! What the hell else am I supposed to do?'

'Do *not* use that tone with me, Jenny Murray,' Mum says, going all calm, so you know there's a storm brewing. But Jenny doesn't see it, or doesn't care.

'He's the one keeps hurting himself, but you're blaming me! If you weren't so damn busy talking to your stupid police and reporters –'

And that's when Mum slaps her. Right across the face. It's not hard, but it's sharp and loud enough a few people hear it and turn around. Deb and Ben are closest, and look at us, worried. It's the first time she ever slapped either of us, and I just stand there, shocked.

Jenny glares back at her. 'Go ahead! Hit me again if it makes you feel better! I can't *feel* it anyway!'

Mum holds a hand up to her mouth, like she's the one who's been slapped, and Jenny keeps standing there, like she's daring her, staring her down, until Mum turns away and walks off toward the washrooms, her arms wrapped around herself.

I want to go after Mum, but I see Mrs Alberti running after her, so I stay put.

'Wow,' I say.

Now Jenny glares at me, 'Shut up! It's your fault.'

'She hit you,' I say. 'She never ever ...'

Deb comes over, 'You OK, honey?' she says to Jenny. 'You want to sit with us a moment?'

Jenny looks at her, says nothing.

'I can make you a cup of tea,' Deb says.

'I don't want your stupid tea,' Jenny says and walks off in the opposite direction to Mum, going I don't know where.

'O-K. How about you, Jack?' Deb says. 'Tea?'

'I should check on Mum,' I say, looking over to the ladies' washrooms.

'I'd give her a moment,' she says, looking over there too. 'Your mum is under incredible pressure.'

'That's no excuse for slapping Jen,' I say. 'She didn't do anything. She should have slapped *me* if she was upset about my stupid face.'

Deb puts her arm around my shoulders and walks me toward their campsite. 'I know, it's not OK, what she did.

But it's not about you, or Jen. It's your dad, the farm, the debt, the funeral, the police, the media …'

'We could have just buried Dad in Yardley and I don't know … got on with our lives,' I say. 'Like normal people. Not this stupid funeral thing.'

She sits me down in one of their camp chairs. Ben is there, but he's quiet. Just puts the kettle on the burner and sits down.

'Most people would have done that,' Deb says. 'Your mum isn't most people. She wants your dad's death to mean something.'

'And what about us?' I ask her. 'Did she ask what *we* want?'

The whole thing with Jenny and Mum just makes me more determined than ever to find out what really happened to Dad. Karsi didn't buy my theory the bank man murdered Dad and he isn't buying my new idea Dad's death might have been faked. He's standing by his police car doing his teeth using water in a cup when I tell him my theory.

'I don't know a soft way to say this, Jack, but I investigated the scene,' he says. 'Wasn't any mystery about it. Your dad lit the fire, your dad died in the fire. You can spend your whole life asking how or why, but it will still come down to that.'

'OK.'

I must sound a bit disappointed. 'Look,' he says, softening a bit. 'These are all fair questions. We asked ourselves some of these things. But we found a body in there and we even asked ourselves, that person we found in your house, was it your dad or could it be someone else?'

'Was he ... was he burned real bad?' I ask.

'He was. A burning roof fell on him. But we figure he was dead by then already,' he says, wincing.

'Then how do you *know* that it was him?' I ask. 'Maybe it was someone else?'

'We know,' he says.

'Did you do fingerprints or DNA?' I ask. 'It could have been an animal.'

'You watch too much TV, mate,' he says. 'Seriously. A man tells the world he's going to burn down his house, the house burns down, the man goes missing, a dead man is found inside the burned-down house ... we don't need DNA.'

'Dental records?' I ask.

'No, we didn't check his teeth,' Karsi says. 'Or take a hair sample. Dr Watson did the post-mortem, he ID'd your dad, he signed the death certificate. He's known your dad since before you were born.' He does the squatting-down thing again. 'Your dad died in the fire he set in his own house,' he says. 'I figure the fire went faster than he expected. He was running out when his heart gave up on him, and that was just bad luck. I'm sorry, Jack, but that's what happened.' He spits out his toothpaste and gives me his serious look, 'I thought you were going to leave your dad's death with me?'

'I know.'

'How about this then, how about you try to work out who's setting all these fires and get back to me with your ideas on that?'

'OK.'

'Right then, detective. Get to it.' He bends down to look in his side mirror and starts picking his teeth with a toothpick, so I know we're done.

Yeah, I'm not leaving anything with Karsi. I've seen this show. It's the one where the local cops completely mess up the investigation because they're lazy or dumb or think they know everything. The police find a body but they don't check DNA, don't check dental records, can't get fingerprints? It could have been a damn roo or a dog or a sheep they found in there.

I have to get a look inside that coffin.

Mum takes Jenny for a long walk after that and it could go two ways, knowing Jenny. Either she comes back, says nothing, and then runs away in the night and joins the navy (don't ask me, she's the one says all the time that's what she's going to do one day), or she'll work it out with Mum and they'll be fine.

I'm watching for signs when they get back, but they're not easy to read. So when we go over to the washrooms to get ready for bed, I ask her.

'So?'

'So what?' she says, making like nothing has happened.

'Did she say sorry?'

'Yeah.'

'And are you two OK now?'

'Yeah.'

'Really?'

'Yes, all right?' she says and stops. 'Just do everyone a favour and try not to burn yourself, cut yourself or break any damn bones until we get to Melbourne, OK?'

'OK.'

'We've got enough problems without your stupid ...'

'I said OK, all right?'

'All right then.' She reaches out and shoves me so hard I nearly fall over. 'I fuckin' love you, you bloody idiot. You know that, right?'

I get my balance. 'Wouldn't know it, the way you've been lately,' I tell her. Then I realise how that sounds and I reach out like a zombie and do a zombie voice, 'Go on, giff me hug.'

She flips me a finger and runs off. 'Hug this.'

Jenny and I pass out in seconds in our sleeping bags after all the drama. There isn't any trouble during the night even though there were plenty of people who never even went to bed, just stayed up drinking. I mean trouble with banks or such, but I hear there was a little punch-up and the police pulled over a man who tried to drive home drunk and hit a fence. Mr Garrett says that probably happens a few times a week in Colac, so it's no biggie.

We get some cereal and then Mr Garrett goes around yelling at people to get up and plenty of them aren't in the mood, but eventually he and Coach Don bully them into action.

Mum sets people to work painting more signs while Mr Garrett and Jenny start getting Danny Boy ready, and Alasdair shows us how to fix our signs to the milk cart, rather than having to hold them or just hang them off the sides. He also shows us not to make them too small and how you needed fewer words and bigger letters. Jenny and Ben make us all Milo.

'Done a few demonstrations in your time then?' Mum asks Alasdair when we're done.

'You mean funeral processions,' he says, tipping his mug at her.

'Of course. Done a few funeral processions in your time?'

'Lawyers are either right-wing nuts or left-wing nuts,' he shrugs. 'I guess I'm the left-wing, public-defender, hopeless-cause kind of nut.'

'Not hopeless, surely,' Mum says.

'Oh, I'll get you to Melbourne,' he says. 'But whether it will make any difference ...'

'Every flood starts with single raindrop,' Mum says.

'Actually, I think the saying is, the first raindrop doesn't feel responsible for the flood,' Alasdair replies.

'I like mine better,' Mum says. 'Besides, we've got real insurance now, don't we, Jenny?' She gives Jenny a nudge.

'What?'

'Got your PayPal thing happening, get us all the way to Melbourne, right? Maybe even help a bit with the costs of the funeral.'

'Oh yeah. For sure now,' Jenny says, taking the praise. If she's still mad at Mum, she's decided not to let it show.

'I heard something about that,' Alasdair says. 'Crowdfunding, right?'

'Yeah,' Jenny says, like it's no big deal, but I know she's busting to tell it.

'How much now?' he asks.

'Let me check,' she says, pulling out her phone. 'I mean, it seems like every time I check, it's ... No!'

Mum sighs, 'It was a mistake, right?'

Jenny looks up at her, a bit pale. 'Thirty-eight thousand,' she says and looks at her phone again, 'eight hundred and fifty.'

'Thirty-eight thousand ... dollars?' Mum asks.

'Yeah, since,' she looks a bit shifty, 'I put some pictures of our house and the video of your poem and ...'

'And what?' Mum asks.

'A ... picture ... of Dad and me,' she says. 'I said all the money goes to the funeral and trying to help us get the farm back again.'

'We can't ...' Mum says and then I can tell she thinks twice. 'We can't just take money from strangers.'

That's not what she was going to say, I bet. I bet she was going to say, 'We can't buy back the farm.' I bet even *sixty-eight* thousand isn't enough for that.

'That's taxable, as income,' Alasdair says. 'By the way.'

'We pay tax on it?' Mum says. 'Even when we're bankrupt?'

'If you're bankrupt, your debtors can seize it. Did you declare yourselves bankrupt?' he asks, frowning.

'Not officially. We've got nothing but debts – we've got no money. The bank foreclosed on the farm,' she says. 'That's what this is all ...'

'I need to set up a trust fund for you,' Alasdair says. 'In the kids' names. Not connected to your dairy business. Move the money there straight away and we need to make sure any other donations get moved to the trust fund, not to your personal accounts.'

'I don't know ...' Mum says.

'Perfectly legal, as long as the money goes straight from the crowdfunding account that's in your daughter's name,' he says. 'Otherwise you might as well give it directly to the bank or the tax department.'

'Won't all that mean fees?'

'I can set it up for you,' he says. 'Gratis. Or, well, it costs a couple hundred in State duties – one-off fees. You'll have to pay those. Or if you don't want me involved, I can recommend someone.'

Mum sucks on her teeth. That means 'maybe probably yes'. 'I'll think on it,' she says.

'Don't think too long,' Alasdair says. 'It helps that the fundraiser is in your daughter's name, not yours, but if your creditors get a sniff there's serious money floating around, they'll get it locked up tight and argue about it later.' He looks at Jenny, 'And that is serious money starting to roll in there. You told people you're going to use the money to "help with the funeral and buy back the farm"? Were those your exact words?'

Jenny thinks for a moment. 'No, I wrote "help with the funeral and help us make a new start".'

'OK, that's good. Keep it general like that. If you get too specific and you use the money for anything else, people can get angry, even sue you for misusing the money.' He must realise he sounds really serious, so he smiles and tries to make a joke. 'No buying ice cream and lollies with it, OK?'

There's a big hold-up when we're all trying to get out of the showground because the Colac police try to say we don't have a permit to march down the street, but the media and cameras are already there and between Alasdair and Sergeant Karsi and Coach Don and a man from the local Farmers First branch someone manages to talk the police into letting us get on our way and it's like being royalty, with people and signs waving and the horse clopping and Mum up front like the Queen of Colac.

'Just sit up the back, you two, and hold your sign,' Mum says as I jump up onto the seat beside her.

'No, why?' I complain.

'Mine or his?' Jenny says. 'Mine's better.'

'As if,' I say. So we end up each holding our own sign which means we don't have a hand to hold on to the milk cart with and we keep falling over every time Danny Boy has to pull up suddenly because of the people in front.

There are tons of police this time, more than you would see at a footy match at the MCG even.

'Look at Darth Vader over there,' Coach Don says, and waves to a policeman dressed all in black, with black sunglasses on, standing with his hand on his belt. 'Thinks a fifty-year-old dairy farmer's wife is going to overthrow the government.' Mum shoots him a look. 'Not that you couldn't, if you wanted to,' he says. He lifts his fist in the air like Mum did the night before. 'People Power, Dawny!' he says with a grin. She smacks him on the shoulder.

People see him doing it and it's freaky because all down the side of the main street people start lifting their fists in the air as we pass them, not cheering, just standing there quiet with their fists raised. Geraldine is in a ute behind us, standing in the back taking photos, and I bet she gets some good ones.

Karsi comes walking back towards us as we get near the end of the main street. 'You just keep going,' he says. 'Head out on the highway. We'll turn people around and get them back to their cars, then anyone who wants to be part of the convoy into Geelong can join us.'

'I reckon most of them will,' Mr Garrett says. 'If they're good as their word from last night.'

'We'll see,' says Karsi. 'Oaths sworn by drunken farmers ...'

'Are you even allowed to drive your car and wear your uniform when you're on holiday?' I ask Karsi.

He looks down at his shirt and dark pants. 'I don't have a choice, didn't bring any other clothes.'

'Impersonating a police officer,' Coach Don says.

'Har,' Karsi says as he walks off again. 'Watch out I don't defect your stupid cart after all.'

Mum decides she wants to sit up back for the first bit, try to have a sleep if she can. She swaps with Jen, but there's no real way for her to get comfortable on Jen's swag because she's either too tall to lie down crossways behind the coffin or too wide to lie down beside it. So she bunches it up and sticks it under her bum and sits with her back up against the side of the milk cart next to me.

'You want to play Spotto?' she asks.

'No thanks,' I tell her.

She nods, closes her eyes, her head nodding with the sway of the milk cart. She looks tired.

'How did you meet Dad?' I ask her. I already know, but she loves telling it. 'You met him at a palace, right?'

Her eyes are still closed, but she smiles. 'The Palais. Magic Dirt gig. Before they became big.'

'I never heard of them.'

'Adalita,' Mum says. 'You heard of her. Their lead singer. She's big still, right?'

'Uh …'

'You and your rap nonsense. I'm talking real rock. Music was music then, gigs weren't like now, all drugs and people sliding up and down against each other and hardly even know each other's names, can't hear each other talking.' Her voice is all dreamy. 'Friday nights at the Palais, all the boys at the bar for a glass of liquid courage or two and the girls cruising around in leather jackets and dark eye shadow. Your dad was with these boys from Yardley who rolled up to the Palais for a drink and a bit of fun and they're all laughing and joking, full of giggles and wind, trying to impress us by acting like they weren't trying to impress us.'

'You liked him because he was tall?'

'Couldn't miss him,' she says. 'And he couldn't miss me either. Up front, jumping up and down to the music, both of us the craziest people in the crowd. Stomped on my feet and said sorry and then after the band, when the DJ came on, he came over and apologised again and asked could he buy me a drink and did I want a dance?'

'Not to Madonna …'

'"Not to Madonna," I said, right.' She cracks an eye open and looks at me. 'Who's telling this story?'

I grin. 'You are. He was a ruckman in Geelong Reserves then, wasn't he?'

'Bragging about it, like that would get him points,' she says, closing her eyes again. 'But he was a tall streak of sunshine, I had to give him that. Had a comeback for everything, could lay me low with laughter, some of the things he came out with. And he was a deadly poet.'

'Did you ever see him cry?' I ask.

She lifts her head up and gives me a look. 'Oh, hell's bells, Jack.'

'I'm just asking.'

She sighs, 'No, I never saw him cry.' Then she looks up at the clouds, 'Not that he didn't have reason.'

'You mean because of Jen and me?'

She reaches over and pulls my head into the pit of her shoulder, 'No, dumbo. You and your sister are the best thing ever happened to us. I'm talking about me.' I'm thinking she might say more, but she goes quiet.

'He cried once,' she says suddenly. 'I nearly forgot. It was just after you and Jen turned five. I wasn't coping. I told him I needed a break and he said he needed a bloody break too and we had a blue. And I got in the station wagon and I took off. Drove up to your Uncle Leo's in Melbourne and I stayed away two weeks and didn't call him. Or even you.'

I've never heard this.

'Then Jen jumped off that stupid rock and broke her foot and humped around on it for two days before your dad noticed and took her to hospital. Leo took the message but I was in the city window-shopping, so it was about ten at night when I got the message. I got in the car and I drove straight to the hospital in Geelong and went running in and your dad was sitting in the corridor outside Jen's ward with you and he looked up and he said, "I wasn't sure you'd come."'

I remember now. But the way *I* remember it, Mum came running in and hugged us and we all went in to Jen's ward and she was sleeping so then we went to a service station and got ice creams.

'He had tears in his eyes that night,' Mum says. 'But he was looking at me, not at Jen.'

After Colac it's a long hot day into Geelong where the only good thing is when we cross the Barwon River, there are some people standing on the bridge waving *#BURN* flags. Which is also the hottest part of the day so we pull in at the next hotel to give Danny Boy some feed and water and we get lunch.

Mr Alberti sees me and Jenny sitting under a tree with our sandwiches and he comes over. 'You kids look hot. You want a Rainbow Fizz?'

Jenny looks at me, but I shrug. 'What's that?'

'You never had a Rainbow Fizz?' he shook his head. 'All right, follow me.' We chase after him as he walks into the hotel. The bar has a wall with four huge TV screens on it so I stop to see if the games are live or replays but Mr Alberti comes back and grabs me and pulls me up to the bar. The girl behind the bar is about twenty-five and has six earrings in one ear and none in the other and curly black hair and black eye shadow and she looks bored. The only other people in there are watching a horse race.

'Light beer and two Rainbow Fizzes thanks luv,' Mr Alberti says.

The girl pours the beer and puts it on the bar. 'What was the rest, sorry?' the girl asks. 'Didn't catch it.'

'Rainbow Fizz,' Mr Alberti says, slower this time. 'It's a kids' drink.'

'Sorry, we don't sell that,' she says. 'We have Coke, lemonade, lemon squash ...'

'You don't just sell it, you make it,' Mr Alberti says. 'Serious, you never made one before?'

'Serious,' she says leaning on the bar. 'You want to teach me?'

'I don't believe this,' he says, and then pushes his hat back, 'OK, here we go. Two tall glasses, fill 'em halfway up with orange juice.' Jenny and I jump up on some stools to watch. 'Right, pour in some grenadine ... slowly.'

As she pours this red stuff, it slides down the side of the glass and sits at the bottom, under the juice. 'OK, now, you got some blue food colouring and lemonade?'

The girl smiles, 'Sorry, maybe in the cocktail bar? This is the public bar.'

Mr Alberti looks worried. 'Anything fizzy and blue will do,' he says. 'Nothing like that? It has to be blue.'

She looks in the fridge behind her and bends down. 'There's this guarana energy drink. Tastes weird, but it's blue.'

'Mum won't let us drink that,' Jenny says. 'It's got coffee in it.'

'Caffeine,' I say.

'Whatever, she'll flip.'

'So, we won't tell her,' Mr Alberti says to her and turns to the girl. 'Pour it in over the back of a spoon.'

As the girl pours, some sort of magic happens. The top of the orange juice turns green and then the blue fizzy drink floats on top. The girl does it to both glasses and then stands there looking a little bit like she can't believe it herself. 'Rainbow Fizz, eh?' she says, and pushes it across the bar and hands us two straws. It's red at the bottom, orange in the middle, then green, then blue.

Jenny squints at it. 'Do we drink it layer by layer or mix it up?'

Mr Alberti is beaming. 'I used to drink the blue and green off the top, then mix the orange and the red,' he says. 'Or else you're sucking pure grenadine off the bottom and that stuff is yuk.'

They both watch as we slurp the fizzy part and then swirl the rest around and it goes a reddy brown. The bottom part tastes like flat Fanta.

Mr Alberti pulls out his wallet. 'What do I owe you?'

'I have no idea,' she says. 'But hey, I learned something new. Let's say the fizzy drinks are on the house.'

'We are going to be so speedy now,' Jenny says. 'No way can we hide it.'

'Don't you dob on me,' Mr Alberti says, looking around like Mum might walk in any minute. 'I got on your mum's wrong side once in my life and I never want to be there again.'

When we get moving again Jenny and me roll out our swags down the back of the milk cart behind the coffin away from Mum and lie down looking up at the clouds and feeling the bumps in the road and clip-clop of Danny Boy's hooves. There couldn't have been too much caffeine in those Rainbow Fizzes because I doze off at some point. I wake up with Jenny thumping my arm.

'You awake?' she asks.

'Am now,' I complain. 'Why?'

'Check it,' she says, pointing back behind us.

We left Colac with what seemed to be about fifteen cars in the convoy, though Jenny said twenty. The ones who are with us all have their headlights on, because that's what you do in a funeral. I start counting and I get to fifty cars all with their headlights on, before I lose them around the bend behind us. 'OK, wow. How many ...'

'I counted seventy, I reckon,' Jenny says. 'Even some with interstate plates.'

Traffic really starts building up after lunch and the police have to help overtakers by pulling us over every thirty minutes or so, but it's a two-lane highway a lot of the time so cars can pass us without getting all angry.

'Oh no,' Mr Garrett says. He's been listening to the radio while he drives along, with an earphone in one ear so he can also chat with Mum and Coach Don with his other ear. He hands Mum an earphone. 'This is not good,' he says.

'What is it?' I ask Mum.

'Shush,' she says, frowning. 'Bugger,' she says, handing the earphone back to Mr Garrett.

'What's up?' Coach Don asks.

'Fools attacked a supermarket in Colac as soon as the police pulled out,' Mum says.

'Who did? What do you mean attacked?'

'Radio says a mob of people stayed in town after the march this morning, drinking at the pub then a few idiots attacked the supermarket on Rae Street.'

'Attacked how?'

'Bottles and rocks. Smashed the windows going into the shopping centre, threw some shopping trolleys in. Spray-painted stuff on the walls.'

'Damn,' Coach Don says, staring ahead. 'Call Alasdair; police are going to be wanting to talk to us again in Geelong, that's for sure.'

Mum looks a bit crumbly suddenly. 'Am I the idiot, Don? This whole funeral thing? The police are right, someone is going to get hurt. Haven't we made our point by now?'

'Front page of the *Geelong Advertiser* and a few photos on page eight of the *Herald Sun* aren't going to change anything Dawn, I told you that. You have to get Farmers First in on this, let them set up that meeting.'

'What meeting?' I ask Mum. I remember the Farmers First man in Yardley running the meeting there, except he didn't seem like he was running much of anything and Coach Don walked out on him.

'Well, hello, nosey,' Mum says, turning around and pinching my cheeks. 'What was that?'

'What meeting, who are you meeting with now?'

'No one, luv,' Mum says. 'Coach Don wants me to meet with the supermarket people and the banks.'

'What people?'

'The people who run them, the supermarkets. But why should they meet with me?'

'How about because they're worried about people all over the country starting to attack their supermarkets?' Coach Don says.

'This was never supposed to be about that, Don,' she says. 'And you know it.'

'Well, it is now,' he says, and he doesn't sound unhappy. 'You can't ignore it.'

'That bloody poem was your idea,' Mum says.

'I never told you to read it on the TV news,' he says back. 'I never suggested you make up your own Farm Power salute.'

She bites her lip. 'I'll ring Alasdair.'

'Whoa, Danny Boy!' Mr Garrett calls from up front and we come to a sudden stop.

* * *

'Is he sick?' Jenny asks as Mr Garrett feels up and down Danny Boy's right foreleg. He unharnessed the horse and led him around, watching him walk without the milk cart pulling behind him. Now he's checking the muscles in his leg.

'Don't know. There's something, but it's not a muscle. I thought maybe he'd thrown a shoe but that's not it either.'

'Told you he was too old for this,' Mr Alberti says. 'What is he in human years, about eighty? Pulling twice his weight from Yardley to Melbourne? Like to see you do that.'

Mr Garrett rounds on him. 'Horse years isn't dog years, you old fool. He's just past his prime, unlike you.'

'Right, you two,' Coach Don says, 'we have fifty cars pulled up on the side of the road and Karsi pacifying some itchy cops dying to book us for something. Can we go on or not?'

'I'll have to have him checked in Geelong,' Mr Garrett says. 'By a vet.'

'But can he pull the cart?' Coach Don asks.

'I reckon,' Mr Garrett says. 'If we take it easy.'

'Any slower and you'll be going backwards,' Mr Alberti says.

Mr Garrett shoots him a death-laser look. 'I mean we should take some weight off. Dawn, Don and the kids should ride in one of the cars.'

'Dibs on Ben and Deb!' I yell and I'm already off before Mum or Jenny can say anything, running up the side of the parked cars to where Ben and Deb's old ute is sitting with the engine running.

I stick my head in the window. 'Can I ride with you?'

'Whoa, you scared the hell out of me,' Deb says. 'Why, what's the hold-up?'

'Danny needs a spell from carrying passengers so we need to find a ride in a car so can I come with you?' I point at the middle seat in the ute in case they think I mean ride in the back with all their camping gear like some sheep dog.

Deb gives me that awesome smile and opens the door and swings her skinny legs out and gives me a royal wave. 'Sure thing, Your Highness. Your chariot awaits.'

'Why don't you turn off the engine if you don't even have aircon?' I ask them when we get rolling again. 'I thought greenies always turn off their engines when they're stopped?'

'Ben is afraid it won't start if we turn it off,' Deb says, reaching over to poke him.

'He's a complicated beast, old Harry,' Ben says, shrugging. 'I'm the only one understands him.'

'You call your car Harry?'

'Or Hazza, take your pick,' Ben says, reaching out to thump the driver's door from the outside. 'Isn't that right, Hazza?' And he revs the engine.

'You just did that,' I point out.

'Nah, that was Harry, just showing he knows we're talking about him.' And he revs the engine again. 'See?'

'Why can't you turn the engine off?'

'Because at the speed your horse and cart is going, I've had to stay in second gear the whole way from Port Fairy, and

Harry has got a dicky water pump, which drains the battery if I don't disconnect it every time I stop the car for more than about five minutes, which is a pain in the backside to do unless we're stopped for the night, so I prefer not to have to do it, so I keep the engine running to keep the battery charged to keep the water pump working which keeps Harry cool. Simple?'

'No,' I tell him. 'Do you have PayPal?'

The good part about going with Ben and Deb instead of riding in the milk cart behind Danny Boy is that they have amazing speakers in the car and can stream music from Deb's phone and she has premium streaming as part of her phone subscription that her dad pays for. They let me play DJ for a while until Deb screams, 'No more misogynistic rap music!' And tries to explain to me what misogynistic means and then takes her phone back and we take turns choosing songs as long as I don't pick rap. I manage to get a bit of hip-hop in there with rap bits in it though, without her freaking out again.

I'm looking for a song and there's a bit of a break and I say to Deb, 'Jenny doesn't think my Dad is dead.' Like it's all her idea, which it was at the start.

'No?' Deb asks. 'What does she think then?'

'She thinks the bank man and Karsi and our doctor and Mum have made a conspiracy to fake that Dad is dead and it's Dad and Coach Don setting fire to the banks and supermarkets,' I tell them.

Deb doesn't look convinced. 'And what do you think?' she asks.

'Where were you that night in Warrnambool when the supermarket burned?' I ask them.

'What?'

'I checked your camp and you weren't in your tent and your car was gone.'

Ben looks at me, frowning. 'We went into the pub for a drink and a counter meal,' he says.

'Pubs shut at midnight,' I tell them. 'The supermarket fire was in the middle of the night, Mum said,' I tell him.

'We met some people and went back their place after the pub shut,' Deb says. 'Wow, you're really the detective.'

'Karsi says that too. What people?'

'Tell him,' Ben sighs. 'He's old enough.'

'They're all friends with that cop,' Deb says to him. 'No.'

'Sergeant Karsi?' I say.

'Yeah, look. Someone burned down those banks and the supermarket, but it doesn't have to be the same person, or group of people,' Ben says. 'Country towns are full of angry people who think the banks and big businesses don't care, city folks don't care, the politicians don't care and their own unions are useless. Your mum has given them a target for their anger, maybe that's all.'

'So it's Mum's fault?'

'No!' Deb says. 'What your mum is doing is personal, not political.'

'Well ...' Ben says, not sounding so sure.

'Anyway, the people burning the banks and supermarkets, that's their own responsibility, their choice, not your mum's fault. I didn't mean it that way.' Deb puts an arm around me and gives me a hug. 'When I was a kid, there were these books called the Famous Five. About these kids who went around solving mysteries, except if you ask me it always turned out there wasn't really any mystery, just stuff they didn't understand. Your mum says your dad died in that fire, that should be good enough for both of you. All right?'

'Yeah. What don't you want Sergeant Karsi to know?'

'My god!' Deb says, putting her hand to her forehead and leaning on the window.

'We met up with some people to smoke some weed,' Ben says, taking his hands off the wheel and shrugging his shoulders, 'OK, Jack?'

I look at Deb. 'Is that all?'

'Yes,' she says, like that's totally the end of the conversation. 'Tame Impala?'

'What?'

'Next on the DJ Deb playlist, you never heard of them?'

'No.'

'You are in for a treat.'

Geelong

Geelong isn't like Colac, with people in their cars parked all along the side of the road as we come in, but Deb says that's because Geelong is a real city and not everyone there even knows about Dad's funeral and if they do, a lot of them don't care. But after Winchelsea, as we pass the Ponds, the crosses start. Little white crosses down the side of the highway all the way to the turnoff into High Street. We pass one family banging their cross in and one of the kids is hanging a milk carton around it, just in case people don't realise what it's all about. Then I see quite a few of them have milk cartons hanging around them.

'That's a good idea,' Ben says. 'Doing it like that, showing it's not some car-crash thing.'

It's about four o'clock in the afternoon so people are still at work mostly, but there's a group of people who look like farmers with their four-wheel drives and utes parked at the turnoff. They give us a big wave and hold their fists in the air. One has a sign, *Geelong Says Welcome to Tom's Funeral!*

I figure we're going to go to another footy oval or showground and I'm hoping, but I don't say it out loud, that they'll put us at Kardinia Park which would be awesome. But the police take us down High Street across the Barwon to the racetrack. Being in Deb and Ben's ute is cool because instead of being the first to arrive, we're one of the last, and when we get there, there's a big crowd and almost more cops than there are people in the funeral procession.

'Holy crap, more stormtroopers here than at a logging demo,' Ben says.

'There's no banks or supermarkets in the forest,' Deb says. 'Got to protect the great Australian Vested Interest from the furious farmers.'

'G'day mate,' Deb says out her window as we drive through rows of police, all standing in the sun, looking hot and bothered. 'G'day. Hi there. Howdy.' Then she turns to Ben. 'Hey, I got a great freaking idea, can you turn around? Have you got the telephone number of that reporter? Geraldine?'

'Yeah, what?'

'Just give it me, and see if you can get us out of here and find a shop or a petrol station. I need to buy some milk.'

I don't know what they're up to, but I jump out and watch for Jenny to come with the Albertis, and then we both wait for Mum by the fence. There's people from the procession, and the people who were waiting at the highway have also come over and the cops and three camera crews and some other reporters hanging around smoking and talking into their phones or taking photos.

'Hope Danny's all right,' Jenny says.

'Yeah. What would we do if he isn't?'

'Mr Garrett said he could get another milk cart if he had to. Maybe he could get another horse.'

'I wouldn't want another horse.'

'Me either. You reckon this place has wifi?'

'You're obsessed.'

'Not everyone thinks all you need is a bit of dirt and a football and you're happy.'

She reminds me I haven't seen Aunty Ell's car and Darren, but then across the racetrack I see her and about five other cars coming through a side gate. The cars pull up and me and Jenny run over.

'Hey, you two,' says Aunty Ell climbing out. 'Your mum here yet?'

'No, did you see her?' Jenny asks.

'I went up on ahead,' Aunty Ell says. 'Had to get this organised. Give us a hand, would you.'

She pushes me back toward her car where Darren is opening the boot and there's a mess of gum-tree branches and leaves in there. She gives Jenny a box of matches and tells Darren to get a little fire going.

'What's going on?' I ask Darren.

'Welcome to country,' he says, pulling branches out. 'Wathaurong mob.' He points over his shoulder at the other cars where a guy who looks like an elder with a long white beard and a black headband is getting out and some others are setting up a microphone and a milk crate and a big speaker.

'He's going to make a speech? What's he going to say?' I ask Darren.

'You never heard one before? It's bloody boring,' Darren says. 'First he says it in language, then in English, blah blah blah.' He lifts up the branches and I grab some and we both go over in front of the microphone and dump them where we're told.

'Yeah, but what's he say?'

'Ah, like g'day grandmothers and grandfathers, aunties and uncles, parents and kiddies, we thank the creator blah blah, thanks to our ancestors, this is Wathaurong country let's all live in peace, no fighting or something, then he'll go grab a branch of smoking gum leaves and wave it around.'

'Awesome.'

'You reckon?' He doesn't sound convinced.

'Is that guy going to play the didge?'

He looks where I'm looking. 'Yeah, looks like it.'

'Can you play one?'

'Get out of it.'

'There's dancers too. Can you do Aboriginal dance?'

'What do you reckon? Let's get out of here before we get another job.'

We run back to the entrance, waiting for Mum to come in. Deb is back from the shops and she's brought a shopping bag full of cartons of milk and some clear plastic cups. There are cops lined up all along the entrance where the cars are coming in and she's going up and down the line offering them all a glass of cold milk. Geraldine is taking pictures from a distance.

Most of the cops just say no and try to look like Easter Island statues, but I can see them looking at Deb out the side of their sunglasses because she's so pretty in her short summer dress and blonde hair and bare feet. She walks up to a group of cops standing on their own talking – they look like those special forces cops who rescue hostages – and taps one on the shoulder and offers him a glass of milk. They're kind of taken by surprise and the one she's tapped smiles and takes the milk and downs it in a single gulp and Deb claps and offers some to the other cops but they've seen Geraldine clicking away with her camera and they say no thanks.

Mr Alberti is also standing by the gates so I go over.

'Have you seen Mum?'

'Oh hi, squirt,' he says. 'Yeah, she's in town talking to the boss cops again with the Melbourne lawyer.'

'Have they arrested her?' I ask, panicking.

'No, mate, not her.' He squats down. 'But they've arrested Don. Suspicion of arson for the bank in Yardley.'

'I knew it!' I say, but I must sound like I'm happy about it, because Mr Alberti frowns at me.

'Don't be a fool. He didn't do it,' Mr Alberti says. 'Police are just trying to scare us off. The Melbourne lawyer says he'll have Don out on bail by tomorrow latest. Police are talking with your mum now. Told her they don't want anyone making speeches. The lawyer says Mum can do what she wants on public land unless they're going to charge her with disturbing the peace and besides, there's a TV crew coming. There's an argument about whether this racetrack is public or private land, so the cops think they have us snookered but he knows his stuff that Melbourne lawyer. I reckon she'll be right. Anyway, they don't dare stop *that* ...' He points to the people setting up the welcome to country. 'TV channels love a good welcome to country ...'

Coach Don arrested? I somehow thought the police were on our side, the way they were helping the funeral convoy up the highway. With Karsi talking to them when they got angry. I never thought they'd really arrest anyone. Now I'm really starting to worry for Mum. Maybe it's better we just stop, maybe I should tell her that. Or maybe the police will stop it and I won't need to.

'Is Danny Boy OK?' I ask.

'He'll be along any minute,' Mr Alberti says. 'Garrett is just a worry wart, loves that horse more than his wife, I reckon. It ain't natural.' He laughs and we both look up the road and now I can see the milk cart with Dad's coffin and

Danny Boy up front hoofing along like he's giving Sunday rides at a carnival and Mr Garrett smiling, just loving it, as people by the gates all lift their fists in the air like Mum and cheer as Dad's coffin gets led into the parking lot of the racecourse.

I don't care what Darren says, the welcome to country is awesome. Mum and Alasdair arrive, and then a guy starts playing didgeridoo and these dancers start dancing a dance I don't really understand but it seems they're mimicking different animals and one is walking around, waving a smoking branch which gives this smell of eucalyptus to everything. And then the old white-haired man gets up on a platform made of plywood and milk crates and speaks in his language first and then he says welcome to Mum and all the people from the procession and points out we're on Wathaurong land and he's heard there's been a bit of trouble on this trip, but he hopes there isn't any trouble while they're here, out of respect for the land and the creator and the ancestors of the Wathaurong people.

Mum is standing next to him and he calls her up. I look over at the police in case they're going to step in and arrest her. Me and Jenny are ready to get in there between them.

'Let 'em try,' Jenny whispers to me. 'They can arrest us all.'

But the cops just cross their arms and watch Mum and watch how the crowd is reacting. The sun is setting now and a few people turn on their car headlights from behind Mum, which lights up the crowd but makes it so she looks like a big black shadow about twice the size she really is.

She looks down at some notes.

'I want to acknowledge the welcome of the Wathaurong people,' she says, 'on whose land we stand, and pay my respects to the local people for allowing us to have this gathering on their land and to their elders present, past and future. Words can't say how much that welcome means to me and I know Tom, wherever he is today, would have loved it.'

'*Wherever he is today*,' I say to Jenny. 'Did you hear that?'

'She means heaven or hell,' she says. 'Suicides don't go to heaven, remember?'

'Believe what you want,' I reply.

'There has been some trouble on this trip,' Mum continues. 'Yes. The police want me to tell anyone who's thinking of repeating that trouble here in Geelong that they should rethink such ideas. Burning banks and attacking supermarkets is no way to honour the memory of my husband Tom, to that I agree.' Mum takes a big breath and straightens her back. 'But neither do I like the way I've been threatened today with such things as fines, and even arrest. One of our travelling party has just been arrested. So I have a message for anyone who thinks they can break my spirit and I'll quote a former Prime Minister on this one: *I will not be bullied!*'

A cheer goes up from the crowd and Mum stands there holding her paper, with her hand shaking a bit and her jaw sticking out. Coach Don isn't there up the front this time, but Mr Garrett is, and him and Pop give Mum a thumbs-up.

Jenny and I look at each other like, *who is this lady and where did our Mum go?*

'There has been some trouble on this trip,' Mum continues. 'Yes. But these are troubled times.' She looks out in the crowd and sees someone and beckons with her hand. 'And I'm grateful you came out to support us, but it doesn't stop here. It's just starting. I want to invite someone up here with me. Ron? That's right, you come up here.'

'Who's Ron?' Jenny asks, standing on her tiptoes and holding on to my shoulder to try and see who Mum is waving toward. A little baldy man with feathery tufts of hair over his ears, wringing a baseball cap between his hands, walks up to the ute, hands his cap to someone and climbs up next to Mum.

'Ron told me he doesn't want to talk in front of all you good people, said he's not a talker. But I wanted you to meet him and he agreed to do that,' Mum says. 'Thank you so much, Ron. Ron lives ... he lived ... in Irrewillipe. Is that right?'

The man nods.

'And today he burned his place to the ground.'

I look around and people are stunned. I thought they'd cheer, but they're just looking at him like, *No Way.*

'Let the bank have the ashes, that's what you said, right Ron?'

He bites his lip, looking at the ground in front of him, and looks up a little bit at the faces around him and nods.

'Thank you, Ron. I know it takes a lot of courage to stand up here, but at least now you know you're not alone,' Mum says and hugs him, and he hugs her back, a little awkward, then he climbs down and walks through the crowd, people patting him on the back. 'Someone get Ron a nice strong cup of tea,' she says, and people laugh.

'Ron forgot his cap,' Jenny whispers and I giggle.

Mum looks around and locks eyes with Karsi for a second, then looks away. 'Now, I mentioned that one of our party has been arrested. He's just an ordinary farmer, like a lot of you. He's a farmer and a father and a football coach and he's done nothing wrong, but this is what happens when you question the powers that be. They do this kind of thing to try to shut you up. Well, we don't have to put up with that either!' There are some big cheers from the crowd now. 'So I want to finish, not with a poem this time. I want to finish with the words of another Australian who got pushed too far; you may know him, his name was Ned Kelly. He wrote some words a hundred and thirty years ago that apparently are still appropriate today, and I quote:

> *'I will not put up with the brutal and cowardly conduct of that parcel of big ugly fat necked wombat headed big bellied magpie legged narrow-hipped splawfooted sons of Irish bailiffs or*

*English landlords which is better known as the Victoria Police,
who some calls honest gentlemen, but I would like to know
what business an honest man would have in the Police.'*

She crumples up the paper and holds her fist in the air and
Jenny and I laugh and a huge cheer goes up from the crowd
and the police look super dark. Their officers are all talking
with each other. Mum is looking at them like she's daring
them to come at her.

'You remember that time she took on that soccer referee?'
Jenny says.

'That time I got hacked and she ran onto the field to give
the ref a mouthful and then ended up taking on the other
team's coach and all their parents too?' I ask.

'Yeah,' Jenny said. 'She's got that same look.'

'This could get ugly,' Mr Alberti says. 'You two go find
Mrs Alberti, would you? Stay by her.'

'We're not leaving Mum!' Jenny says.

'Your mum's not the one needs looking after,' he says,
pointing as the Wathaurong elder helps her down off the
milk crate and reporters with cameras and microphones and
a bunch of other people crowd around her.

'They could arrest her!' I say. 'They already arrested
Coach Don!'

'For what? Quoting Henry Lawson and Ned Kelly? No,
mate, they'll go after other people first, like Don, Garrett
and me. They know we've still got a hundred and fifty

kilometres to Melbourne. They'll try to pull the pin on this parade before then, that's for sure now.'

It's not fair how we're parked with Mrs Alberti and she won't let us go anywhere until things settle down, she says, because it doesn't look to me like anything is settling down. The police are going around telling anyone who isn't directly connected with the funeral party to go home. That gets a few people to leave but then someone starts letting the air out of people's tyres and everyone is saying they can't go anywhere because their tyres are flat. They think that's really funny, but the police don't. They bring in a tow truck but then decide it would be a dumb idea to try to tow anyone's car, the mood the people are in. So they end up pulling back to the entrance to the racetrack just checking everyone coming in and out and filming licence plates.

About midnight a police officer with one of those loudhailer things gets up on a crate. There are about a hundred people still hanging around. 'Can I have your attention please,' he says. 'We all want a peaceful night here tonight. If you're having a drink, please don't drive. And if you're going into town, you'll find police helpfully stationed outside every bank and supermarket and government office in case you get lost and need directions.' He says it like he's making a joke, but no one laughs. He gets down off the crate and hands the loudhailer to a man in overalls with those glowing green stripes on them.

'George Argyle from the SES, folks. Arrangements for tonight,' the man says. 'The jockey club has kindly agreed to keep the toilet and changing facilities open all night for your convenience, but please clean up after yourselves. The local SES has camp beds, blankets and towels down by the toilet blocks that you can hire for a small donation if you need a bed for the night. Not much, but better than sleeping on the ground or in the back of a ute. There's some St John's volunteers at the toilet blocks too in case anyone feels unwell. That's about it. Any questions, come find me.'

Other nights have had the feeling of a family barbecue or party about them, but not tonight. People are gathered in small groups in the headlights of their cars or on fold-up chairs around camping lights. Mum is still with reporters, like she's been all night. If she were here, she'd be telling us it's time to go to bed.

'Mrs Alberti, is it all right we go to sleep now? We're really tired,' I say.

Jenny looks at me like, *are you crazy? Who wants to go to bed now?*

Mrs Alberti is busy fussing with their beds in the back of their ute, so she just looks up and says, 'Of course, dear. I'll tell your mum where you are. Off you go, do your teeth, mind. And remember your checks.'

'I'm *not* tired!' Jenny says, but I grab her arm really hard and haul her off.

'We're not going to bed,' I tell her. I show her the key I swiped from Mr Garrett's toolbox. The one that opens the coffin lid.

Mr Garrett is off with Danny Boy, who's getting checked by a vet so the milk cart is basically all alone in the middle of the parked cars. There's no one near it, which isn't too surprising considering there's a big black coffin sitting in the back of it with just a battery-powered lamp on top.

'Now's our chance,' I say. 'Get up there.'

'No,' she replies. 'You're mad. I'm not looking.'

'If you're right, then you'll be right and I'll be wrong and I'll shut up. Now get up there or I'll go tell Mum it was *your* idea.'

'No, we're going back to Mrs Alberti.'

She thinks just because she was born like five minutes before me she can be boss of me. But we're both about the same size and weight so she only wins about half the fights. This was her idea first, she's cornered, she knows it, and the only way to shut me up is to do what I ask. I just stand looking at her.

'Oh dammit! I'll help you,' she says. 'But there is no way I'm looking inside that coffin.'

'You help me get the lid off,' I tell her, 'I'll do the looking, fraidy cat.'

I climb up the back of the milk cart and she follows me up. I look around but no one is paying any attention to us and there's no light shining right on us, there's just the lamp on top of the coffin which we shut off without anyone noticing. I'm so right, this is the perfect time for what we need to do.

'You get the clips on the left,' I tell her. 'I'll do the ones on the right and the one with the lock.'

The clips are like brass screws with monkey ears. First you loosen the screws and then you can flip them up out of the eye of the lock. There's four on my side and three on Jenny's side plus the one that's a locked lock. I do mine faster and crawl over to her side and she's doing the last one before the lock.

'OK, do you have your phone?'

'No, I left it with yours, charging in the Albertis' camper, remember?'

'Bum bum bum. We need a light,' I say. I look at the battery-powered lamp, which I'm afraid someone will notice if we start swinging it around. 'A smaller one.'

'Can't you see enough to put the key in?'

'No, to look inside the coffin! It's dark here, it's going to be even darker inside, right?'

'Shall I get my phone?'

'No, it'll take too long. Someone could come. We'll have to use the big lamp – I won't turn it on until it's inside the coffin.' I reach for my pocket and pull out the key again. 'Here goes.' The key goes into the little lock and I give it a half-turn and lift the last clasp off. 'You go to that end. We have to lift off the lid but like, just enough to slide it, enough so we can see in, not so much that it falls completely off in case we can't get it back on again.'

'OK.'

'You know what I mean? Just slide it ...'

'I get you already!'

'OK, go then.'

I go down to the bottom end of the coffin with the lamp and she goes to the top. I grab the clasp at the end and test it to see how heavy the lid is. I'm thinking of those vampire films where the coffin lid weighs like a ton and creaks when the vampire opens it. If this lid creaks, I'm going to scream. But it won't creak because it isn't on hinges, right?

Then I think about the smell. I don't want to, but I can't help it. Dead bodies smell, right? This coffin has been out in the sunshine for days now. I'm thinking of dead roos by the side of the road. How they smell after a couple of days. I can't get it out of my head.

'I don't want to!' Jenny whines.

'Shut up and lift,' I tell her. 'Now!'

The lid isn't heavy at all. It's like lifting one of those table tennis tops they have at school that even Jenny and me can carry without needing help. I lift it using the clasp to get a hand under and then slide it about halfway off to the left, while Jenny slides her end about halfway off to the right, so it's sitting diagonally across the coffin.

I can see there's blue shiny cloth lining the inside of the

coffin. That was Dad's favorite colour, blue. I wonder if that's on purpose.

I realise I'm holding my breath. Jenny is looking away so it has to be me who looks inside. Suddenly I can't. But I can't hold my breath forever. I let it out and have to drag in a huge lungful of air.

It smells OK.

I mean, it doesn't smell like roadkill. It doesn't smell like anything really, except maybe ...

'Corn,' Jenny says. 'Smells like cattle feed.' And she looks in the coffin.

So I have to look. I push the lid a bit further over so I can see most of my end of the coffin. It's dark in there all right but I put the lamp inside under the lid of the coffin and turn it on.

In the bottom of the coffin where the feet should be, I can see a big brown bag of feed, with another further along.

'Maybe he's under the bags?' I whisper to Jenny. 'Maybe they put them in there to hold it down, the body.'

'Look how low down they are,' Jenny says. 'There's nothing under them. That's all there is, is a couple of feed sacks!'

'Maybe further up,' I tell her. I try putting my head in so I can see the middle of the coffin where the lid still covers it and there's a small box shape but nothing else. There's no way a body could be squeezed in here even if you folded it at the knees. Maybe he was burned so bad, they put his body in feed sacks?

I reach out to give one of the sacks a push.

'Oh my god. Oh my god,' Jenny says, really loud.

'Keep it down,' I hiss at her. 'Someone will hear!'

I push a corner, gently, and then with a bit more force and it dents and I can feel the grain moving around inside. I prod a bit more.

'It's just feed grain. Why?' It comes out of me like a wail. 'Why trick us?'

'I don't know, Jack,' Jen says. 'I don't *know.*'

I don't know what else to do, so I yell up the moon and I hear Pop's voice from out of his car window, 'Goddamit, I'm trying to sleep here!'

A torchlight shines in our eyes and there's another voice, 'What in hell are you two doing up there?!'

Mum. We're busted.

'You were trying to do *what*?!' Mum asks. She's sat us down on the prickly grass behind the milk cart.

'Jack didn't believe Dad was inside,' Jenny says. 'He wanted to see for himself.'

Mum sighs, 'Oh, Jack.'

I'm about ready to explode at her. But Mum's got the torch on us and Jenny's looking at me like *don't make this worse*, and I decide it's better if I just shut up.

Mum sits down in front of us, turns out the torch. It's just the light from the other campers now and it flickers on her face. 'Look, I know this is tough on you. Losing the house, losing your father, leaving Yardley, all in the space of a few days? But we have to do this while your dad's death is still in the papers, while people are paying attention. You get that, right?'

'But it's *empty*!' I accuse her, not able to keep it in a second longer. 'He's not in there!'

'He's in there,' Mum says, looking up at the coffin. 'Just not like you might have expected.'

Jenny and I look at each other, confused.

Mum leans forward, reaches out, takes Jenny's left hand and my right hand, and holds them, 'There's laws about burying bodies,' she explains. 'You only get a couple of days. And the whole point of this is to take it slow.' She holds our hands tight. 'So we had your dad cremated, and we put his ashes in a box inside the coffin, with some feed bags for the weight.'

'Who's *we*?' Jenny asks. 'Does everyone except us know?'

'No, just me, the funeral home and Karsi,' she says. 'It was his idea. To get around the law. The others don't need to be bothered with it, it's just a detail.' She shakes our hands once or twice, looking into our faces, 'So yes, he's really dead. And he's really in there. OK?'

'Yeah,' Jenny says.

I don't say anything, and Mum shakes my hand one more time, 'OK, mister?'

'Yeah, OK,' I tell her. But what I'm thinking is, no. Not OK. She's letting everyone think it's his body in there, but it's just his ashes? Well, if she's been lying about that, what else is she lying about? And how far is it from 'your dad's body isn't in there, it's just his ashes' to 'actually, the real truth is, you were right Jack, he isn't dead at all.'

Mum groans as she gets up, 'Right, enough nonsense. Checks and bed, you two.' She looks over at the coffin, 'I have to get that lid back on before anyone notices.' She lifts Jenny up and holds a hand out to me, but I get myself up. I give her the key and trail off behind Jenny, towards the toilets.

Jenny can believe he's dead, if that's what she wants. I want *proof*.

'Wakey wakey, sleepyheads,' Mum's voice says next morning. 'Porridge when you're ready.'

'Cold or hot?' I ask. Then I remember I'm mad at her for hiding stuff from us and she smiles at me but I don't smile back.

'Hot from Maynards' camp stove,' she says. She's squatting down under the milk cart. 'With raisins. We're leaving in thirty minutes.'

Jenny is lying in the bottom of her swag, just her hair sticking out. The magpies are singing like crazy this morning. Like it's a farewell song, just for us here at the racetrack.

'Magpies are singing us goodbye,' Jenny says, crawling out of her swag.

'Good morning, miss. They are, aren't they? Put your shoes on.'

'Will there be a march, like in Colac?' Jenny asks.

'No chance of that. Police want us straight out of here. They're sending us on back roads out of Geelong.'

'Did anything happen last night?'

'Nothing much,' Mum says.

'You mean apart from your mum getting the whole of the Victoria Police against us?' comes a voice from up front of the milk cart, which must be Mr Garrett. I can hear Danny Boy shuffling around and snorting, so Mr Garrett must be about to harness him. He gets all impatient before he gets the harness on.

He isn't the only one snorting. 'And what do you think I should have said, John Garrett?' Mum demands. 'Stood idly by and said nothing, as they pick us off one by one? You want to join Don in a prison cell? I am bloody sick and tired of bullies and when I see them, I'm going to call them out!'

'Well you did that,' Mr Garrett says. 'It's a wonder Tom lived as long as he did around you, if he had a weak ticker.'

'Oh shut up, you,' Mum says, but she's only fake annoyed at him, I can hear that.

He comes around to the front of the milk cart and lifts a newspaper off the seat and hands it me. It's the *Herald Sun.* On the front page is a picture of Deb standing on her toes pouring milk for one of the police in riot gear. She looks so small, and he looks so scary in all of his black kevlar, but he's smiling.

Mr Garrett taps the page. 'Just made the front page of the Melbourne paper. Nothing much at all.'

I get my shoes on and start shovelling down the porridge Mum has brought. Then I need to go to the toilet but can't decide whether to run for the toilet or finish the porridge and I know Mum will go off if I try to do both and the way I feel, if she starts having a go at me, it'll get out of control, I know it. So I sit with my legs crossed in front of Danny and eat my porridge and try not to think about the toilet.

'How's Danny Boy?' I ask Mr Garrett.

Danny Boy hears me and lowers his head and starts snuffling at my bowl.

'He's all right, aren't you, mate?' Mr Garrett says, patting his neck as he slides the harness over. 'Watch he doesn't slurp your … too late.'

You forget how long a horse's tongue is sometimes. He's lucky it wasn't hot.

'Give me that, you,' Mum says. She must be a mind-reader because she says, 'No, there isn't any more. Go do your teeth.'

'Yuk. I thought horses only like raw oats,' I say to Mr Garrett while I try to find my toothbrush and see if Jenny is finishing her porridge or not, but she is.

'Horses like what horses like,' he says. 'I had one used to like meat pies. I called him Hannibal.'

'I know him,' Jenny says. 'The Roman with the elephants.'

'Yeah, different Hannibal,' Mr Garrett says.

* * *

'How's this for a treat, kids?' Mum asks. I was thinking she'd be mad the police were making us go the back way out of Geelong, along the Portarlington Road by the swampy ground. There's just us and the cars in front and behind and there's no one waving signs or giving salutes or anything. But you can see the ocean, and the sun is shining, is what she's trying to say.

'I think you hit a chord,' Mr Garrett says to Mum. He's got an earphone in one ear and it's plugged into a small radio. 'The Ned Kelly thing is all over the radio.'

'You think?' she says, smiling. 'Dad taught me that quote.'

'I thought your dad was a city fella?'

'He was also a troublemaker,' she says. 'He memorised that quote so he could say it to a policeman one day as a clever insult and he'd be able to get away with it because he could say he was quoting Ned Kelly.'

'Did he ever use it? Like, in a real argument with a copper?'

'Yeah.'

'And?'

'He got an eighty-dollar fine.'

They keep blabbing on and I tune out because Mum has just reminded me Coach Don has been arrested, Mum will probably be next, Dad is either dead, or not, and my sister is a useless co-investigator. I have to keep reminding myself I might have Dorotea's analgesia but I'm pretty much the only sane person on this damn milk cart.

But then a car comes up alongside us and he's tooting on his horn and the passenger is waving like crazy, but not angry, more like frantic. He pulls in front of the horse and cart with his emergency blinker lights on and two people jump out. One is the Melbourne lawyer and the other is the reporter, Geraldine. And the back door opens and Coach Don gets out too, with a big grin on his face like the Cats just won the premiership.

Mr Garrett has to pull Danny Boy up into a crash stop and there's dust and stones flying and the cars behind have to jam on their brakes but no one is angry. Mum hops down and hoofs over to Coach Don and gives him a big hug and a kiss on the cheek and Mr Garrett gives him a little wave. The Highway Patrol car and other cars up front keep going; they haven't realised yet we've stopped. Jenny looks at me like, *what's next?* I just shrug.

'Where are you headed?' Coach Don yells up to Mr Garrett. 'Melbourne's that way!' he says, pointing back behind us.

'Police want us to go via Queenscliff, keep us off the freeway,' Mr Garrett yells back. 'It still works. Plenty of towns to pass through.'

'It's not even the right side of town for the cemetery.' Coach Don scratches his head. 'It means we have to go right through St Kilda and Southbank to get there.'

'Right up St Kilda Road through Fed Square actually,' comes a voice and it's Karsi. 'Hey, Don.'

'Hey yourself,' Coach Don says and they shake hands. 'You have anything to do with this idea?'

'Highway Patrol wanted us on back roads north, sending us via the You Yangs, but that would take forever. I suggested the Nepean Highway instead and that kept them happy. But they're still hoping you'll give up before Melbourne. I guess you're not. Giving up, that is …'

'I'd guess not,' Coach Don agrees.

Geraldine is taking photos and the Melbourne lawyer is talking to Mum and Mr Alberti has turned his car around and him and the police escort car are coming back to see what the hold-up is.

'Where's our next stop?' Jenny asks. 'Did you hear?'

Mum gave us a map a couple of days ago and I pull it out, tracing my finger around Port Phillip Bay. 'How long's the ferry trip?'

'There's a ferry?'

I show her. 'From Queenscliff to … Sorrento? See?'

'Can you take a horse on a ferry?'

'Mum!' Jenny calls out. 'Can you even take horses on the ferry?'

All the grown-ups look at each other. The policeman driving the escort car pulls up alongside and leans out the window. 'What's the hold-up?'

'Can you take a horse and cart on the Queenscliff ferry?' Mum asks him.

'I dunno,' says the policeman, and he and the police lady in the car have a talk. 'I can ask, but it's your responsibility to sort it out with the ferry operator.'

'It was your boss told us we'd have to go this way,' Mr Garrett points out.

'We're the Victoria Police,' the cop says, 'not a bloody travel agent. Now get moving again, would you, you're backing up traffic.'

Coach Don and Mum and the Melbourne lawyer climb up into the cart. Mr Garrett whistles at Danny Boy and we get rolling again.

'Call the ferry company,' Mum says to Coach Don, 'would you?'

'I'll look it up!' Jenny says, pulling out her phone, all puffed up because it was her idea the ferry and the horse might be a problem. 'Can I use data, Mum?'

'I've been thinking about why the police were so happy we decided to come this way. I'm willing to bet,' Alasdair says, 'they've already checked and think they know what the rules are about horses on the Queenscliff ferry.' He's changed his clothes since he first turned up. When he first arrived he was wearing a suit and waistcoat and shiny black shoes and a white shirt and a blue tie. Now he's wearing black jeans and a blue shirt with a white t-shirt underneath and working boots that still look new but not shiny.

'Course they have,' Coach Don says. 'That's their plan, send us all the way down the Bellarine and then we get to

Queenscliff and find out we can't get on the ferry. We've lost a day that way and we have to waste another day getting back to Geelong and then it's back roads all through bloody Werribee and Sunshine to get to Melbourne – we'll never make it in time. That's their bloody thinking and we fell for it.'

'We're not out of it yet,' Mum says. 'Call the ferry company.'

'I'll make a few calls too,' Alasdair says. 'We have a guy who's an expert on traffic and carriage law.'

'Here's the number,' Jenny says, handing her phone to Coach Don.

'How much does the ferry cost?' Mr Garrett asks. 'Isn't it about seventy bucks? We'll lose a few of these hangers-on if they have to cough up.'

'And what if the ferry is already booked,' I ask. 'Remember that time …'

Everyone is firing questions at her suddenly and Mum holds up her hands. 'Jenny has money. Don, you have to book for twenty cars,' Mum says, tugging on Coach Don's arm. 'And a horse.'

'*Summary Offences Act 1966*, section 8,' the Melbourne lawyer is telling the manager in the ferry's small ticket office. He hands his phone to the manager and shows him something his office sent through to him.

The manager is a little round guy with stains on his shirt, which isn't buttoned up at the top even though he's wearing a tie, because his neck is too big for the shirt. He has a big smile but I don't see what's funny. The Highway Patrol police are smiling too, so whatever he thinks is funny, they think is funny too.

All I know is he's saying we can't take the horse on the ferry unless it's in a horse float. He doesn't even look at the lawyer's phone. 'Company policy, sorry. No uncontained livestock on the ferry.'

Mr Garrett is reading something written on a poster on the wall of the office. 'Says here you allow pets,' he says.

'On a leash,' the man says. 'And a draught horse is not a bloody pet. It's livestock.'

'You really do want to read this,' Alasdair is saying, pointing at his phone.

The manager crosses his arms. 'Why don't you read it for me?'

'OK,' he says. 'Um. Section 8b, amendment 137, 1974 ... Here we are: "Any person who, being the owner, driver, guard or conductor of a public vehicle for the conveyance of passengers who wilfully delays without lawful reason any passenger ..."'

'How about No Horses Allowed Unless in A Float, there's your lawful reason,' one of the Highway Patrol cops calls and they laugh. There's two of them, a man and a lady cop, who've been with us since Colac. Karsi is standing up the back with his arms crossed but he's not saying anything.

'No, that's a company policy, not a law,' Alasdair says and

keeps going. '"... wilfully delays without lawful reason any passenger shall be guilty of an offence."'

'You going to arrest me?' the manager asks the police, who just keep smiling.

'Actually, *I* can arrest you,' Alasdair says.

The manager looks at him, going a bit red, 'You?'

'Absolutely. Section 458 of the Crimes Act, my friend. I have just as much power to arrest you as the boys in blue over there.'

The police shuffle a bit, but they don't argue with him.

'I have to call head office about this,' the manager says.

'Of course, before you do, though, you might want to read this too,' the lawyer says, starting to hand him the phone, but then deciding against it. 'Or I could just read it for you. I'll do that, shall I? Here, *Federal Transport Compliance and Miscellaneous Act, 1983.* You'll like this. A girl tried to get on the ferry to Tassie with her Shetland pony and they wouldn't let her. The horse got injured as they tried to turn it around and so the case went to court. Turns out the definition of passenger conveyance in the Act hasn't been updated since 1842 and it includes,' he shows the manager, 'it includes "passengers conveyed on horses, donkeys, camels and oxen" so the ferry company was forced to pay out damages *and* allow the girl and her horse on the ferry next time, as long as she rode it on.'

'No, really?' Coach Don says. 'Camels?'

'And oxen. She had to clean up her own mess,' the lawyer says. 'But yeah.'

'Anyway, it doesn't matter,' the manager says, spreading his legs and leaning forward. 'We're fully booked.'

'Booked?' Mum asks. 'But we called and —'

'Fully booked, sorry,' the man says, spreading his hands. 'Wish we could help.'

Mr Alberti has been hovering up the back of the group but he leans in. 'Fully booked, one o'clock on a Thursday afternoon during school term?'

'Yeah, sorry,' the man says. He turns around and picks up a piece of paper. 'Twenty cars and one ... *passenger conveyance*? I can get you on next ... um ... Monday 6 a.m.'

'Monday,' Mr Alberti says with a growl.

'Earliest,' the man says, smiling again.

'What about just one vehicle?' Coach Don says. 'The horse and cart.'

'Ah well, one vehicle ... oversize?'

'Oversize?'

'Longer than five metres?'

'It's eight metres,' Mr Garrett says. 'Horse and cart.'

'That's eighty-eight dollars, not including passengers,' the man says, like he's hoping we don't have the money. 'Eleven dollars a metre.'

'All right,' Coach Don says. 'Book it on.'

'Can't, sorry, oversize vehicle spaces are even more tight, let me see ... Tuesday 10 a.m.'

'Bullshit,' Coach Don says, stepping closer to the man.

The Highway Patrol policeman steps forward, 'Let's all just calm down, all right?'

The manager steps behind the policeman and the female cop says maybe everyone should go out and get some fresh air and think about things, and people look at Mum and she says, 'Yeah, we'll do that. Come on, people.'

I'm talking to the female cop whose name is Natalie. I want to know how you get to be a cop, like do you go to university or what. She's nearly as cool as Deb.

'Are you for or against us?' I ask her.

'The police don't take sides,' she says. 'But my parents were farmers.'

Karsi is walking past as she says it and he winks at me. 'Thought I smelled a funny smell.' He goes to talk to the other cop.

She sticks her tongue out at him.

'Being a cop is more fun than farming, I bet,' I tell her.

'It's not all fun, but yeah, it's different. And it's police officer, by the way. Not cop.'

'Sorry.'

She leans toward me so no one else can hear. 'What your mum is doing is awesome,' Natalie says. 'Really. She has some guts.'

'Thanks. Can I see that stick, the one on your belt?'

We're standing outside the ferry building, which is this big creamy-painted place with green roofs. Inside, all the grown-ups are arguing about what we should do, like maybe Mum could get just the coffin on the ferry but then what's she going to do from the other side? Jenny and me are like, yeah, but what about us? So they pushed us out. Jenny is hopping along the rocks of the breakwater. She loves hopping on rocks and if Mum saw her she'd freak and yell at her to get off before she breaks a leg but the whole reason she's doing it is because Mum isn't watching. Natalie puts her hand on her baton, like she's going to take it off and show me, then she looks past me, 'Wait a minute. I've got an idea. *Hey*, excuse me, can I have a word?' she calls out as a big truckie who's just pulled up in his cattle truck goes to walk past her and into the café.

He looks like she's caught him doing something. 'Uh, yeah?'

'Your truck's empty, right?' Natalie says, walking past him and toward the cattle truck. It's big and it's got bars and slats down the sides but you can see it's empty and you can smell it's empty too.

'Is there a problem?' he asks. Now he really looks nervous. 'You need to see the papers, or ...'

'No, how wide is it?'

'Standard single,' he says, '4.3 by 2.5.'

'And how long?'

'The whole rig or just the trailer?'

'Trailer,' she says, peering through the back gate.

'12.5, why?'

She walks around to the wheels at the back. 'How long since you had the tyres checked?'

'Oh come on,' he says. 'I've got to pick up a load in Boneo and get back before dark. The tyres are fine, but if youse waste my time checking them ...'

She gives him a look. 'At this stage, I'm just asking. You booked on the next ferry?'

'One o'clock, yeah.'

'Good. I might have a favour to ask.'

Geraldine walks up to her with phone held out in front of her ready to record but Natalie puts up her hand. 'Not happening,' is all she says. 'But get ready with your camera.'

The truckie's name is Dave. 'The whole thing, horse and cart and ... all?' he's asking.

'How wide is your milk cart?' Natalie asks. Everyone looks at Mr Garrett.

'Two metres, wheel to wheel,' he says.

'Half a metre to spare,' Natalie points out.

Her partner isn't looking so sure but he knows Sergeant Karsi and he's waiting for him to say something now that he's worked out what Natalie's idea is.

'Sounds like an option,' Karsi says. 'You know any law against putting a horse-drawn cart inside a cattle truck? With the horse? Coz I don't.'

'Well I do,' the manager says from behind the police. 'It's an unsafe load is what it is.'

'Shut it, you,' Natalie says. I'm thinking I totally want to be a police officer when I finish school.

'And how am I supposed to charge for that?' the manager whines. 'A vehicle inside a vehicle?'

'I said shut it,' Natalie says. She turns to Mr Garrett and the truckie. 'You have forty minutes to get that horse and cart loaded on that semitrailer in a manner that poses no risk to public safety or to the horse.'

'What about the rest of us?' Mr Alberti asks, but the manager has run outside after the others, still arguing about something.

Jen and Mum have gone into the café to get some ice creams but I wanted to stay and watch the horse get loaded. Danny Boy is not real thrilled about walking up the ramp into the cattle truck, but Mr Garrett puts bigger blinkers around his eyes and after about three goes gets him up into the truck and puts a feedbag around his nose. They tie up some hay bales and a couple of spare tyres from people's cars to the insides of the cattle truck so he can't turn around and he can't hurt himself.

'First time he's been on a boat,' Mr Garrett says. 'First time for a lot of things.'

The men are working out whether to shove the milk cart up into the truck with the coffin on or take it out and put it in afterwards. Natalie and her partner are standing by their car having a bit of an argument, so I slide over to listen.

'We were supposed to deal with the problem,' he's saying.

'We *are* dealing with it,' Natalie says. 'Five minutes past one, they're on that ferry and there *is* no problem any more.'

'For us,' he says. 'You're just passing it on to Melbourne.'

'Tell me you want to work out what to do with a two-tonne horse and cart, twenty cockies in their utes, two cars full of journalists and a dead man in a coffin. There's a reason the inspector isn't here,' she says. 'He doesn't want anything to do with this, so he handballed it to you and you were dumb enough to say yes sir, thank you sir.'

He drops his hat up on the hot roof of their police car and runs his hands through his hair. 'That Searoads Ferry manager is going to call up Geelong, tell them your good idea. How he was just doing what we asked him, trying to hold them up, and you cut the grass from under him.'

'You're the ranking officer on the ground here.'

'We need a story.'

'Tell 'em that lawyer scared the crap out of us and we had no way of checking he wasn't right. He threatened a citizen's arrest of the Searoads manager, the media would have loved that, so we intervened to get the protesters onto the ferry and out of Geelong.'

He looks at her. 'I guess that'll fly.'

'You guess.'

'I guess it'll have to.'

'So, you go call it in while I go to see how many of these cars we can get on the next ferry.'

'How are you going to do that?' he asks, looking at the car park which is starting to fill with a few more cars in nice neat lines but doesn't look totally packed to me.

She has a great smile and she looks down at me. 'I'm willing to bet the ferry isn't fully booked, but just in case, me and my offsider Jack here are going to go around to the other cars and tell them there's an emergency situation and would they mind waiting for the next ferry instead, aren't we, mate?'

The ferry is this amazing big white catamaran with bright blue and green decks and yellow traffic stripes and the truck with Danny Boy and the milk cart and the coffin goes on first and then all the cars behind it and we get ten of the cars from our convoy with us because there were some people who said they couldn't afford to miss the ferry and Natalie didn't want to argue with them in case they made a fuss, but there were five who said no worries, they could wait. So Mr Alberti and Deb and Ben and Geraldine and Alasdair and the reporter from Portland and Sergeant Karsi and Mr Garrett and Coach Don and Aunty Ell and Darren and two cars full of Wathaurong people and a couple of others who joined in Geelong, we all make it on board.

There's hardly time for a packet of chips before we're unloading at the other side and Dave the truckie is pretty keen to get on his way so he pulls up as soon as he can once he's off the ferry and everyone jumps out of their cars and begins pulling the milk cart out of the truck and this big crowd comes out of the Hotel Sorrento where we're stopped and the milk cart gets a bit stuck, but then they free it and the crowd gives a big cheer but they give an even bigger cheer when they see Danny Boy backing out of the truck and down the ramp and he tosses his head and his mane like he's loving it.

Geraldine is loving it; she's got pictures of the horse with the big stone pub in the background and the hotel guests standing there cheering with their glasses raised.

'Hold him, will you,' Mr Garrett says to me. 'I have to check him for knocks.' He starts running his hands down Danny Boy's legs and lifting his feet and Danny Boy is tossing his head but I've learned how to hold his rein tight so he can't carry on too much. 'Good on you,' Mr Garrett says. 'Let's get the harness on him before he starts doing somersaults for the crowd.'

The guests from the pub are standing on a big grassy area that looks over the car park and Jenny says, come on, grab a bucket, and we go running up there and tell them who we are and ask if they want to help with the cost of the funeral and they're all happy to throw something in the bucket. As we walk back down to the milk cart, Jenny is looking in. 'About twenty bucks, I reckon,' she says.

'That's pretty good, right?' I tell her.

'I just checked my GoFundMe page,' she says, and looks around so no one can hear.

'Yeah?'

'It's gone mental.'

Mental? I'm thinking, OK, it was at thirty thousand, so maybe now it's double …

'One hundred thousand plus three thousand dollars,' she says.

'You mean a hundred and three thousand.'

'Whatever. I bet we could rebuild the house for that. I bet we could pay off the bank.'

'Did you tell Mum?'

'She doesn't believe it's real money,' Jenny says. 'She thinks it's like a school walkathon or something where people say they'll pay you twenty cents a kilometre and then they never pay up. She doesn't get the idea of PayPal.'

'That's a lot of money, Jen, you have to –'

'What are you two nattering on about?' Mum says, creeping up on us. OK, so she probably doesn't actually creep up on us, probably she just sees us talking and walks over, but she scares the pants off me appearing like that.

'Just counting,' Jenny says, holding up the bucket and looking at me with her death stare.

'Yeah, we got twenty bucks,' I say. 'Maybe more even.'

Mum looks in the bucket. 'I'd say you got nearly fifty,' she says. 'Well done, you two, go give it to Coach Don eh, he can put it in the kitty.'

Then there's another cheer from the grassy verge by the pub and it's the Melbourne Highway Patrol arriving. They're not as friendly as Natalie.

* * *

Coach Don wants to push on a bit and see if we can get to Mornington, which he says we have to if we want to get to Carlton by Sunday.

Mr Garrett isn't happy though because he says Danny Boy is high as a kite after the trip inside the truck inside the ferry and he doesn't want him to have another turn and it'll soon be five o'clock, shouldn't they pull up stumps and consider themselves lucky to be in Sorrento? Sorrento to Melbourne, they can do it in a day with a really early start.

'Rec reserve is just down the road, isn't it?' Karsi asks one of the local police and he says yeah, and Mum says, 'I think we all need a bit of a breather, don't we? We're nearly there now.'

'What are you saying, Garrett?' Mr Alberti asks. 'Sorrento to the CBD in one hop? I did it in five hours on a bike when I was younger, and that was with a headwind. But is it doable in a day by horse?'

'Danny will get us there,' Mr Garrett says. 'Saturday night or Sunday morning, we'll see how he goes. But tonight he needs to rest.'

'Are we going to Federation Square when we get there?' Jenny pipes up. 'I thought the whole point was Mum would give a speech in Federation Square.'

'Where did you get that idea?' Mum asked her.

'Coach Don said something about Federation Square back in Yardley ...'

Mum looks thoughtful. 'We'd need a permit, wouldn't we?' she says.

'No, actually not,' Alasdair says. 'You'll be lucky to get any sort of crowd, and permits are really only needed if you think it's going to be a huge crowd and you want police to organise crowd control – or if they insist, which they really can't.' He shrugs, 'Freedom of political expression.'

'Really? I thought there'd be all sorts of rules,' Coach Don said.

'I'll check with Fed Square management,' he says. 'But as long as you're not erecting fences or trying to plug into power, pretty much anyone can stop up anywhere on public land and hold a gathering.'

'Bet they hand out parking tickets though,' Mr Alberti grumbles. 'Bloody bombers never miss a trick.'

'You can bet on that,' Alasdair says.

'I'll get on to some people,' Karsi says. 'It'll be better we let them know exactly what we're planning, even if we don't need a permit. Might want a couple of extra cars for the escort.'

'What about tonight?' Mum asks.

'Rec reserve, straight up the road about two hundred metres,' Deb says. 'We just went up and checked it out. There's some people finishing cricket training and they said there's a number we can call. Police can probably get them to open up the clubhouse so we can make some food and take showers, like usual, eh?'

In the end it turns out we wouldn't have been allowed to leave the town anyway. The Sorrento police have already organised for us to pull up at the reserve and there are some people from the cricket club there and they've opened up the change rooms for showers by the time we get there and are pulling sausages out of a big fridge and they've opened the bar.

The clubhouse is a big two-storey place with a balcony but Mum says we have to stay on the ground floor and not go exploring and we'll all be having an early night so don't get any ideas. The club is called the Sharks and pretty soon there's lots of people in the bar. Most of the cricketers have stayed on and I recognise a few people from the pub balcony who gave us money. Geraldine is interviewing people to see if they heard about the funeral horse and cart and most of them say they have but I don't know, maybe they're just saying it to get their name in the Melbourne paper.

'I support the farmers,' one of them is saying to her. 'All right? I think it's really sad what happened to the lady there.' He's pointing with his beer glass. 'But this shit, sorry, this stuff with burning down businesses? I'm not saying I have sympathy for the banks, no way, but there's people who work in that supermarket, what about them? They have to live too, just like the farmers.'

'Fuck the banks,' says the guy next to him, really quiet. 'Fuck big business.' He's just standing at the bar, looking up at a telly and not really in the conversation.

Geraldine looks over at him. 'You don't feel the same?' she asks. 'Would you like to tell me what you think about this funeral procession?'

'I just did,' the man says. 'You can quote me on it.'

Geraldine looks a bit disappointed, but then she sees another group of men and goes over to them instead.

'Fuck the fucking banks,' the man says again and looks down at me. 'Sorry, kid, but you come into a bar, you're going to hear stuff.'

'It's people's jobs, Rhys,' the first guy says. 'You burn down the banks, where does it stop? Supermarkets too? You work at the servo. How about if they burned that down? Whole town goes up in flames and you're out of a job, how about that?'

'My dad died,' I tell the first guy. I don't know why. Anyway, I've said it.

'Oh shit,' the man says. 'I'm sorry, all right.'

'Don't be saying that to people,' the angry man says to me. 'I might agree with what your mum is doing, but it's not the fault of people here your dad died.' He puts a hand on my shoulder and gives me a little push. 'Go find your mum, eh.'

I don't go looking for Mum. I decide it's more interesting following Geraldine around and working out who's with us and who's against us. After talking to another ten people she notices me standing there. 'What's up?'

'Six-four,' I tell her. 'With the two other guys, that's seven-five.'

'Seven-five what?' she asks, putting away her recorder.

'Seven who support us, five who don't,' I tell her.

'Hadn't looked at it like that,' she says. 'I'll call that a majority in my next article, shall I?'

The cricket club captain gets up on the bar and announces that the money from the sausage sizzle and the bar will 'go to the widow', and this gets a cheer. Jenny and me are sitting in a little office where a lady said we could use the internet to check Jenny's Facebook and GoFundMe and things.

'What are you doing?'

She pulls on her bottom lip and clicks on a page. 'How do you make a petrol bomb?'

I reach for the mouse. 'Don't even joke about it.'

'I'm not joking,' she says, pushing my hand away. 'Is it like, just petrol in a bottle or something? How do you light it without blowing yourself up? Can you ...'

'You are not going to google "petrol bombs",' I say. 'You moron. I bet the police are already watching your Facebook ...'

'Wow, paranoid much?' she asks.

'They would be,' I say. 'They'll be watching all of us, just waiting for an excuse to arrest us.'

She sighs. 'So because you're afraid, we shouldn't do anything, we should just sit on that stupid milk cart behind that stupid horse all the way to Melbourne and then bury Dad, if he's even dead, and then what?'

'I don't know, find a house and a school in Melbourne I guess.'

'You think too small, Jack,' she says. She clicks the mouse, pushes her screen so I can see it. 'One hundred and twenty-two now,' she says. 'Thousand. I moved about two thousand of it out of PayPal to Mum's bank account so she can give it to the people who need money for petrol and food and the ferry.'

'She'll ask where it came from.'

'She won't. She never checks how much is in there. I asked her how much we had and she said she has no idea, but one day she'll go to the machine and it will say no and we'll be broke and that'll be that.'

'Could I get new soccer boots?' I ask her.

'Sure,' she says. 'After we buy back our farm.'

'OK.'

'And the cows.'

'Yeah yeah, I get it.'

'And rebuild the house.'

'Shut up.'

'And buy all new furniture and plates and glasses and knives and forks and a telly because Mum and Dad sold ours.'

'So funny.'

'Oh, and a soccer ball, because you'd need something to kick with your new boots.'

Luckily before I hit Jen, Geraldine comes up to us. 'You two just going to sit there arguing all night, or do you want to come out to the road and plant your crosses?'

* * *

I swear it wasn't Jenny. I know she was talking about it and for a minute, when we heard about it, I looked at her like, *you did not, did you?* but she shook her head. It wasn't her.

But someone burned down one of the banks on Ocean Beach Road overnight and according to Mr Alberti they must have had balls like a Brahman bull because there was a police car parked right out the front and whoever it was piled a huge stack of wood up against the back door and set it on fire and then the door caught fire and then the ceiling inside caught fire and in about ten minutes by the time the policeman out the front knew what was happening the whole back of the bank was on fire. But the fire brigade put the fire out before the whole building went up and the shops next door were OK.

Apparently there were sirens going for hours and you could smell the smoke from where we were camped but Jenny and I didn't hear a thing.

And that's not the big news, according to Deb. She's been sitting in her car with Ben, listening to the early morning radio news, thinking they might hear about the fire in Sorrento some more.

'There were two other fires,' she says, coming over to the milk cart. 'One yesterday afternoon, one last night, up north.'

'I know,' Mr Garrett says. 'Someone in the shower block was saying. Supermarket in Gruyere and a bank in the Fleurieu.'

'Gruyere's in the Dandenongs,' Mum says. 'Where's Fleurieu?'

'South Australia.'

'You started something now, Dawn,' Mr Alberti says, and he sounds scared. 'This is really something now.'

'I didn't start this,' Mum says and she looks at Coach Don. 'I didn't start any fires.'

'Don't give me your evil eye, woman,' Coach Don says. 'You think I have some sort of magic X-Man rocket plane that can transport me from Sorrento to the Dandenongs and over to South Aussie and back again while you're asleep?'

'Did you hear?' Karsi says, running up. 'Apparently there was a phone call before the fire in South Australia. They said someone sprayed the bank window with your hashtag.'

'What's a hashtag?' Mum asks.

Karsi looks at us. 'It's what the kids have put on all their crosses, #BURN. It's on the banners on the side of the milk cart. People were waving it on placards in Colac. How could you not have seen it?'

Mum gets annoyed. 'Don't patronise me, Hussein Karsioglu. I've had just about all I can take from you lot,' she says and she stumps off in the direction of the ladies' toilets. Jenny runs after her.

Jenny and I felt a bit funny doing the thing with the crosses last night, but Geraldine said it was important to keep up routines. She even suggested we set fire to it because that

220

would make a good picture but I pointed out there was a fire ban and we'd get in trouble and she dropped it.

After breakfast Jenny and me get the harness on Danny all by ourselves in a world-record twelve and a half minutes, and even Mr Garrett is impressed. Danny looks like he's had a good rest because he's stomping and snorting and wants to get rolling before Mr Garrett even has himself sat down. We have about fifteen cars in the procession, because some more have come across on the morning ferry from Queenscliff, but Mr Alberti, Coach Don, Mum and Alasdair have to go to the police station down by the wharf to talk to police about the latest fire, and say they'll catch us up later.

Aunty Ell sends Darren to ride with us for company and Mr Garrett has Ben up front with him but they aren't talking much, mostly they just listen to Ben's phone which has a radio app on it.

As we pull out of the reserve onto the Nepean Highway, I look to see if our cross has fallen over in the night, or if it's still standing up, because we didn't dig it in too deep. It was kind of awkward after Geraldine's dumb idea of setting fire to it, so we just wanted to get it done and get back to the camp.

'Bloody hell,' Darren says.

'Wow,' Jenny gasps. 'Hold this, I want to get a photo,' and she gives me the bread roll she's eating and jumps down off the back of the milk cart. She'll have to jog to catch us up but we're used to jumping on and off when we need to go to the toilet and Danny Boy never goes much faster than a quick walk so it's easy to grab on and jump up using the steps at the front if one of the adults gives us a hand-up.

There's a *forest* of white crosses in the grass on the side of the road by the stone gates at the entrance to the racetrack. Big ones and little ones and some people standing there looking at them, and some flowers too, that people have put there. Geraldine is there, taking video, talking to a lady who's putting a bunch of flowers down with the crosses and taking her photo. Half of the crosses are just plain white, but half of them have *#BURN* written in the middle or at the top.

Jenny catches us up at the roundabout going down to the main street where there are some people standing and they don't look too happy. One of them calls out something rude and gives us the finger and he bends down and picks up a rock and throws it after us but he misses by a mile.

Jenny is going to yell something at him but Ben has turned and he pulls Jenny up onto the milk cart then puts a hand on her shoulder. 'No, mate,' he says. 'That's what he wants you to do – don't let him think you even noticed him.'

'He threw a rock!' Jenny says. 'What if he hit us?'

'He didn't,' Ben says. 'You have to realise, there's a few people who know what we're doing and they're with us. And then there's most people who have no clue who we are and only see we're driving a horse on a main road with a coffin in the back in a procession full of cars with their lights all on, so maybe they work out it's a funeral, but that's all. Then there's a few, like him, who think it's our fault these idiots are setting fire to banks and supermarkets and they can't get angry at those people because the police haven't caught any of them yet, so they get angry at us.'

'Yeah, but what are we going to do if one of them does hit us with a rock, or something worse?' Jenny asks again.

'We're gonna love 'em to death, aren't we, Ben?' Mr Garrett laughs. 'You bloody tree huggers,' he shakes his head. He turns around to Jenny. 'I got a licensed twelve-gauge shotgun in the box under my feet, girl. Anyone hits you with a rock, I'll put a dozen pellets into their backside and see if they still want to throw rocks after that.'

'Way to be a role model, mate,' Ben says.

'Can I try the gun next time we stop?' Darren asks.

'No. And the box is locked, right, Garrett?'

'Yep, combi lock. Code is 000,' Mr Garrett says with a grin.

'It is not. That isn't the code, Darren. Don't listen to him.' But then they both stop stirring each other and listen to Ben's phone as the radio program gets cut by a news bulletin.

… interrupt the program for a news update. Victoria Police have advised that a third fire yesterday involving a milk truck that was parked overnight in a fenced lot in Goldwins' Dairy Co-op in Rochester is believed to have been deliberately lit. The truck tyres and cabin were set on fire and the hashtag #BURN was spray-painted on the body of the truck. Police are reviewing CCTV footage and are asking for anyone with information about the fire to contact Crime Stoppers.

'It's a crowning fire now,' Mr Garrett says, almost to himself. 'Jumping along the tops of trees faster than the wind. We have to face it.'

We get to Dromana mid-morning and there's a park there by the beach with a playground and something like an ice-cream van that also sells coffee and everyone decides we'll stop for a few minutes because there's a toilet there too. There's just enough room for about fifteen cars and the milk cart. The police park on the main road. It's one of those cold blue-sky days, so no one is up for a swim. The playground is a sad one made for kids under five and even they'd reckon it was boring. Just a wooden castle with a yellow plastic slide and a set of swings.

'Swing me!' Jenny says, like she's about four again, and runs for one of the swings. Darren takes the other one and I push them both – one left-handed, the other right-handed, both complaining I'm not pushing hard enough. Then we go down to the water to throw stuff as Mum and the others arrive. Mum comes over, stands watching us, breathing in the air with hands on her hips and a smile on her face. A real one. The first real one I've seen since the house went up. She's so pretty I almost forget again that I should still be mad at her about the coffin. Don walks over too, and she puts a hand on his shoulder.

'I recognise this place,' she says. 'We stopped here once, Tom and me and the kids. For ice cream.'

'Where have you been? Did you get arrested?' I ask her.

'No, hon, but the police have a lot of questions right now,' she explains. 'There's been a lot of banks and things being set on fire. Three or four people have tried to burn their own properties to the ground too, like Ron did. City people, not country. People with houses who can't pay their mortgages.'

'Copycats,' Jenny says.

'I guess …' Mum says. 'Anyway, every time they do it, people are using that sign you made. The BURN one.'

'*Hashtag* BURN,' Jenny says.

'Well anyway,' Mum says. 'This is bigger than your dad's funeral now. Bigger than just dairy farmers. Centrelink sent out thousands of debt recovery notices last week and some protesters lit a fire in a Centrelink office.'

'Are they going to let us finish the funeral?' I ask.

Mum looks at Coach Don. 'You just spoke to Karsi. What do you think?'

'There's a lot of pressure to shut us down now. Political pressure,' Coach Don says. 'I'm getting mixed messages. Fed Square management has given permission for a memorial speech, but Vic Police are saying it could draw in thousands of people and they don't have the manpower. Karsi said the Highway Patrol wants us to hold here. I reckon they're shaping to try to force us to hand over the coffin.'

'Where's Alasdair?' Mum asks, looking up and down the convoy.

'On his way,' Coach Don says. 'He was up in Melbourne talking to the city council – he thinks they'll support us, if we can get there.'

'Did the police tell you directly that we can't go any further?' Mum asks. She looks up the road where the police are climbing out of their patrol cars, fanning themselves with their hats. A couple are waiting in the queue for coffee and ice cream.

'Well, not in so many words …' Coach Don says.

'But not a direct order,' Mum says, deciding something. 'Back on the cart, kids.' She yells out to Mr Garrett who's filling a bucket with feed for Danny Boy, 'Saddle up, Garrett, let's see if they're serious!'

He looks at her and frowns, then grabs another bucket. 'Get some water, girl!' he yells at Jenny and throws it to her. 'Wet the horse down.'

Coach Don starts running down the line of cars telling people to get back in and get ready to move.

Jenny and I fill the bucket with water from a plastic barrel at the back of the milk cart. It slops everywhere as I run around to Danny Boy, who's sweating hard from the morning sun and he tosses his head as soon as he can smell the water, nearly knocking the bucket out of my hand as he sticks his nose in. He nearly empties the bucket in a single draw, but I pull it away and throw what's left over his flanks. Jenny refills it and does the same on the other side of him. His whole hide shivers but he looks pretty glad about it.

'Pour some over yourselves too while you're at it,' Mum yells, and motions with her finger over her head to show she means it. Jenny and I look at each other and shrug, fill up our buckets again and start tossing water at each other and laughing.

'Enough of that! All aboard!' Mr Garrett yells and I pull away, throw my bucket up on the milk cart and climb up at the back which is not easy because it's moving, jerking forward with big jumps as Danny Boy gets up to a quick walk. I pull Jenny up after me.

The traffic police in the ice-cream queue are a bit slow seeing us pulling back into traffic and we're about level with their empty cop car before they realise. The people in our convoy are quicker and are already rolling.

'Get a move on, Garrett!' Mum yells. She's sitting in the middle of the drivers' bench on the left of Mr Garrett and to the right of Coach Don, looking ahead like she can will Federation Square closer just by giving the horizon fierce looks. 'I want to see what they're willing to do to stop us!'

The police have finally decided they aren't getting coffee or ice cream this afternoon after all and run for their cars. One of them quickly pulls up alongside and an officer puts an arm out the window waving us down. 'Pull that animal to the side of the road, driver!' he yells on the police car's loudspeaker. But he has to drop back as he runs out of lane because of approaching traffic. Mr Garrett taps his ears like he can't hear, sets his jaw and gives the reins a shake. 'Gee up, Danny!' he yells and Danny Boy lifts himself into a trot. 'Let's give 'em a run for their money, boy!' Right at the back, Ben and Deb are weaving left and right in their old ute so that the police cars in the back can't overtake them.

Now it's getting crazy. It's probably the world's slowest police pursuit. There are twenty cars behind us on the two-lane road and the police car near us has its lights and siren on, and the police officer is trying to overtake but it isn't safe because of the traffic coming against us so he has to stay behind and wait for a wider piece of road.

'Looks like they're serious, Dawn!' Mr Garrett yells. He looks over his shoulder at Jenny and me, then Mum and Coach Don. 'I don't think we have an option here.'

And right then the police car pulls out into the oncoming traffic and a car coming the other way has to slam on its brakes and it skids to a stop broadside across the road right in front of us and Danny Boy tries to go around it to the right but the police car is right next to him so he swerves left and the milk cart goes up on one wheel and before I know it I'm half flying, half jumping over the side, and Jenny lands right beside me and we both fall into a ditch. I mean, it sounds worse than it is, because after all Danny Boy is hardly a racehorse. The adults up front all have something to hang on to so they stay in their seats and the police in the patrol car pile out and run up the road waving their arms to stop anyone else driving into us.

And Mum is jumping down from the cart and running towards us and I grab Jenny because the look on Mum's face is scarier than when that car was coming straight at us.

The police pull everyone in to the side of the road so that traffic can get past. No one hit anyone so there's no accident to clear up. It's still sunny but cool, so it isn't too bad being stuck out here. I mean, I'm thirsty, but the sun isn't too hot today.

Mum gets totally paranoid after we jump off the cart, so she makes Jenny and me do a full body check of each other to make sure there are no cuts or scratches or anything broken and then she checks us both again herself just to be sure.

As everything is getting organised, Geraldine comes roaring down the road in her little blue car and Alasdair jumps out and runs up the road in his suit with his tie flying behind him, while Geraldine fast-waddles along behind him. The grown-ups are up front arguing with the police and two TV vans with their cameramen and reporters. Me and Jenny listen for a while but it gets boring because Alasdair is using long words, and the police are using loud ones, and people keep telling us to get further up the footpath so the traffic can go past in the one lane that isn't blocked but there's nowhere to stand so we go and sit on the gutter in the shade of the milk cart.

Darren comes up and sits beside us. 'This sucks, eh?' he says, throwing a stone.

'Yeah, we got this far, why do they have to stop us now?' Jenny asks. 'It's just stupid. I mean, it's just a few more hours, and the memorial, then the funeral and it's all finished.'

'You don't know?' Darren asks, looking at Jenny and me like we're space aliens just landed on earth.

'No, what?' I ask him.

'The fires in Sydney?'

'Yeah, we know about that,' Jenny says. 'The Centrelink? That's like, so yesterday.'

He leans his head back. 'Wow, you *don't* know.' Now he leans forward, 'Yesterday it was one fire in a Centrelink in Parramatta. Today there's like ten, all over the country – some banks, government offices, two politician's offices. There's full-on rioting in Corio!'

'Is that in Melbourne?'

'I think so. There's five more farmhouses around the country have been burned to the ground too, by people just torching them and walking off.'

Suddenly the milk cart jerks forward and we have to scoot backwards on our bums so we don't get rolled over by the back wheels. I jump up and there's a policeman who has grabbed Danny Boy by the harness and is trying to pull him around, except Mr Garrett has put the brakes on. Danny Boy is tossing his head, not sure what's going on.

'Hey,' Jenny yells. 'Let go of him! You're scaring him.'

The cop looks at us, annoyed. 'I know horses. Just tell me how I get the cart moving,' he says. 'This little sideshow is over. I have to walk him across the road to that beach carpark until we get a horsebox here to take him away.' He walks down the side of Danny Boy, looking under the milk cart. 'Must be a brake …' he mutters to himself.

'Don't show him,' Jenny whispers to me, like I would have. 'Let him work it out.'

But he finds it. Climbs quickly up into the driver's seat and pushes down on the foot pedal Mr Garrett uses to set the brake, and then hops down with a big smile, and winks at Jenny, then takes Danny Boy by the bridle and gives him a hard tug so he'll start moving. Danny Boy isn't having it. He tosses his head, letting out a loud snort, and makes the policeman let go.

'Hey!' Mr Garrett shouts from up ahead where he's been with all the other adults, arguing. He's only just seen the policeman trying to move the milk cart and he comes running back toward us. 'Stop that!' He's got his riding crop in his right hand still.

The policeman sees him and puts a hand on his hip near his gun and his other hand up with his palm out. 'Stop right there, sir!' he yells at Mr Garrett and Mr Garrett slows down but he doesn't stop. 'I said STOP!' the cop yells and he pulls his gun.

Jenny grabs my arm, and Darren looks around like he's looking for something he can hit the cop with. That's what he says later anyway.

Maybe it's the near-death accident, or all the shouting, or standing in the sun too long, or maybe it's the sudden galloping, but right about then is when a vein in Danny Boy's head blows out.

He's all caught up in the harness but he drops to his knees on his front legs first, then gives a big heaving huff and falls over sideways.

The snort heard round the world

Danny Boy probably saved Mr Garrett from getting shot, but that's not what people are worried about right now.

Mr Garrett is cradling Danny Boy's head in his lap, sitting on the road with dozens of people in a circle all around him. He's crying, which is a good thing because he looks like if he was trying to hold it in, he'd probably pop a cog himself.

Jenny goes over and stands beside him and I stand beside her and we're looking down at Danny Boy. He was huffing a bit before but now he's completely still and his eyes have this kind of bloodshot jelly look about them. I'm wondering, shouldn't we close them, like they do to dead people in the movies?

Jenny is standing with her knuckles in her mouth next to Mr Garrett, who is down on his knees and moaning kind of quiet, so only we can hear. I don't know what to do, so I'm looking at Jenny and that's when I see it.

'Your face!' I say to Jenny. No, it can't be.

She looks at me, sniffing. 'What?'

I reach out my hand and wipe her cheek. It comes back dry, but her eyes look wet. I want to show her, but it's not like I can take a picture or anything, 'You're nearly crying!'

She pushes my hand away. 'Not funny.'

'No, seriously!'

She reaches up her hand to her face and rubs her eyes.

'Whatever,' she says, and puts a hand on Mr Garrett's shoulder and they're both there together and he puts his face in his hands and really lets go.

I ball my fists up and walk away.

I've got that feeling again, like someone is blowing up a balloon, inside my chest. I just need to get away from it all, but there's nowhere to run. It's not fair! She didn't love Danny more than me. And I looked after him nearly as much as her. People are going to be looking at us thinking *she's* the only one who's sad!

There's a house with a metal fence and a lady standing there with some water in a jug and some plastic cups, like she can't decide whether to come out and help or stay inside and just watch the show, and she sees me and she holds out a cup. 'Would you like some water, darlin'?'

She sounds English. I look away at Jenny and Mr Garrett and the police everywhere and the farmers and TV crews and I look past her into her front yard and I turn to her, 'Can I just sit down, on your grass?'

'Yes, of course, luv,' she says. She takes my elbow and I sit on the dry brown ground and I take the water from her but I don't drink it, I'm so angry. I pound the ground with my fist and I pound it again and again until I can feel my arm shaking and she's looking at me kind of scared and she squats down and she takes my arm and stops me pounding my fist and she says, 'What is it, luv?'

I bring my knees up and bury my face in them and she puts an arm around me. 'Is it the horse? I saw him drop. It's a terrible thing, you must be really upset.'

I look up at her and give her a glare. 'If I was upset, I'd be crying, wouldn't I?'

'Well ...'

'Well I'm not. Because *someone* has to hold it together, don't they?' I say to her.

'I suppose ...'

'So that's me,' I tell her. 'I'm that guy.'

She's looking around us now, like she is looking for help. 'Now, see now. We all take these things differently ...'

I laugh. 'Oh yeah, you could say that.'

Then she looks relieved and I see it's because Mum is coming in the gate. Mum stands looking down at me, looking at the lady. 'What's all this then?'

'He's a bit upset, the poor thing,' the lady says. 'Just wanted to sit down for a minute.'

'Thank you,' Mum tells her.

'Would you like some cold water?' the lady asks, holding out a cup.

'That would be nice, thanks,' Mum says, and takes a cup and sits down next to me. I don't want to look at her, so I put my face in my knees again.

She doesn't say anything. It's a thing she does, just waits you out. I know she won't move until I say something.

'It's just not fair!' I say into my knees.

'It's the horse,' the lady says. 'I think he's upset about …'

'It's not the horse,' Mum says to me softly. 'Is it?'

'She's nearly crying!' I tell her. 'Jenny. That's the *second* time!'

'Ah,' Mum says, looking out the gate at Mr Garrett helping Jenny up from the ground and looking around him like he's wondering what to do now as some people walk towards them. 'OK, right.'

'I'm just as sad as her!' I tell Mum. 'It's so unfair. What if she can cry one day and I never do?'

Mum knows if she tries to hug me now I'll just up and run, so lucky for her she doesn't. She pulls up a piece of dry grass and crumbles it between her fingers. 'You're the same, but you're different, you know that,' Mum says. The lady with the water jug just stands there frowning, no clue what we're talking about. Tough.

'But it makes people think she cares more!' I say. 'And she doesn't!'

'I know, Jack,' Mum says. 'But it's like –'

'Don't tell me it's like her periods,' I say to her, even angrier now.

'Like that,' she says. 'You can't feel your insides, like when you have an upset stomach, but she's starting to feel hers. This is the same. You'll catch up.'

'But you don't *know*!' I yell at her. 'I might never!'

'Don't say that,' Mum says.

'I read online, there's types of analgesia where people can't cry and they never do, ever, in their whole lives,' I tell her.

'And Dorotea's is different,' she says. 'Some people get some feeling back as they grow up, some end up able to cry.'

'Some! Not all!' I yell. I stand up. I've heard it all before. I don't want to hear it now. 'How long are we going to be stuck on this stupid road?' I see Jenny with the crowd of people. 'Danny Boy is dead! Everyone is just standing around, no one is *doing* anything!'

I leave Mum standing there with the lady with the water jug and I go to find Pop because I know he'll be somewhere telling people what they should be doing.

Coach Don is talking angrily with the cops, and one of them is trying to tell people to step away while Karsi is telling him to calm down, let things just cool down a bit.

Alasdair is suddenly without anyone to talk to and he comes up and kneels down beside me. 'You were near the horse, can you tell me what happened?' He takes my arm. Puts a finger to his mouth, like I should talk quiet.

I look at him. He's on our side, right? I look for Mum, but she's still in with that lady.

'A policeman tried to move Danny Boy and Mr Garrett saw him and started running over, then Danny Boy collapsed,' I tell him as Jenny joins us.

'Did the policeman touch Danny Boy?' Alasdair asks. 'This is really important. Did the policeman make any sort of contact with Danny Boy?'

'Contact?'

'Did he touch him, grab him, try to move him physically?'

I think back. 'Yeah, he grabbed his harness first, pulled on that. Then he realised the brake was set, so he hopped on the milk cart and let off the brake. Then he grabbed the bridle and Danny Boy threw him off, and Mr Garrett saw that and that's when –'

'He hit Danny Boy with his club,' Jenny says. She sounds angry.

I look at her like she's crazy.

'Are you sure?' Alasdair asks.

'*He* couldn't see everything,' she says, nodding at me. 'I saw it *all*. He let off the brake and he smacked Danny Boy with his club on his hindquarters to try to get him moving. He hit him *hard*.'

I'm thinking back. Did he? I don't think he did. Maybe I didn't see?

'Thanks,' Alasdair says quickly, standing up. He looks around until he sees the Vic Police officer with the most stripes and he walks straight over to him and starts talking. We follow like a pair of ducklings.

'Captain, I'm representing these people and you have a real situation here,' Alasdair is saying to the cop. The guy is wiping his brow, hat in his hand. He's got other cops trying to talk to him, and Coach Don is hovering too, looking dead set on having a go at him while Ben holds him back.

'Oh, I do?' the cop says, looking at Alasdair through narrow eyes. He takes a breath and looks around him. 'Really? I just see a coffin I need to get carted off to Melbourne General Cemetery, one dead horse I need to clear off the road and a host of traffic violations. With respect, I don't see any "situation", sir.'

Alasdair looks down at us and indicates with a wave of one hand, 'These children just told me they saw your constable strike that horse before it fell dead.'

'They *what*?'

'They saw your constable strike that horse with his baton, and then it fell down dead,' Alasdair told him. 'I'm thinking unlawful killing of an animal. That sound like a "situation" to you now, officer?'

'He didn't,' I whisper to Jenny. 'Did he?'

'Just because you didn't see it,' she hisses at me. 'Shut up.'

The police officer wipes his hand across his face, looks down at us, looks at Alasdair like he wishes him all kinds of hurt. Lots of people look at Alasdair like that but he doesn't seem to care.

Right then Mum comes up and stands between us with her arms around our shoulders. 'What's all this then?' she asks.

Jenny jumps in before I can say anything. 'We saw a policeman hit Danny Boy and make him fall down, now Alasdair is telling it to the policeman here.'

The officer hears her. Mum says nothing, just looks up at Alasdair and the policeman.

'The word of two minors isn't going to hold against one of my constables,' the officer says.

'More trouble than this is all worth though,' Alasdair says and he looks over at the TV crews standing behind some yellow tape and filming everything in sight. 'What say we stick to the plan I just agreed with the senior inspector and the mayor's office, all right? The city works people are already preparing things downtown; make a call if you need to. We're talking a quick memorial speech in Federation Square, then tomorrow we bury the poor man at Melbourne General and this is all over.'

Two more TV crews pull up now and jump out, filming the growing crowd. Traffic is backing up again with only one lane open and some of the drivers start leaning on their horns. Then a photographer sees Mr Garrett standing with Danny Boy, and Karsi in his police uniform with his arm over Mr Garrett's shoulders, and the photographer ducks under the police tape to get the shot, which means all the other reporters try to get past and the one policeman there can't hold them back. A reporter jams a microphone in the policeman's face. 'Officer? Can you tell us what has happened here? We heard the horse has been shot?'

'It has *not*,' the captain growls at her, then he rounds on Alasdair, 'I'm going to make that call.'

While his constables herd the reporters back, the officer turns his back and talks quickly into his mobile phone. He has to yell a bit to make himself heard over the reporters shouting questions, but then he turns back to Alasdair.

'All right. You will organise to get that dead animal moved. You will get that cart with that coffin lawfully hitched up to a motorised vehicle and you will tow it to Federation Square under escort. You have an hour to get there, get your memorial service underway, or I will start arresting people for unlawful assembly, public nuisance and about a dozen other things I can think of.'

The tractor guy Trevor is the one with the right tow hitch to be able to connect up to Mr Garrett's milk cart. The police block off the road so he can come around and hook up, and meantime Mum goes over and sits with Mr Garrett. She puts an arm around him and rocks him a bit, side to side.

Darren is looking at his mobile. 'There's a mob going to be at Fed Square,' he says. He's got his phone in one hand, a cricket ball in the other.

'How many?' Jenny asks.

'Could be ten, could be a hundred,' he shrugs. 'Who knows. I just got a message from a kid I met here last year and my mum has been on her phone the last two days telling people to come with flags and everything.'

'Awesome,' Jenny says.

'Really? Could look a bit weird, only five turn up.'

'Still awesome they'd even bother, for someone they don't even know,' she says.

'Yeah, well, my mum, she had this thing for your dad ...'

We both look at Darren like, *what?*

'No, not a *thing* thing,' he says. 'Come on, no. Yuk. No, there was this time my olds had this party and it got a bit out of control. This guy started busting up stuff, in the kitchen like, you know ...'

Jenny and me both look at each because, no, we don't.

'... throwing plates and glasses. Dad was trying to calm them down but they weren't listening to him. Mum and me were hiding in her room until it blew out, but these people kept going, so Mum called your dad. He came over and helped Dad shut it down. Things like that, is what I mean.'

'Yeah,' Jenny says. 'Parties, eh.'

And I look at her like, *oh, so you've been to a party like that?* But she just shrugs.

'Yeah. So, you want to play Droppit until we go?' Darren is looking at me. 'Your hand's OK now, yeah? Just try not to catch it with your face this time.'

'Ha ha, not funny,' I say. And we go down the road aways to a place we can throw the ball. Leave Jenny there just watching.

Tough.

Let her go cry about it.

It's lunchtime by the time they work out how to hitch the milk cart to Trevor's tractor and get all the right connections for the tail-lights and stuff. We're not allowed to ride in the milk cart when it's being towed, so for the trip up to Fed Square we sit up in the cab of the tractor with Trevor.

'What will they do with Danny Boy?' I ask him. Last we saw was Mr Garrett and some police standing waiting and waving quietly to cars as the funeral convoy pulled away behind the tractor.

'The horse? That was his name?'

'Yeah.'

It's not as noisy in the cabin as you'd think, and it has a fantastic radio you can connect your mobile phone to and play music and really cool leather seats.

'Well, they … he's a *big* horse, right? So they can't just get a few guys and carry him. They'll have to get something like an earth mover – a bobcat, you know?' He sucks on a tooth, I can see he's trying to think how he would do it. 'Or maybe better, you get a heavy hauler with a little crane on the back, you can make a sling, lift him onto the trailer with that, but you need to be, you know, discreet, driving a dead horse around.'

'They'd put him in a semi?' I hadn't thought about that. I thought it would be a horse box. But that would be stupid, lying him upside down in a horse box, legs in the air.

'Yeah, could be a flatbed, but I'm thinking more like an open top, so they can lower him in, and people driving by, they can't see him in there. More respectful like that,' he decides. 'For everyone.'

'And do they bury horses? In a cemetery?' I ask. 'Could they bury him next to Dad if we wanted?'

'What? No, they … No.'

Jenny looks at me with her eyebrows raised like, *just stop asking questions*, then sighs and looks out the window.

It takes most of the afternoon to get through St Kilda to the city centre because the police have us driving in just one lane and the convoy stretches back about a mile and is growing all the time. Jenny and I start counting, and we stop at about fifty cars because the rest get caught at a red light and we lose sight of them. People out shopping stop and watch and I'm wondering do they even know or do they think it's just a normal funeral for like, a big Greek family or something, because the police made us take down the banners on the sides and back of the milk cart but all the cars have their headlights on.

Mum asked Alasdair if they could make us do that and he said we'd won the big fight, so there was no point starting small ones.

Trevor lets us switch around the radio to hear if we're on the news and there's plenty on the radio news and traffic news about Danny Boy and the funeral and telling people to avoid the city centre if they don't want delays because the 'biggest funeral cortege the city has seen in years is arriving in town'. We hit a talk channel where the two people on the air are arguing about whether this funeral procession is bigger than the one for Gough Whitlam, and then they start arguing about who's to blame for the outbreak of fires and the riot in Sydney; is it Mum, or is it the banks, or is it the politicians for not doing anything about the problems of ordinary folks or is it ... blah blah. Looking out on Punt Road though at people going in and out of the shops and fast food places, you wouldn't hardly know there was anything happening different to any normal Saturday.

But at least some people know, because as we pass a service station there's a family there on the pavement and their kids are holding up signs saying *#BURN!* They wave at us like it's Moomba or something. And then when we turn the corner onto Brunton Avenue by the MCG Jenny says, 'Lookit!' and there are people standing there in the parklands and some are holding signs and some are just waving or holding fists in the air like Mum did.

MELBOURNE WITH THE COCKIES!
NO FARMS, NO LIFE!
#BURN MOFO #BURN
WELFARE RELIEF OR #BURN!

'People look angry,' I say. 'Are they angry at us for blocking traffic?'

Trevor smiles. 'No, mate. They're angry at a lot of things, but not us.'

'They're angry about *everything*,' Jenny says. 'You should see the messages people leave on my GoFundMe page. I had to delete some in case they shut my page down.'

'It's not just one thing, right?' Trevor says. 'Like, why I'm here. I'm not a farmer, turns out I'm not much of a businessman either. But I'm bloody fed up with useless politicians and banks and drought and bloody power shortages and rivers running dry and ...' He's thumping his steering wheel and he looks at me and must see something in my face. 'Hey, sorry ... it's not like it's all bad. Things will probably come good again, right? Just ... not everyone is an optimist like me.'

Jenny has tuned out and is waving back to some kids who look like a scout troop waving their troop flags, and then we turn onto Flinders Street and it looks like it's thousands of people there, but the news reports are saying a few hundred.

'Hey, we're on the wrong side of the road!' I suddenly realise.

'It's OK, we're just following the police car,' Trevor says.

'But maybe it's a trick,' I say. 'They want us to commit a crime so they can arrest us.'

'I don't think so,' Trevor says.

'Yeah, they could have arrested everyone back where Danny died,' Jenny says. 'They're not going to do it now in front of all these people.'

'They just want to get us into the Square in the fastest way,' Trevor says. 'See, there's another cop car up there ahead, turning the traffic away.'

I lean over to Jenny and whisper, 'They could get you for lying to a policeman, about Danny Boy.'

'I saw what I saw,' she says, not caring if Trevor hears. 'And besides, if I lied, which I'm not saying I did, but if I lied, I lied to a lawyer. Everyone does that. I bet it's not even a crime.'

And then we're there and the sun is shining off the crazy buildings like it's trying to blind everyone.

At Fed Square, it's what Mum calls bedlam. The police make us take the tractor and milk cart and drive it onto Swanston Street and park in front of all the flags so that all the other cars can come in behind us. The convoy goes all the way back around the corner on Flinders Street and people just pull up behind each other, turn off their engines and leave their cars right there.

A cop bangs on the door of the tractor cabin and Trevor opens his door.

'OK, you're good here, you can shut down your engine,' the cop says.

'It has to run down on automatic,' Trevor says. 'Give me a minute.' And he closes the door. He stands up and looks through the cabin's back window. 'This is no good,' he says. 'You're a TV crew, you want a picture of the milk cart with

247

the arts centre in the background. You can hardly see it parked over here.'

People are starting to gather around the milk cart, looking in on the coffin. One lady leans in and touches it, like she's trying to see if it's real. Trevor opens his window, 'Hey! Be careful, I have to turn around.' He sits down and puts the tractor in gear. 'Belt up, don't want you falling over,' he says, and Jenny and I reach around for seat belts.

Really slow and careful he turns the tractor left to where the police have dropped the security bollards so that they can get their cars in, and he drives up over the footpath and it feels like we might tip, even though the gutter there is only about ten centimetres, but then we're up and past the parked police cars and the milk cart is bumping over the footpath too, and people are waving hats and flags and cheering as Trevor takes the milk cart and Dad's coffin all the way to the bottom of the steps leading up to the Square. A couple of police look like they think they should stop him, or do something, but in the end they stand scratching their heads or they put their hands on their hips and just watch.

When he gets to the bottom of the steps Trevor stops the tractor and shuts down the engine. 'End of the line!' he calls out happily. 'Mission accomplished.' And he holds out his hand for a big high five so we land him a couple and jump out to look for Mum.

* * *

Which isn't easy, I tell you. We see a bunch of people getting out of cars. They're pulling flags and banners out of the boots and taking selfies. More are coming down from the Koorie Heritage Trust building. Aunty Ell sees us and comes over. 'Well, here's double trouble,' she says. 'Hey, you. Where's your mum?' She looks around.

'We thought maybe she was with you,' Jenny says.

'No, hon, haven't seen her, I been too busy saying hi to people,' she says. 'Not a bad turnout, eh?'

'All these people knew Dad?' I ask.

Aunty Ell smiles. 'Bless you, bub, no. These people are here for what your dad represents.'

'What's that?'

'Fighting spirit. Someone has to fight for the people who have no voice.' She looks north to where the Parliament is. 'No one over there's going to do it.'

'You want to get something to eat?' Darren asks. 'There's a 7-Eleven here somewhere.'

'Yeah, I … No, we have to find Mum,' I say.

'OK, later, eh?'

'Later,' Jenny says.

We take a few steps and I grab Jenny's arm. 'You want to split up? I'll go up and down the convoy, you go to the top of the steps and see if you can see her from there. I'll meet you back here in ten.'

She looks at me like I suddenly grew a brain. 'That might actually work. OK. Race you!' And she dives into the crowd.

I see people starting to put white crosses on the ground, leaning them against the steps.

I have this idea Mum would be talking to the police, or other grown-ups we know, but I run all the way down the convoy and around the corner and I see Mr Alberti and Mrs Garrett but they haven't seen Mum. I'm starting to worry by the time I get to the back of the convoy where the crowd thins out.

Maybe she really has been arrested this time. I wonder if it's because Trevor drove the milk cart right in front of the Square. I wonder if maybe she's in the Parliament, talking to some politicians – there was some talk maybe she'd have a meeting with the governor even. I run all the way back to the milk cart and am still standing there looking around when Jenny runs up. I can see straight away she hasn't found her either.

'We have to try again,' she says, panting.

'No, wait,' I say, getting my breath. 'I know where she is.'

'So, let's go,' she says.

'No, I mean, I didn't see her, but I bet I know where she is …'

'What? How?'

'She's with Dad' I say.

'At the milk cart?' she asks, frowning. 'No, I went by there. There was just –'

'No, idiot. *With* Dad,' I say. 'If he's still alive, then he'll be here in town somewhere. He'd have to be!'

'Here?' she asks. She looks at me like she doesn't know what I'm talking about and then she catches up. 'No, Jack, that … would be crazy. He'd be arrested in a heartbeat.'

'Maybe. But close, right? He'd want to see this!'

She puts her hands to her ears. 'Shut up! Just stop, all right?'

'Hey hey,' says this voice and I turn around and there's Mum. Just Mum. 'You two, arguing all the time. I thought twins were supposed to –'

'Mum!' I yell. 'I thought you'd been …'

'Now now,' she says. 'Don't get het up just because of all this hullabaloo.' She pulls me and Jenny closer. 'The police want us to get this done quickly, before things get out of hand.' She looks around at people laying crosses on the steps, Aunty Ell's mob carrying didges and a bunch of what Mr Garrett would call ferals banging on some bongos. 'Not that they aren't already.'

We go down by the milk cart and when people see Mum they start forming a circle, expecting something. Aunty Ell is there too, and the bank man from Yardley, Gary, he's up on the milk cart next to the coffin, setting up a big speaker and a microphone. Someone hands up a power cord and he plugs it in and then gives Mum a signal. He must have driven up today.

Coach Don is there and Mr Alberti and Mrs Alberti and Mr Garrett and Mrs Garrett and Mr and Mrs Turnbolt who must have come up from Yardley for the day because I didn't see them in the procession after the first day, and the Maynards and all their kids and Aunty Ell with Darren. Plus there's about three camera crews there and maybe ten reporters with microphones which they start handing up to the bank man on the milk cart too, so he can fix them with tape to the microphone stand. Geraldine is just one of the mob now, but she's standing with Karsi and she gives me a big smile and a wink and I give her a little wave back.

Jen starts on one side counting the crowd and I start on the other. There's too many people so I count them in clumps of ten. I decide there's three thousand two hundred and fifty and she says five. And it's all types. There's country people, you can see them a mile off, but there's also city people in suits and skirts and a mum with a whole soccer team of kids and some political party handing out pamphlets, and cops, but not as many as you'd think, and at the edges a lot of people who were just walking past and have stopped to see what's going on.

'I never thought it would be like this,' Jenny says, holding my arm. 'When we left home I really never thought anyone would care. It just felt stupid back then, but now it's …'

'I know,' I tell her. 'Me either.'

'Time, Dawn,' Coach Don says. Someone has pulled some hay bales off the back of the milk cart so Mum can use them like steps, and she gives Coach Don's hand a squeeze and takes a big deep breath and she steps up onto the milk cart and has to steady herself on Dad's coffin, but then she turns around and faces the microphones and people go quiet.

Mum looks around at all the faces. 'I can't ...' she starts, and then she chokes up a bit, but she takes another breath. 'I can't thank you all enough for coming out here and showing you care. I know most of you didn't know Tom, don't know who he was ... and we have to keep this short. Tom's mother was from the Widjabul people of the Bundjalung nation up by Lismore. Some of her people are here today and they wanted to make a musical tribute.' She looks down at Aunty Ell and gives her a big smile and looks down at a little piece of paper she has in her hand, 'And these are the boys from the Wathaurong Boys' Didge Group. When you're ready, Aunty.'

People back away a bit to give the didge players some room. There are seven of them, boys and men, and behind them stand seven girls. The men and boys start with a low hum on their instruments and then one of them bends his head and starts playing a higher tone. After a few seconds the others join in, and the sound gives me goosebumps. The girls have clapsticks and play in time to the rise and fall of the didgeridoos. Then the girls take the beat alone and hold it before the boys join back in and it's like the buildings around us are leaning in, like the whole city is listening. Then the group leader gives his didge five or six big growls and the others follow and it's done.

People clap and the didge players stand up with the girls and smile shy smiles and then they pick up their stools and their instruments and they walk out to the back of the crowd.

Mum wipes some tears from her cheeks. 'Well, that was beautiful, thank you. I know Tom loved that music and I'm sure wherever he is, he's smiling right now.' She takes the paper up again and looks at it. 'Like I was saying, I know most of you here never knew Tom and you came here for a lot of different reasons. You came to support the farmers who are breaking under the weight of drought and debt,' there are cheers from a lot of people in the crowd, 'or you're here because you're buckling under the weight of your mortgage or you have no job and the bank is breathing down your neck and you think there's no one in the world who cares ...' More cheers, this time from people who look like city people. 'Or you're here because you're worried about the planet, about how the climate is changing around you and the government in its big fancy house down there is doing nothing about it.' Now there are boos, and I see Ben and Deb standing over the other side of the crowd, fists in the air with a group of people who look thin and serious like Ben, and some farmers too.

Mum looks around, sighs, 'My husband was like you. He took it in his head to burn our house down instead of hand it over to the bank, and the damn fool died. Now I have no business, no home ... and no husband,' she says. She looks down at Jenny and me. 'But I still have love. Love gives you hope, right? Love gives you strength.' Now she looks out at the people again, and she lifts her voice, 'Love gives you *fire*.'

People with *#BURN* signs hold them up and cheer. Mum stands there and lifts her fist in the air and now everyone, all three thousand two hundred and fifty, have their fists in the air too.

Jenny looks at me like, *holy moly, is this our mum?*

Mum looks over at Karsi, who's making a movement with his hand like, *calm down, girl.* But she looks at her paper and looks up again. 'We've had a bit of a tradition on this trip. My husband was a bit of a poetry lover, and our family friend Don started this off by reciting a poem in memory of our Tom. So I'd like to finish the same way.' She takes a pause and the crowd go quiet. 'It's another verse by Lawson, and it's called the Bush Fire.' Her voice cracks but she keeps going to the end.

'Ah, better the thud of the deadly gun, and the crash of the
      bursting shell,
Than the terrible silence where drought is fought out there in
      the western hell;
And better the rattle of rifles near, or the thunder on deck at
      sea,
Than the sound—most hellish of all to hear—of fire where it
      should not be.'

People are dead quiet. I hear a car sound its horn but it must be ten blocks away.

'My husband lost his life to fire,' Mum says after a moment. 'People have been taking his example, burning their own properties, burning the property of others. I understand why, but that's never going to fix things. We need to come together over this. This isn't about city versus country, farms versus factories, coal versus wind, this is about Australians coming together to solve our problems not just for this crisis, but the one after this, and the one after that. So we can keep food on the tables of this nation, people in jobs, and no one has to walk off their farms ever again.'

She looks around, like she's looking for something. I'm serious, it's so quiet there's a pigeon goes overhead and he poops right in front of me and you can hear it splat on the ground, it's that quiet.

'Close your eyes,' Mum says. 'Close your eyes and be still.' And people do. I mean, I don't, but people all around are closing their eyes. Right next to me is this lady who looks like she just walked out of a bank, in a blue suit and red shirt and tight ponytail, with a briefcase, and she's standing with her eyes closed and her chin up and she's not moving. 'How are you feeling? Worried? Pissed off, angry, scared? Alone?' Her voice rises. 'Now open your eyes. Look around! Because you're *not* alone!'

And people open their eyes and start smiling and it's still quiet until this guy up the back yells out 'Hell no!' really loudly and Mum raises her fist into the air again and everyone starts laughing and clapping and Mum decides that's enough and starts climbing down again.

I hear a man lean over to his wife and say, 'She should run for Parliament.' And I'm thinking, yeah, probably I've got the most kick-arse mum in the entire universe.

'She couldn't talk her man out of killing himself, you think she can do better as a politician? I don't think so,' his wife says. 'Let's go eat.'

People are still clapping, and Mum climbs down and journalists jump on her and people are trying to clap her on the back and Coach Don and Mr Alberti are trying to keep a space around her and Darren weaves through them all and comes up to us.

'That didge music was deadly, eh?' he says. 'That was my idea.'

'No, really?' Jenny says, looking at him a bit different and I realise it's a look I've seen a few times now and finally I work out what's happening. Seriously?

They start teasing each other which is super awkward so I get up on the milk cart and start looking around. Most of the crowd is leaving now and police are waving them off the roads and back onto the footpaths and a cop with a loudhailer is telling people which streets are the fastest out of town. I can see a big line of cops standing out on the road, but they've got nothing to do, there's no one near them. Trevor is arguing with a couple of police who want him to get Dad's coffin off the Square.

What I'm really looking for is Dad. If I'm right, if he is alive, he'll be here for sure. He wouldn't miss this. Mum's big speech? No way.

I just see families, farmers standing around in groups, someone selling pies, a few people collecting for charities working the crowd, lots of police.

Then across the lights, over by Young and Jackson, I see a dark shadow. A man, standing under a tree, mostly all I can see is he's smoking a cigarette. The little red light of it in the shade. He's tall like Dad. Smokes in long draws like Dad. My skin goes cold. He's a hundred metres away, maybe ten metres up the street, just leaning against the tree, watching.

I fix the spot in my head, jump down from the milk cart and grab Jenny. 'Quick, come!' I take her arm and try to pull her away.

She shrugs me off. 'No. What?'

'Just *come*,' I tell her, not wanting to say it in front of Darren.

'No. We have to wait for Mum,' Jenny says. 'We can –'

I groan and leave her there. Every minute I waste he could be walking away.

The crowd is thinning out but I still can't run in a straight line. I have to dodge and weave up the footpath, get across the lights, counting trees and looking up ahead to where I think he's standing. It looks like he's still there, then I lose sight. A cop at the intersection grabs my shoulder and says, 'Wait for traffic to clear, matey.' He holds everyone up for a few minutes so some cars can go over, then waves us through. I'm off like a shot, the tree is up ahead, people walking under and around it. I can't see …

He's gone.

I look up and down the street but there's no one leaning up against any of the trees here.

When I get back to the top of the steps, Darren is gone, Mum is down in the Square talking to Karsi and some other police, and Jenny is checking her GoFundMe and Facebook pages.

'Three thousand four hundred and twenty followers on Facebook,' she says, sounding a bit disappointed.

'That's pretty good,' I tell her and try to cheer her up. 'That's more than the Cats have, I bet, and they're a football team.'

'No, I got way more than them,' she says. 'That's three thousand new followers *today*. I was hoping for maybe ten.'

'How many total then?'

'Eleven thousand, three hundred and three,' she says.

'And how much money?'

She thumbs across to her GoFundMe page and bites her lip. 'It kind of stalled around a hundred and twenty thousand for a couple of days there, but I think Danny Boy helped, all those posts I made of him …'

'You've been posting about Danny Boy?'

'Of course. It was terrible! You think I'm going to be quiet about it? Holy …' She goes a bit quiet. 'One hundred and sixty-nine thousand and some!'

I go on my phone and look at what she's been putting up. Photos of Danny Boy lying in the street and Mr Garrett sitting with him. Karsi in his uniform holding Mr Garrett while he's crying. Luckily she hasn't written anything about a cop hitting Danny, which I'm pretty sure never happened. I check the website for the *Geelong Advertiser* and there's a story by Geraldine, with a big *EXCLUSIVE* across the top, where she's interviewed Mum: *HERE'S WHAT THE YARDLEY DAIRY WIDOW IS DOING NEXT*, the headline reads. I read a few sentences.

'Did you read this?' I look further down the article.

'What?' Jenny asks, not looking up from her phone. 'Show me?'

I hold the phone for her so she can see the headline and the picture of Mum that looks like it was taken this afternoon.

'No.'

'It says we're moving State!' I tell her. 'Says she wants 'a fresh start' somewhere new.'

'A fresh start?' Jenny says, kind of quiet as she reads on. 'What does that mean? What about the farm?'

'That's later.' I take the phone back, scroll down the bottom. 'See she says here – *"I've got dairying in my blood now. I'm not giving up on that. But there's too many memories in Yardley."*'

'What about Uncle Leo's? What about staying in Melbourne a while?'

'Nothing about that.'

'Bloody hell, this family is so bloody messed up!' she half yells.

We're both kind of stunned. What the hell?

'OK,' she says. 'OK. I never really wanted to live with Uncle Leo anyway.'

'Yeah, but what State? Where else has dairy farms? Why are we leaving Victoria?'

'I don't know!' Jenny half yells. 'You just keep asking and asking your stupid questions like I have the answers! I. Don't. Know. Jack.'

She looks back down at her telephone and it really annoys me and I reach out and swat it out of her hand. She looks at me like she wants to hit me back. I know exactly what she's feeling. But she picks up her phone, checks it isn't cracked, and then yells up at the buildings, 'She drives me mental!' she says.

'Me too.'

'She never tells us anything.'

'It's like we're just little kids, we're just supposed to go along with everything, we get no say in anything!'

'I know! Oh, let's burn our house down, don't worry about where we're going to live, oh, your dad died, let's put his body on the back of a horse and ride all the way to Melbourne to bury him!'

We're really getting into it now, and it feels good. I stand up. 'Yeah! And why would we stay in Yardley where we got friends, or Melbourne where we got family? No, let's move to another State!' A paper cup blows past and I kick it and it flies through the air about ten metres and hits a man on the head and he looks around confused but Jenny grabs me and we turn the other way. It's so stupid, we can't help laughing like idiots, and I have to grab her for support.

We straighten up. 'I thought I saw Dad earlier,' I tell her.

'Where, *when*?'

'Saw who, dear?' Mrs Turnbolt says, coming up behind us.

Jenny is looking at me like, *you did not just say that*. We both turn around and smile.

'Uh, Darren, playing the didge. He was one of the ones with the didgeridoo, but she won't believe me,' I tell Mrs Turnbolt.

She stands with her purse clenched in front of her, as though it will protect her from the big city, 'That was a nice touch, wasn't it?'

'Mrs Turnbolt, can you tell Mum we're just going to get a drink at the 7-Eleven?' Jenny asks. 'We have our own money.'

She frowns. 'Well, she sent me up here to fetch you down, we'll be leaving any minute ...'

'We won't take long, we'll go straight back to the milk cart after,' Jenny says.

'I guess that's all right.'

'OK, thank you,' Jenny says and grabs my arm and pulls me down the stairs, hugging me in close as soon as we've gone a couple of metres.

'You think you saw *Dad* and you're only telling me now?' she says.

'I don't know!' I tell her. 'It was in shadow and he was a long way away under a tree ...'

She grabs my arm again and pushes me towards the shop. 'In there now. You tell me *everything*.'

'Dad gave up smoking,' she says after I tell her what I saw. 'Last year.'

'So he started again, without Mum around to pester him,' I insist.

'He wouldn't have stayed across the road, he'd want Mum to be able to see him,' she says.

'He wouldn't want to be recognised,' I disagree. 'Too many people up front who might know him.'

'So why come at all? It makes no sense. Dad's dead, all right, his ashes are in that coffin, Jack.'

I stare at her. 'What? It was *your* idea,' I say and mimic her voice. '*What if Dad's alive? What if it's him and Coach Don lighting the fires?* Remember that?'

She just looks down at her cup and sucks on her straw. 'That was a hundred miles ago. Lots has happened since then.' She says it like she knows something.

'What are you saying? Jen?' She ignores me, just looks away out the window.

I go to grab her hand and that's when I notice it for the first time. The back of her hand is kind of blue, and there's a weird lump sticking up under the skin.

'Stop,' I say, holding her wrist and pulling it toward me. 'This isn't good.'

She looks at her hand, turning it, flexing her fingers. The little lump slides around under her skin. 'Oh damn, I think I broke something.'

'When?'

She looks at it again, poking at the lump. It looks kind of like it has a sharp end on it, like it might break through the skin if you pushed too hard.

'I don't know, it's been kind of funny since we jumped off the milk cart this afternoon, before Danny Boy died,' she says. 'But we did our checks, then it was the memorial … I forgot about it.'

'It must have been when we fell out.'

'Yeah, I kind of landed …' She thinks back. 'Yeah, I think I landed on this hand.'

I push the bone and watch it move. 'That is definitely broken.'

'But I can move my fingers OK,' she says.

'We have to call Mum,' I tell her. 'Go to hospital.'

'We're leaving now,' she says. 'Uncle Leo's.' She makes a face.

'Then tell her when we get there.'

Jenny looks at her wrist and then at me. 'How about we don't? Until after the funeral tomorrow.'

'But if it gets infected?'

'The skin isn't broken, it's just a little bone or something, I'll be careful with it,' she says. 'Just like, tomorrow morning and then after the funeral we can get it looked at.'

'OK.'

'OK.'

And I reach over and pull her head toward mine and touch my forehead to hers and there's a deal there, that whatever all this is, whatever is happening, it's still her and me. Like it always has been. And screw the rest.

Melbourne

'Seems like things are quieting down,' Mum says, watching news reports on the TV. 'Here in Melbourne anyway. They're still rioting in Sydney and there's a fire in Perth now.'

We got a cab to Uncle Leo's in Carlton. He's a nice bloke, but his house smells like fried food and he's kind of shy and awkward which makes everyone around him shy and awkward. The good part is he isn't home, he's interstate for work for a week. It kind of tells you a lot about our family that he didn't even cancel that to come to the funeral. But it's good that we have the place to ourselves for a while.

There were nearly twenty people in here earlier. Karsi went off with some other police to 'do paperwork', but the Garretts and the Albertis and the Turnbolts and the Maynards and Coach Don and Geraldine and Alasdair were here, and even Pop had his chair pulled up on the steps and people were sitting around the door talking with him. They were all talking and smoking and drinking beer like no one was ever going home. Except Ben and Deb, who I haven't seen since Federation Square, so I guess they're off planning something. They talked about starting a thirst strike; I didn't even know that was a thing. Mum says they're more likely just trying to find somewhere to stay, and then Coach Don says that's a good idea, he still has to go and find a room somewhere and suddenly everyone is gone.

'Come with me, meathead,' Jenny says and points to the door.

'Where are you going?' Mum asks. 'It's late.'

'Just around the block,' Jenny says. 'You can't expect us to sleep this early.'

Mum points down past the little kitchen. 'There's real beds down there. You haven't slept in a real bed since I don't know when.' She looks straight at Jen. 'You need to sleep, miss.'

'Can't we just take a walk, then get ready for bed?' Jenny asks. 'Just me and Jack. Mum?'

Mum smiles, so I know Jenny's won. 'Oh all right. Stay together and don't wander too far.' She watches us all the way to the door.

Jenny grabs the sleeve of my jumper and pulls me outside. When we get outside she pulls her phone out of her jeans pocket and hands it to me. It's on her GoFundMe page and it's showing $169,480 now.

'I'm going to cash out,' Jenny says. 'End the campaign.'

'How do you do that?' I ask.

'You just do it in the app, and the money goes to into your PayPal. The plan is, tomorrow Alasdair is going to help me move it from PayPal into this special bank account he set up. Mum and him agreed.'

'Wow. That's amazing, you know that?'

'I know. People can still give money, but I figure after the funeral, all the publicity dies down, there won't be that much more.'

'And then how do we get the money?'

'It's in a trust – we can't get it until we turn eighteen.'

'No soccer boots then?'

'No, I have a better idea.' There's a low wall alongside a small park with dead grass and rusting swings, and she sits down on it. 'But you have to promise this is just between you and me.'

'OK.'

'No, I freaking mean it, Jack. You can't tell anyone, all right? Even Mum. Especially Mum.'

She's never sounded this serious. I sit down beside her.

She puts an arm around my shoulder. 'This is my plan. We are getting out of this mess.'

'I am *not* joining the navy,' I tell her, guessing where she's going. 'Besides, they wouldn't even take us. As soon as they found out about the Dorotea's –'

'Not the navy, dummy,' she says. 'I mean really out, way way out. Like other side of the world out.'

I frown. 'Just tell me.'

'Where's the one place in the world people won't look at us like we're freaks, with our gloves and big boots and stupid routines?'

'I don't know.'

'Yeah you do. Sweden. As soon as we can get that money, we're going to get passports and plane tickets and we're going to move to Dorotea. It's where this stupid disease comes from, it's like semi-normal there.'

'Sweden?'

'Yeah, we'd arrive and people would be like, oh, you have analgesia? Whatever, so does my cousin, so does my teacher, so do I ...'

'Yeah, but *Sweden?*' She's scaring me. She's so serious and it's so crazy. 'Mum would never let us.'

'Mum couldn't stop us!' she says fiercely. 'We'd be eighteen, we'd have our own money. Enough money to live on for years! We'd get jobs over there – they have a dairy in Dorotea, I researched it. Or work in a café or something, anything.' She turns me to face her. 'We'd be normal, Jack. First time in our lives.'

'Can we use the money for that?'

'People gave that money so we could get a new start – this is a new start. And I raised it, not Mum, not anyone else.'

I can see she'll explode if I don't say yes. 'OK.' I say it, but I'm not feeling it yet. Sweden?

'Seriously? You can't just say it and not mean it. You have

to mean it and you have to keep it quiet for five years. Can you do that?'

'Why do we have to keep it quiet? Why couldn't Mum come if she wants?' I ask her.

'We tell her, she'll use the next five years to talk us out of it,' she says. 'You can hear her, right? We need the money for *food*, we need the money for *rent*. Or, it's not your money, you asked people to donate it for the funeral. Or, you need it for medical bills, how are you supposed to pay for hospital and specialists, blah blah blah.'

'Yeah, but maybe she's right. How are we supposed to pay for doctors?'

'Sweden has free healthcare. You can look it up. And Dorotea has a special clinic for people with analgesia because it's like ground zero for people like us.' She still has her hands on my shoulders and she shakes me. 'You *can't* tell her, all right?'

She's right. If we told Mum, she really would spend the next five years working on us.

'Come on, it's not like she hasn't kept things from us,' she says. 'The coffin full of cattle feed? The whole thing about moving interstate? When was she going to tell us that? When we're on a bus headed for Adelaide?'

'OK. You're right. I'm in.'

She kisses me, full on the gob, and hugs me. 'Yes! Yes, yes, yes.'

I wipe my mouth. 'But you have to promise to go to the hospital tomorrow with your hand.'

'Deal,' she smiles. 'I was going to anyway.'

'Yeah, right. Because I'm not going to Sweden with someone who had their hand amputated because they wouldn't admit to Mum they broke it.'

And then we're walking back and I realise I said it and you can't take something like that back and I wonder what I just said yes to.

It's my first time at a cemetery. I expected it to look like in the zombie movies with dead trees and tombstones and wilting flowers. But the trees are still green, there's grass mown nice and neat, lots of tombstones but with some big flowery bushes around the sides. I guess cemeteries are allowed more water than ordinary houses. There's even a beehive set up against one wall, with bees flying in and out.

'I guess they live off all the flowers people leave here. How do you think the honey tastes?' Mr Alberti asks.

'I don't know but I'm dying to try some,' Coach Don says.

'Ouch,' Mr Alberti nudges him as Mum walks up.

I wanted to come with the tractor and Trevor pulling the milk cart that Danny Boy brought nearly all the way, but early in the morning Trevor pulled it to the gates of the cemetery, which is where it is when we all arrive. Mum and Jenny had a big fight about what she was going to wear but lucky for her we don't have that many clothes any more so she got to keep her jeans but had to wear a black top that Aunty Ell had borrowed from someone and it looks quite cool like it's actually meant to go with boots and gloves. I have dark blue jeans and a red T-shirt that make me look like some kind of Demons supporter and everyone keeps saying it.

The council has opened the oval next door for parking and there are about twenty cars parked there already when we arrive at ten o'clock, with some people from Yardley standing by the gates with the milk cart. The whole town is here, it seems like, including a lot of people and families who weren't in the procession but just came up for the day.

Coach Don walks over to Mum. 'So here we go, Dawn. End of the road.' He holds out his arms for a hug and Mum gives him a good one, hanging on a beat too long so he starts to pat her back and then kind of shuffles back when she lets him go.

'Yeah, well. End of this road,' Mum says. She grabs me around the shoulders. 'Still a long road ahead.'

A lock of hair has fallen out from behind her ears and Jen reaches up and tucks it back in. 'I'm a mess, aren't I?' Mum whispers to Jen.

'You're allowed to be a mess at a funeral, Mum,' Jen tells her.

Geraldine waves, and the reporter from Portland is there too, but the police have the cameras and reporters penned up on the other side of the gates so they can see us pull the milk cart in at ten-thirty for the eleven o'clock service.

'Can we have a moment, Dawn?' Coach Don asks. 'While we still can?' He nods over to the side and I see them all standing there. The Albertis and the Maynards and the Turnbolts and Aunty Ell and the Garrettses, Pop and Ben and Deb. They've gotten changed out of their feral forest-people gear. Ben has washed his hair and put it up in a ponytail and Deb is wearing a dress I haven't seen before, and shoes. I realise it's the first time I've seen her with shoes on. We walk over and Mum puts her hand on Mr Garrett's arm.

'I'm so sorry about Danny Boy, John.'

'Don't you worry about him,' Mr Garrett says, looking at Mrs Garrett who nods. 'He had the time of his life. Crowds cheering him, ride on a ferry, high-speed police chase.' He looks down at Jen and me, 'These two fussing over him like he was royalty. He died happy.' He looks up at Coach Don, like he's expecting something.

Coach Don coughs. His face is usually brown with the sun and cracked from frowning and smiling, but right now it's a bit flushed, everyone looking at him. 'Yeah, well, it's just we read what you said about quitting Yardley.'

Mum looks surprised, but she doesn't deny it.

'And we get it,' Coach Don says. For some reason he looks at Jen. 'You've got more than enough on your hands without hanging around Yardley. Best to let history be history.'

'And memories,' Mrs Alberti says, jumping in. 'Best to let the bad ones go, start making new ones, eh Dawn?'

Mum nods, but I'm waiting because they're building up to something.

Pop can't take it. 'Oh for God's sake show her will you!'

They step aside and there's a little car behind them on the driveway and they're all looking at it. I mean, it's been here the whole time, but I didn't even notice it. Which is pretty amazing, since it's bright yellow.

Coach Don holds out a set of keys. 'So we got you that. It's a big city, you'll need a car.'

'Only fifty-five thousand on the clock,' Pop says. 'Small car of the year in 2012. Six litres per hundred ks.'

'It's got a CD,' Mrs Maynard says. 'You can have these to get you started.' She pulls some CDs from her purse. Mum takes them, not knowing what to do with them, so Mrs Maynard takes them back again. 'I'll just … you can get them after.'

'It'll get you where you're going,' Mr Maynard says. 'I gave it a solid road test yesterday afternoon. It's in good nick.'

'You're all …' Mum says. She takes the keys from Coach Don and then gives him a big hug. 'You're too bloody much.' She finishes hugging and wipes her eyes, then stands and looks at it a moment, then turns to us. 'People will be playing Yellow Spotto with *us* now, eh kids?' She looks at the faces around her. 'But you can't afford this. I can't take it.'

'We can and you will,' Mrs Garrett says.

'My dad paid the rego,' Deb says. 'I told him about you and he volunteered.' She looks at Ben and he frowns. 'OK, he was voluntold,' she says.

'I gave it a professional once-over too,' Karsi says. 'Even I can't find anything to defect on it.'

It's just about the smallest, yellowest car I've ever seen. All I'm thinking is, wherever we're going, I hope it's close. And will Mum even fit?

Pop must see my face because he rolls up next to me. 'Don't worry, you can't hardly see the colour when you sit inside it. That colour is why we got such a good price.'

'No, I like it,' Mum says, overhearing him. She turns to Ben. 'Did you pick the colour?'

He claps Mr Garrett on the shoulder. 'We picked it together, right Garrett?'

'Did we my arse,' Mr Garrett says but he pats Ben's arm and holds it there around his shoulder, leaning on him a bit.

'Well I like it. It's like a sunrise. It's like a new day,' Mum says.

Mrs Alberti hears that and rushes in for another hug and a big sob.

'All right, Mrs A,' Mr Alberti says, deciding enough hugs have been had. 'We ready, Garrett?'

'Let's get this done,' Mr Garrett says. He looks up at the coffin on the milk cart then at the front where Danny Boy should be. 'Not quite the way I imagined bringing Tom Murray home, but ...'

'You take the front, John,' Coach Don says quietly, 'We'll be behind you.'

There are six men pulling the milk cart with Dad's coffin in it, through the big stone gates and then around the bend, past this huge weird monument to Elvis, to the big stone church in the middle of the cemetery. Mr Garrett up front, Coach Don on the other side, Karsi in a black suit instead of his uniform, and on the other side of him Mr Alberti, Mr Turnbolt and Ben.

We pass these buildings that don't have doors or windows, about two storeys high and ten metres deep. Along their walls are marble plates with pictures and flowers on them and it takes me a while to realise there's dead people behind them. I'm wondering are they in coffins or just their ashes and I'm wondering do they have to pay more than the people outside under the ground and if you pay more to be low down or high up.

'Who are you looking for?' I ask Jenny, noticing her getting fidgety and looking around. 'Darren is here if that's what you're stressing about. I just saw him with Aunty Ell. Jeez, you'll see him after.'

'Good, yeah,' she says and looks at me like, *just drop it* so I shrug and look at the back of the milk cart. She's wearing a long-sleeved shirt with the cuffs pulled down over her wrists, like it's a fashion thing, but it's just to hide her hand from Mum, because it's totally blue-black now even though she put foundation on it to cover it up.

She's really jumpy and I wonder if maybe she has a fever because of her broken bones. I should have checked.

It's a nice sunny morning, going to be a hot day. We walk with Mum behind the milk cart, and all the others walk behind us. I stop counting at a hundred people. We go really slow, and Mum has to stop at one point and lean on Mrs Garrett, so it takes about fifteen minutes to get to the chapel. It's funny listening to the crunch of the wheels on the road without the sound of Danny Boy's hooves clip-clopping as well. A couple of photographers nearly go over backwards crouching down on the road in front of the milk cart and Mr Garrett gives no sign of slowing down, but they get out of the way before we run them over.

Mr Garrett has been holding his hat in his left hand, but he puts it on his head as the milk cart comes to a stop and he motions the others to lower the big poles they've been pulling the milk cart with. We wait at the back as he comes around and climbs up into the milk cart and drops the gate at the back so that he can lower down two ramps for people to use when they're getting the coffin out.

Mum lets go of Mrs Garrett's arm. 'We'll go inside now,' Mum says to us. 'While the men are getting the coffin down. There's something we have to talk about before the service.'

I look at Jenny like, *what?* But she just looks away.

Inside we walk through a lobby and into a long narrow chapel with grey carpet and four small benches on each side and big skylights up front over the altar so everything is bright and white. People from Yardley are already filling up the seats but they left space at the front just for us and we take the left side. Mrs Alberti is still crying and Mr Alberti is holding her and Mrs Maynard is patting her back. Mum waves to a couple of people and I'm sitting and waiting for her to just bloody sit down and explain and Jenny is still not looking at me. What the hell?

Then I realise, whatever is coming, I don't want to know. I don't want to hear it.

Maybe it's about What Happens Next. We move interstate? Or worse, maybe we get some little apartment in Melbourne and she can work as a waitress because that's what happens in movies to People Who Screw Up And Lose Everything.

She turns to me. 'One thing,' Mum says. 'Before the coffin comes in, I wanted you to know something.' Why is she talking to me? Why not both of us? Jenny's knuckles are white. She's holding them in her lap so they don't shake. She's looking at the ground. Whatever it is, she already knows.

'After the service we have to go to the police station,' Mum says, and waits.

'I know,' I say straight back at her. Then I realise I haven't been listening. I thought she said hospital. I thought she was talking about Jenny's hand. I was already feeling relieved, if that was all it was about. We were going to be told off again for not being careful, I could deal with that. But then I realised she said police. 'Wait, what?'

'You know?' Mum asks, frowning.

'No, sorry, I thought you said … did you say police?'

'Yes,' Mum looks at Jenny, puts a hand on her leg, but she's still looking down at the floor. 'Alasdair will meet us there. Jenny has to give a statement.'

Alasdair? I jump in, 'Is this about the money?'

'No,' Mum says. 'It's about the fires.'

Now Jenny looks up. 'I didn't light the first one,' she says. 'I don't know who did. But I did the others.'

'How did you …? How did the police …?' My mind is whirling.

'Karsi came to me last night,' Mum says. 'While you two were out having your walk. They saw Jenny on a CCTV camera in Warrnambool. He's a good man Karsi, he said it should be me who asks her. So I asked your sister this morning while you were having your shower.'

I look at Jenny. 'You didn't tell me. You should have told *me*!' I can't keep my voice down and I don't care. People look over.

She's pale. 'I almost did, Jack. A hundred times. But you would have stopped me,' she says.

'You let me think it was Dad! You helped me look in the *coffin* …'

Mum looks at me strangely, but Jenny just shrugs. 'You ask so many questions. I just wanted you to be asking the wrong ones.'

'Why didn't they arrest you?' I ask her. 'Last night?'

'It's sensitive times, Jack,' Mum answers. 'Fires, riots, banks, supermarkets, you name it. Karsi talked them into letting us get the funeral over with, but then we have to go in to the station at Southbank.'

People are really staring at us now. I don't care. If Jenny lit those fires, then … there is no Yardley conspiracy. No fake death certificate. No one out there hiding in the shadows. I'd been holding onto that hope like I was hanging by one hand off a bridge. And it's a double burn. Because Jenny knew it the whole time and she was the one going around lighting those fires and she never told me. Why not? Hide it from everyone else, hide it from the whole world, but not me! Why? How stupid am I?

I let out a big wail as it hits me that Dad isn't going to miraculously walk back into our lives.

Jenny is just sitting there, looking at the ground, and before I know it I'm on my feet and punching her. A couple of people stand up and two rows back Mr Maynard says, 'Hey there, Jack!', but this time the heat is rising in me and I don't care. I don't want to let her get away with it. Jenny just curls into a ball on the pew, doesn't fight back. I really lay into her. Mum wraps her arms around me, so I punch her a couple of times too, then someone grabs me from behind. I'm thrashing and kicking, but they're too strong.

'Sssssh, easy Jack,' a voice says in my ear. It's Karsi. If I could break free I'd run for it, but he doesn't let me go. He's got me from behind, one arm around my chest, the other around my waist, lifting me so my feet are nearly off the ground. People are looking at me like I'm a baboon in a zoo.

'Just let me go all right?' I tell him. I can't fight him, so I go limp but he keeps holding me. 'Let me go!'

He loosens his grip, but he's standing between me and the aisle, so there's no way out. All the heat is gone. Now I just feel stupid, so I sit down. He sits next to me, like some kind of bodyguard.

Someone handed me a bible as I walked in and I dropped it when I stood up and when I sit down again I sit on it and pull it out from under me. I think about throwing it, but there's nothing to throw it at except the coffin, so I just sit and look at it. It's thick and black and I just focus on the cover to block everything out – the gold-on-black letters, brown worn corners – not reading, just staring. As I look at it, a drop of something falls on the top. I wipe it off, but another drop falls. I look up at the roof of the chapel to see is it leaking, then I realise it's me.

I look around to see are people still looking, and I see Coach Don watching. He's crying too, got his hanky in his hand.

Reaches across the aisle and hands it to me.

And beyond

Mum lit a spark with Dad's funeral and Jenny turned it into a wildfire. A wildfire that spread from bank to bank, State to State and it's burning still.

We had to move out of Uncle Leo's place because he said Mum was turning it into a refugee centre. Which wasn't really fair because mostly it was the telephone calls that annoyed him, Mum on the phone all day and night. But we did get people turning up at the door with nowhere to go and there was this one morning where this guy and his son, they were unemployed shearers, were making breakfast in Uncle Leo's kitchen and Uncle Leo came in and looked at them and said, 'Who are you?' and they explained and Uncle Leo just sat down and nodded and he ate the fried eggs they'd made and they all talked about Gippsland and the drought and then he went out back where Mum had just finished her shower and they had a full-on shouting match.

So Mum took a part-time job at Farmers First, talking to politicians and helping organise demonstrations, and we moved into a little flat in Fitzroy and the Garretts come to visit now and then and Coach Don has been up twice and we went back to Yardley once because Mr Garrett got a new horse and everyone from the funeral procession went around to see it. But it's strange going home when your home isn't there any more, so I don't want to do that again. But I miss my soccer team.

I don't know what happened to moving interstate. I asked Mum if that's happening, if that's what we're doing when Jen gets out, and she said you say things out loud sometimes that you should just keep in your head because suddenly it's a thing and if you don't go through with it right away everyone is asking why. Like, *hasn't she got enough to do these days without thinking about that?* So who knows.

Karsi is the one from down there we see the most. Well, he's not from down there any more because he got transferred from Portland to South Melbourne. Mum said it's because he got in trouble for helping us, although it was nothing they could sack him for. He takes me to the footy whenever the Cats are playing and once he took me to Kardinia Park and we saw them there and Mum came too. Every Sunday they go for Chinese, never the same one twice. He makes Mum laugh which is good because if he's not around she does a lot of sitting and looking at the door, like she's waiting for someone to come in.

We've got a bit of money now Mum has a job. So we can afford to go to the football, and I joined a cricket club down the road. I never played in a proper club before but it turns out you can be a pretty good batsman when you're not scared of the ball. But school was weird at first.

The first school I went to, it's not like I grew up there, so I had to explain to people about five times a day why I wore gloves and steel-toed boots even when I was wearing shorts and I mostly sat in the library during breaks and lunch because I sprained my ankle playing handball on the bitumen playground and didn't realise for a couple days and it turned black and yellow and Mum went mental. That's wasn't the worst though.

It was weird being at school without Jenny. It's always been us and suddenly it was just me. Growing up, when some kid was being a dick to one of us, he had to take on both of us. I didn't tell Mum how tough it was because she'd have been down there like a flash, talking to teachers and parents and making it worse. But after school I would hang with these deadly Koorie kids from another school who are Darren's cousins and after a few months I talked Mum into letting me move schools. Being at their school is much better because just the fact I'm Darren's mate is good enough for them.

Doing my checks on my own, that's another annoying thing. But I've got Jenny's phone while she's inside and I found a way with a selfie stick and the camera so I can do it myself. I killed myself laughing in the bathroom the other day and Mum asked me if I was OK, but it was just because I imagined someone walking in while I was bent over with the selfie stick between my legs and the phone poked up my clacker. It's kind of stupid, but I can do it, because it isn't forever. Jenny will be out in a couple of years and I can keep the Sweden thing secret that long because Mum has no idea. And because Jenny says the thought of getting away, just us – it's what keeps her going in there.

Everyone has their theory about why she did it, but when things calmed down and I asked her, she just said, 'Because Dad would have.' I'd almost convinced myself it was him, so maybe he would. But I don't think that was the whole reason. Mum says people do crazy things sometimes when they're upset and angry and hurt and that it was her fault too because she didn't see what was happening to Jenny. Alasdair's theory was it was the analgesia. Because when you can't cry, how do you show the world you're hurting? That's what Alasdair told the court when she was being sentenced, anyway. The *Sun* and the *Geelong Advertiser* ran a crusade to get her off, but she'd done too much damage for the judge to just let her go. The police tried to say she lit the fire in Yardley too but the Turnbolts and I witnessed that she was with us all night and couldn't have got into town and back again without us knowing. Which actually she could have, because both of them are deaf and I was asleep, but the police had to drop that one and she'd pleaded guilty to the others so they had more than enough to get her convicted.

If Jenny had been an adult, she would have got fifteen years or upward, the judge said. But as a kid, and because she said sorry, she only got three years at Malmsbury Detention Centre. Mum and I talk with her every day and we visit her twice a week. We'd go more often except petrol is expensive, even in our little yellow car. Sometimes I go on my own on weekends if Mum is busy, but it's three hours and three trains. Alasdair tried to get her community release but that didn't work, and we petitioned to have her moved to Parkville which is only fifteen minutes away but Malmsbury is the only one with medical officers who can take care of her when she gets hurt. She got beaten up pretty often in the start; kids testing how much she could take, but they got bored with that pretty quickly and mostly leave her alone. She makes money now, tricking the newbies into betting she can't push a needle through her hand without crying. That kind of thing gets you big-time respect in a place like Malmsbury, so she's doing OK. Better than I expected.

Once they let me go with her to her room, which she shares with this girl called Bernie from Nutfield who stole a car in Perth and drove it all the way to Melbourne without a licence and tried to sell it. It wasn't the first car she stole. It doesn't look like a prison cell with bars; it has a normal grey door with small windows in it, two beds, a desk for doing homework and a sink. They're allowed to put stuff on the walls, so Bernie has a big poster of a red Ford Mustang which she says is the sweetest ride she ever stole. Jenny has a huge Swedish flag and she's trying to learn Swedish phrases but it's a crazy language. I'm glad Swedes all learn English in school.

You ask me who did the Yardley fire, my guess is Pop. I know, crazy, right? Old guy in a wheelchair? I bet the police never even considered it was him because of his legs. But I can totally see him in a balaclava, throwing petrol bombs at that bank from the window of his car. Plus, he drives that model of Hilux.

It's six hundred and forty-two days until Jenny gets out, if she doesn't screw up in there and gets max time off her sentence. And I looked it up; being in gaol won't count against her for her Sweden visa, because she's a minor and crimes don't count if you're a kid.

I've been looking online about Dorotea too, and it's way, *way* up at the top of Sweden. I was showing Jenny and she said well, at least we won't have to worry about getting too hot. There's not many dairies; just fishing, forests, shops and internet companies and I don't see us fishing so we decided I'll be a teacher and she'll start her own internet company. Or, since I can cry now, or cried once at least, I'm thinking I could also be a social worker, like Aunty. Or I might join the police.

We only talk about it on my solo visits though, because Mum still doesn't know and we haven't decided when to tell her. Or what to tell her – because Jen is still like, she isn't coming, but I don't see why she shouldn't, if she wants to.

I get these urges to tell Mum about it. I nearly did, a couple of times. The other day she was in the little kitchen in our flat and she was making me baked beans after school, and she'd just finished talking to someone on the phone (like usual, because she is always either just finished or just about to) and she was singing a Cold Chisel song and the sun was coming through the high window over the sink and lighting her up and I nearly cracked and told her.

Nearly told Karsi once at the football too. And Pop, when we were down to see Mr Garrett's new horse. OK, I nearly cracked maybe a dozen times. I didn't though, because I know that if I tell Pop, then it's like telling the whole of Yardley.

What keeps me going, helps me keep our secret, is this insane video I found on YouTube. Someone recorded it with a camera on a headband as they were cycling through this forest in Dorotea in the snow. They have these crazy mountain bikes that have skis on the front and the back is like tank tracks instead of tyres, so you can ride them uphill in the snow and then ski down the other side. So this girl is screaming down this slope in the forest, dodging the trees on her bike and a moose walks right out in front of her and she drops the bike and she slides Right Under The Moose.

When I'm about to crack, I think of that video. Me and Jen are totally going to do that.

About Dorotea's analgesia

Congenital insensitivity to pain, or congenital analgesia, is a real hereditary disease. It usually presents in a form even more debilitating than described here. Dorotea's analgesia is fictional, but it is based on a form of the disease experienced by people in one particular region in Sweden known as Norbotten, where an unusually high number of people share a mutation in their DNA that leads to analgesia.

If you'd like to learn more, just go to www.pubmed.gov and search for 'Norrbottnian congenital insensitivity to pain'.

Acknowledgments

I love a challenge and there can be few challenges more tempting to an Australian author than trying to win the HarperCollins Banjo Prize! It's a huge opportunity to be published, but even more, a huge vote of confidence in the future of Australian writing. So my first thanks go to the management at HarperCollins Publishers Australia for creating the Banjo Prize and then putting in all the work it takes to sort through the hundreds and hundreds of manuscripts and then read and judge the contenders. I saw the prize announced on a writers' blog in about March of 2018, and entries were due at the end of May. At that point, *Taking Tom Murray Home* was a rough first draft that I really thought twice about entering. But I hammered away at it for two months and on midnight of the last possible day to enter, I sent it in. And it was *very* rough, I am the first to admit. So thanks also go to the fantastic editorial team at HarperCollins, from Catherine Milne to Nicola Robinson, freelancers Julia Stiles and Nicola Young, and not least designer Laura Thomas for her beautiful cover.

This book was born on a road trip through southwest Victoria with my family a few years ago, and at the time I wrote my journal notes, I had no idea it would turn into *Taking Tom Murray Home*, so I had to go back and check a lot of details before publication to be sure I got them right. In summer 2019 I re-drove the journey Dawn and the kids take from Yardley (based loosely on the town of Heywood, in Victoria) to Geelong and then up to Melbourne, speaking to locals along the way. Huge thanks for expert advice, as well as letting me spend time with her beautiful Clydesdales, goes to Kim Wood of Heartwood Horses at Bannockburn. A large part of making *Taking Tom Murray Home* believable was getting the character of Karsi right, and showing how the police might deal with such a crazy stunt. So I have to also thank Victoria Police, in particular media adviser Rochelle Jackson and Leading Senior Constable Leo Finnegan, for their help with a question that started with 'OK, so tell me what you'd do; this guy burns down his own house and then ...'

Another important part of making the book believable was imagining and describing the challenges of living with analgesia. For help in this, I'm incredibly grateful to my brother, neurologist Dr Mark Slee, and his physician wife, Dr Rose Smith, for helping ground a fictional condition in medical fact.

Few things are more valuable when you are setting out on any learning journey (and starting out as an author has been that) than a good mentor. I first started banging out ideas for manuscripts in 2013 and completed my first full-length manuscript by the end of 2015. It was an attempt at a light-hearted crime novel, so I showed it to a bloke I'd met at football and cricket matches and backyard barbeques over the years, Kelly Award-winning crime writer and musician, Dave Warner. He read it, and didn't laugh at me. He's given me huge encouragement, as well as tips and advice along the way, and so I owe a big thanks to Dave.

When you are wondering whether it is all worth it, you need people who believe in you, and for that I would also like to acknowledge Carl Pritzkat and Sharon Rice at the US *Publishers Weekly* magazine, for reading and recognising my early work, and encouraging me to keep plugging away. (If you're interested, you can pick up ebooks of that early work free via my author page on Goodreads.com)

I was raised in the city, but my parents are from country stock and grew up in the mid north and far north of South Australia. We spent our childhood Easters and summers on the wheat and sheep farming properties of our relatives and it ground a love of the outback into me. My parents were both avid writers and readers themselves, so huge thanks go to Denys and Teresa for giving me a love of books, writing and good Australian yarns, because without that childhood this novel would have been impossible.

The first draft of this book was written over six intense months of intercontinental travel, when it felt like I spent more time in planes and lounges than at home with my family. The final draft was written over two months of a Danish spring when I should have been out in our garden with my wife, trimming the apple trees and raking out moss, but instead I was locked in the glasshouse or up all night tapping away at the keyboard. To my wife Lise, my son Kristian and my long-suffering proofreading daughter Asta, I owe thanks for your boundless encouragement, your understanding for the many lost hours I spent on the book, and being the best cheer squad a would-be author could hope for.

Copenhagen,
June 2019.